STACY M. JONES

The Missing Link

For all my readers who have loved this series as much as I have.
It's been a joy to share these stories with you.

Acknowledgments

Thank you to the detectives and forensics teams I've had the pleasure of working with through the years and the knowledge and expertise shared with me while writing this series. Special thanks to 17 Studio Book Design for bringing my stories to life with amazing covers. Thank you to Dj Hendrickson for your insightful editing and Liza Wood for proofreading and revisions.

Thanks to my wonderful readers who have embraced this series and fell in love with Riley's adventures. While this is the last book in the series, Riley will hold a special place in my heart. I think we will all miss her.

CHAPTER 1

For nearly an hour, I sat at my dining room table, going through the images and documents Cat O'Connor, the host of the podcast Rock City Killers, had provided for her next series. It was a case from 1995 in our city of Little Rock, Arkansas, that police and the prosecutor's office believed they had solved.

Cat and the families of the three missing young girls weren't so sure. Their bodies had never been found, and the man convicted of the crime, Randy Stock, had maintained his innocence even this many years later.

Randy was soon to be released from prison. He had been serving a sentence for kidnapping but not murder. With no bodies recovered and nothing to indicate the girls were deceased, there was no murder case to be charged. After reviewing some of the case file, even the charges of kidnapping seemed flimsy. But the prosecutor's office had secured a conviction. I was stumped.

That was the point of the podcast and why Cat was taking the case. For her and the families, there were still many questions to be answered. First and foremost, if the girls were deceased, where were their bodies? There had been numerous searches over the years, and more than a few detectives had tried and failed to obtain the information from Randy. The man professed his innocence over and over again. With Randy's release, the podcast was timely.

It didn't escape me that Randy could be guilty. He had been seen speaking to all three of the victims on the day they had gone missing. The girls were last seen on a Friday afternoon in early May 1995, right after school let out. Each had been riding their bikes to and from school. The girls lived a few blocks from each other and the school.

The girls were last seen at a local store not far from the school. It was a local deli of sorts. The kind of place where teachers stopped for coffee in the morning and bought lunch in the afternoons, and kids stopped after school to get snacks.

The owner had run the shop for nearly fifty years. He was a staple in the community and the one who had gone to the police to tell them the girls had been in the store the afternoon they went missing. He was also the one who had seen the girls speaking to Randy right before they rode off on their bikes. But he hadn't been suspicious of Randy, just commented that he held the door open for the girls and said hello. The police took that and ran with it.

It was later in the afternoon when the girls hadn't arrived home that one of the mothers started to get worried. She went to search for the girls and found their bikes on the only stretch of road where there weren't any houses. It was a narrow half-mile between the school and the start of the neighborhood where they all lived. All three of the bikes had been tossed carelessly in the grass. Just behind the fence line at the side of the road was a local farm.

The mother went to the farm, searching for the girls. The owner had been in his barn and told her that he hadn't seen the girls but had heard some girls about twenty minutes prior. He was so far from where the bikes were found that to him, it sounded like children playing after school. He hadn't heard calls for help or anything alarming – just young girls chattering. He hadn't been able to make out what they were saying and it stopped shortly after that.

The mother called the school to see if the girls had gone back there.

The person who answered assured her that the girls weren't there. She later second-guessed herself on taking the time to make that call when it should have been obvious to her that they didn't go back to the school. As she explained to the detective assigned to the case, she had panicked. No one questioned why she had called the school, but she felt like she had wasted time when they could have been searching for the girls.

The mother then called the other parents and 911 to report the girls missing. Unlike a lot of cases, the police didn't make them wait or say they were overreacting. The bikes on the side of the road, coupled with the farmer having heard the girls had been enough to spring the community into action.

Cat's file contained not only official reports but local news clippings from the time. The case had garnered local and national attention. Because I was so young, I don't remember the case at all. I was young then, too young to be watching the news, if it had even made national news all the way up in New York.

My partner, Cooper Deagnan, had promised Cat that we would help her with the investigation. Cat didn't just want to rehash the case, she wanted to know more about what had really happened to the girls. She wanted to *solve* the case and find the truth once and for all.

A lot of people said the case had already been solved and the man responsible was behind bars.

Randy was among the last people to speak to the girls outside of the deli. His statement to the police was that he held the door open for them on their way out. One of the girls dropped her candy bar and he picked it up and handed it to her. She thanked him and went to her bike. He watched the three of them huddle together near their bikes before getting on them and riding off. That was it, the totality of his interaction with them.

Randy had been working as a lineman for the electric company and had just gotten off work – a long shift and he was tired. He had stopped at the deli for a sandwich, had that brief interaction, bought what he had come for and went home. Another witness said that Randy had lingered outside the shop for too long, staring at the girls. I wasn't sure what was true.

The detective didn't believe him.

When the detective asked him what the girls had been discussing, Randy explained he hadn't been close enough to be able to hear them. He couldn't remember what they were wearing or what color bikes they were riding. He was barely able to pick them out of photographs. Randy said over and over again, other than holding the door and picking up the one girl's candy, he had no interaction with them. He was tired from a long day of work and hadn't paid any attention to them – that was the only explanation he had for not remembering the details.

The problem was that in the absence of information, the detective thought he was being evasive and lying. Randy had rubbed the detective the wrong way and had been on his radar from the start. I'd go as far as to say that the detective got tunnel vision in the absence of other credible leads.

I couldn't see anything in the case file that would have made me suspicious of Randy. He's not the person I would have been focused on. I had searched through the whole file, hoping to find something, anything that would help me to understand how Randy had been not only arrested for kidnapping but convicted. There was no physical evidence, not that anyone thought to take possible fingerprints off the bikes. No one saw Randy leave the deli and chase after the girls. There was no physical evidence in his truck or his home to indicate the girls had been there.

There was nothing. Zilch.

The detective had a theory. Randy was a sexual predator and struck when he saw an opportunity. He was headed into the deli when he saw the three girls on their bikes. He went into the store to give them enough time to leave and give himself an alibi. Then he chased them down, grabbing them one by one from their bikes, and throwing them into his truck. The detective assumed he brandished a gun to get them to comply so easily. The weapon was key. Otherwise, why would the girls comply? There were three of them and only one of him. Surely, one of the girls could have gotten away.

Randy did have a gun that the cops found when they searched his home. A Beretta handgun that, after they tested it, hadn't been recently fired. That was okay because no one was saying that Randy had shot the girls, only that he had used it to threaten them into the truck. The problem with that was that this was Arkansas, and the majority of people had a handgun for protection. Having a gun wasn't uncommon. Randy owned it legally. He had no criminal record, not even a speeding ticket.

The detective explained it away by saying that Randy was a good predator, one of the best who never got caught. But no other victims came forward once Randy was arrested. There was no outpouring of relief from the community, indicating that the man had not terrorized anyone. The detective again explained it away by saying the victims were too scared to come forward, even though he was now locked up.

Once Randy was arrested for the kidnappings, he hadn't been given bail. The prosecutor reasoned that if he got out and he had killed the girls, it was a chance for him to dispose of evidence. He was too much of a risk to the community. The judge listened.

When it came time for prosecution, the case was light. The detective testified to his theory, with the defense attorney objecting throughout his testimony as speculation. The judge allowed it. It had set up the possibility for an appeal, which ultimately also failed. They put on another two witnesses who saw Randy outside of the shop while the girls were there. Randy had been living alone, so there wasn't even an alibi for what he had done that night.

The prosecution's case had nothing. Literally nothing – no forensics, no witnesses who saw Randy take the girls, and no bodies. Their whole case was based on a detective who had tunnel vision and a wild theory that couldn't be substantiated. What had swayed the jury was the outpouring of grief for the parents who had taken the witness stand.

It was a heart-string case and someone needed to pay.

If I had been on that jury, there is no way I'd have convicted.

Randy had served his full sentence and in days would be released back into the public. He had a sister living in Dallas, but that was it. The few friends he had were long gone. Randy had no one and no reason to speak to me. If he was the one who had killed the girls, and that was still a big if, he had an incentive not to disclose where the bodies were located. He hadn't been convicted of murder, so a murder case was still on the table.

Double jeopardy did not apply.

If the bodies were found, they could arrest him for murder and send him to prison all over again. This time for life. He had every reason not to want to speak to me or anyone.

Yet, when Cat wrote him a letter explaining the podcast and requesting his participation, he promptly replied. Randy was looking forward to getting out of prison and clearing his name. Instead of shying away from the case, as a guilty man who still faced criminal prosecution might, he encouraged us to march on with the podcast. He offered an interview and whatever else we might need. He said he had no money but could get a job and help us.

Cat wrote back, assuring him no financial support was needed. She worked with him on a time and a location for me to interview him when he gets out of prison. She was working with Cooper now to set up interviews with the others who had testified at court and all the families of the victims.

They seemed happy that Cat was doing a podcast. Their goal was not the same as Randy's. They wanted to find their loved ones. Cat explained that all she was after was the truth and that she had retained private investigators to help find the evidence she needed to uncover the truth.

It was an undertaking for all of us, and the clock was ticking.

There was just one caveat to the whole thing for me – this case pitted me against my husband, Det. Luke Morgan, who was the head of the homicide unit at the Little Rock Police Department. He was a kid in Little Rock when the case happened, but it was his department that I was blaming for the terrible investigation.

The detective who had worked the case was retired, but Luke had already been forced to stand in front of the press with a statement that came down from the brass that he fully supported the detective on the case and that they were looking for any evidence that Randy Stock had killed those girls. If anyone in the public had that information, they could share it with law enforcement.

The prosecutor's office wanted Randy to remain in prison. They were ready to try him for murder, except this time it wasn't going to be so easy. They had no new evidence, so for now, Randy would walk free.

It put us squarely on opposite sides. While Luke would never tell me not to take an investigation, the tension in our home had started to rise. We had agreed to disagree and not talk about the case. It wasn't ideal, but it was workable for now.

I pushed aside the anxiety that filled my body thinking about Luke. I refocused my attention on the file, knowing that the only thing I was after was the truth.

CHAPTER 2

L uke brushed a hand over his bald head, the stubble scratching his fingers. He needed to go to the barber shop for a clean shave soon. He had been shaving his head for so long now that he couldn't remember when he had first started. The balding had started near his thirtieth birthday and showed no signs of slowing. Luke was never one to fight nature, so he shaved it off and never looked back.

Someone, an old girlfriend, told him that Black men can carry off bald. He didn't know if she was just filling his head with compliments to get back in his good graces, as the relationship had soured, or if it was one of the things she said that had been true. Either way, he lived with it, and Riley liked it, so he didn't complain.

Rubbing his head to feel the prickle of the stubble was now more of a nervous tick when he was stressed. He stared down at the decades-old case file, not sure what he could do with it. Detective Lyle Tucker had handled the investigation initially in 1995 when three twelve-year-old girls, Samantha Albright, Kathleen Elliott, and Violet Yeaton, went missing.

They were never found.

Luke had been instructed by the higher-ups, far higher than his direct Captain, to give the case a once-over and see if there was anything he could find that might help the prosecutor slap a murder charge on

Randy Stock's investigation. The prosecutor's office didn't want the man back in the community. The families of the young girls didn't think he had served enough time. Luke didn't disagree with them.

The problem was that the case against him was flimsy to nonexistent. Luke had no idea how, unless some new evidence came to light, he was going to be able to arrest Randy for murder. While he knew there was no hope that the girls were alive, he had no evidence that they were deceased either.

If Luke was going to be transparent and honest, which was the last thing the brass wanted, the Little Rock police didn't have a kidnapping case either. Randy had been in the wrong place at the wrong time, and Lyle Tucker had wanted to make a name for himself. The prosecutor was up for reelection and needed a win. People made their careers on the back of… Luke couldn't finish his thought.

He wanted to say *innocent man*, but he had no idea if Randy was innocent. He could very well have done something to the girls. He couldn't go as far as Riley and Cooper and say that he was innocent. He knew that's what they were thinking.

His boss now, and former partner, Captain Bill Tyler, hadn't wanted Luke dragged into the case. He didn't want Luke to have made that statement to the media. He'd fought as hard as he could to stop it from happening. He had also looked at Luke regretfully when he assigned him the case. Luke didn't blame Tyler. He knew why it was being given to him instead of one of the other homicide detectives.

If Luke had the case, there'd be a fair and balanced outcome. He wasn't looking to make his career. He was exactly where he wanted to be and had nothing to prove. That didn't mean he didn't have a lot riding on him.

Luke had read the case file, as thin as it was, several times. He had a handful of statements memorized and knew all the players involved. The lack of evidence left him with almost nothing to go on. His head was bent low over it one more time on the off chance he'd find a new nugget of information when Tyler's booming voice echoed through the detective's bullpen.

"Luke! My office now." Then he disappeared behind the half-open door.

Luke closed the case file, pushed out his chair, and double-timed it into Tyler's office. "What's going on?" he asked, sitting down without being asked.

Tyler leaned forward in his chair, his forearms resting on the desk. He pinched the skin in between his eyes, an outward sign of stress. "I just received a call. We have two missing girls in Hillcrest. They were leaving Walls Elementary School earlier today. There was a half-day and the girls walked together towards home. One of the mothers works from home. The girls never arrived. She called the school and was told they left and didn't return."

"Could they have gone to another friend's house?" Luke asked, trying to deny the rising fear spreading through his belly.

"I don't know. We don't know what we don't know right now. I think we do need to take this seriously."

"Of course." Luke didn't understand one thing. "Why has this been bumped up to you? Isn't this something for the uniformed officers until we know more?"

"I wish that were the case," Tyler said with regret in his tone. "The media is already on it and has already speculated that the case is similar to the missing girls from the Randy Stock case."

Luke didn't understand that. "How can they possibly make the connection? He's not even out of prison yet."

Tyler threw his hands up. "His upcoming prison release has his case back in the news. The statement they forced you to make put a spotlight on us. The call has already come down that they want you on this case too."

"It's not even a case yet," Luke argued, knowing it wasn't Tyler's fault and there was nothing they were going to be able to do. He saw the pinch in Tyler's features and he conceded. "I'll go out there right now. At least with a detective on the ground from the start, we won't miss anything."

"Hopefully by the time you get there, it will have all been a misunderstanding and the girls are safe at home." As Luke got up to leave, Tyler yelled, "Call me if you need anything."

Luke waved over his shoulder as he tried to shake off the feeling that had fallen over him. It was a mix of dread and fear. He grabbed his keys and cellphone off the desk and headed for the door. While he made his way to Hillcrest, he tried to call his current partner, Det. Derek Granger, and update him on the development. Granger was wrapping up a case downtown and had been out of the office most of the day. The phone went straight to voicemail and Luke left a detailed message.

A few minutes later, Luke navigated down the small, narrow Hillcrest streets, dodging several police cars pulled over to the side. He found a place to park and made his way toward the school, nodding hello to several officers.

As Luke got close to the school, he heard his name called twice, loudly, from down the street. He turned to see Granger, all six-foot-four and close to two-hundred and fifty pounds of mostly muscle barreling towards him. For a man who looked like a defensive tackle on an NFL team, Granger could move.

He waited for Granger to catch up with him. "You got my message."

"I was already on my way up here when I got the call. What do we know?"

"Not much," Luke said with a sigh. "They had a half day of school, and the girls walked home together. I don't even have the girls' names yet." Luke filled him in on the few sparse details that Tyler had shared with him. Together, they walked toward a group of people, a mix of men and women surrounded by three uniformed cops.

Luke approached them and pulled his badge out, which was attached to the chain around his neck, from his shirt. "I'm Det. Luke Morgan and this is Det. Derek Granger from the homicide unit. We've been assigned to the case."

One of the women, who identified herself as a teacher, paled. "Why would we need homicide detectives already? We don't even know what's happened."

"Ma'am," Luke said as calmly as possible, "we don't know anything at this point. We are here to ensure the girls are found as quickly as possible. The Little Rock Police Department is offering our full support. Whatever you need, we are here to ensure you access it."

A murmur of appreciation rippled through the group.

"Has there been any developments?" Granger asked one of the men, who was a teacher at the school.

"No," he said with a shake of his head. "We don't know anything more than the girls left when the bell rang at the end of the day. They had to walk a few blocks from school to home, but they never made it. One of the mothers, Gail Herin, rushed over to the school, thinking her daughter, Jenna, and the girl's friend, Scarlett Evans, might have stayed late. Both girls are excellent students and participate in several after-school activities. But they had already left. We rushed to help and started walking the streets, following the path they should have taken. Cops are in the school right now searching."

"Are the parents of both girls here?" Luke asked, looking toward the front door of the school.

The man said, "In the principal's office, talking to one of the cops. Scarlett Evans's mother is a lawyer with the prosecutor's office."

"Amelia Evans?" Luke didn't hold back the shock in his tone.

"That's her. She's there inside if you want to speak to her."

Granger cursed softly under his breath. It echoed what Luke was feeling. He knew Amelia well. She was a long-time assistant prosecutor, handling homicides and sex crimes. She was a solid attorney who rarely lost a case. She was also someone extremely ethical, but by the nature of her profession, had a target on her back.

Luke and Granger made their way toward the school. Before entering, Granger put his hand out to stop Luke. "Why don't you interview Amelia and the other parent while I call in a search and rescue dog. If we can't get something with their scent, we can get a lot clearer on the direction they went."

"That's a good idea." As Granger walked off, Luke headed into the school alone. He found his way through a maze of hallways, asking a teacher for directions to the principal's office along the way. He entered into a large administrator office and was met with a flurry of activity – a woman on the phone barking orders to someone on the other end, another woman standing near a copier preparing flyers to go out with the photos of the missing girls and their biographical information, and the din of questions and answers by cops and the people they were interviewing.

Luke flashed his badge to the woman on the phone and was directed to an inner office. Luke didn't bother knocking on the door. "Amelia," he said softly as he entered when he saw his friend sitting at the round table with the uniformed cop.

She raised her head as a tear streaked from her bright blue eyes to her rouged cheek. "Luke, I'm so glad you're here. Scarlett is missing."

"We're here for whatever you need." There was a lot he wanted to say to her but not in front of the principal and the two uniformed cops who also occupied the room. "Let's clear the room and allow me to speak to Amelia privately."

No one questioned Luke's authority. The one cop who had been interviewing Amelia when Luke arrived said he'd email his notes. Luke thanked him as he walked out the door. When they were alone, Luke went to the table and slid his hand across it, offering her a gesture of support.

"You know I hate to ask this, but it's the most obvious question."

"Are there any threats against me?" Amelia asked, finishing for him. "Several. There are always threats. Most of them are harmless. The most pressing is my ex-husband."

Ex-husband. Luke hadn't realized. "I'm sorry. I didn't know you got divorced."

Amelia shrugged. "I tried to keep it quiet. Given Christopher's work, there are threats against him, too. The divorce was messy. We spent some time in family court working out a custody schedule. I was concerned about his drinking, which is what led to the divorce. If I'm going to be honest with you, I didn't want him to have Scarlett unsupervised unless he got some help."

Amelia's husband, Christopher Evans, was a well-known criminal defense attorney in Little Rock. He took high-profile cases of the most unscrupulous defendants. The kind other defense attorneys didn't want to touch – sexual assaults, domestic violence, homicide. Luke understood. Everyone had the right to a defense.

Luke was familiar with Christopher's drinking. He'd been ordered into treatment once already by a judge and nearly lost his license to practice in the state. He had cleaned up his act for a while. That was the last Luke had heard.

"Do you think he'd take Scarlett?" Luke asked, knowing this would be the best outcome in the situation.

"I don't know what to think," Amelia said, still on edge. "I'll give you all his information. He's been living in an apartment in West Little Rock since the divorce."

Luke went over everything about Scarlett and her friend. When he was done, he asked, "Where are Jenna Herin's parents?"

"They went home," Amelia said. "Gail passed out in the office and was rushed home by her husband. She's not okay, Luke. Not that I am either, but she was distraught, more so than I've ever seen a parent."

Luke knew he wouldn't get much information from her in that condition. "I'll go talk to Christopher. Let's hope for the best."

CHAPTER 3

"What time is your meeting?" Cooper Deagnan asked his wife, Adele Baker, as he rinsed out his coffee cup. He assumed she didn't hear him and asked the question again. Adele had a meeting with a potential new client at midday. She hadn't had court that morning, so she did something she rarely did and slept in. Her work as a criminal defense attorney in Little Rock was a tireless job.

Adele was half-dressed, sitting on the couch with her feet up and her laptop on a small blue laptop desk perched at the top of her thighs. With her head bowed, she murmured something Cooper couldn't hear.

"What?" he asked, walking over to her.

"At eleven. Should be quick. The case is a simple, straightforward burglary charge. Are you meeting Cat and Riley?"

Cooper checked his watch. "I need to get down to Cat's studio soon." He stood there for a moment looking at her. "Are you feeling okay?"

Adele raised her head. "A little tired."

"Can you cancel your meeting and rest?"

"If I still don't feel well this afternoon, I'll come back and rest. I promise."

Cooper knew she pushed herself too hard. But he also knew he couldn't lecture her to take better care of herself. He let it drop and focused on what he was feeling about the case. Cat had approached him about helping her. When he first heard about the case, he was all in. Now, the closer they got to starting, he was having cold feet, and that rarely happened.

Adele shifted the laptop off her thighs onto the couch next to her and gave him her undivided attention. "What's going on, Cooper? You were excited about helping to solve a cold case when you first heard about it."

Cooper had been mulling it over for weeks and he still wasn't sure. He slumped down in the chair across from the couch. "I don't know. Part of me wonders if they got the right guy and we are helping a child killer. In all my years as a detective first and then a private investigator, there are cases I don't touch. I'm not helping someone accused of harming children. I don't do it." He knew Adele had a similar policy unless she felt strongly that the person was innocent.

Adele stared over at her husband, her features softening. "You're not helping a child killer. You're ensuring that the parents have justice. The girls are still missing. If you were able to find them or find definitive evidence about what happened, think of the good it would do. You don't owe the guy anything. He served his time. If he's innocent, he will be cleared based on the evidence you find. If he's guilty of murder, then you testify and make sure he never sees the light of day." She waited a moment for him to absorb what she said. "Can you live with that?"

Cooper hadn't thought about it that way. He had read over the case file before passing it off to Riley. Then he got in his head about it. He was prone to overthinking and had gone down some deep rabbit holes, talking himself in and out of helping Cat with the case.

"I don't know if he's guilty or not, but the last thing I want to do is clear a guilty man's name."

Adele said she understood that. "Is he guilty? When you were going through the case file, you said the evidence was light."

"There's barely any evidence," Cooper said with a sigh. "There's no evidence to point a finger at him or anyone else, for that matter. Those girls are gone, never to be seen or heard from again. He was there, one of the last people to see them alive. If not him, then who?"

"That's your job then." Adele cocked her head to the side and offered him a smile. "You're way overthinking this. Go into it like you go into every case. Do your best and let the chips fall where they may."

Cooper wanted to do that. There was just one catch every time he tried. "There are children's lives at risk if I get it wrong."

Adele offered him a sympathetic smile. "Why don't you go to the prison and speak to him before you jump into the case. You read people well. Maybe you'll be able to get a sense of him. If you get a creepy vibe, tell Cat you can't work on the case with her. I'm sure Riley will still help her, and you can focus on other things."

Cooper considered it for a moment. It wasn't the worst idea. He knew Randy had been moved from the state prison to the local jail as he was about to be released. Cooper wasn't sure why he had been moved. Cat had provided that nugget of information a few days prior. He checked his watch again, knowing that if he was going to do this, he needed to do it now.

Cooper pushed himself up from the chair. "I think I'll go to the jail now."

Adele wasn't surprised at his reaction. "I think you should."

"What happens if we find Randy is innocent? Can he sue someone?"

Adele nodded. "He most definitely can. If he didn't take those girls, then the man lost decades of his life, his freedom, for a crime he didn't commit. You said yourself there isn't much evidence. I'm sure the case will be strong, if it comes down to it."

"Who would handle a case like that? You?"

"There are civil lawyers for those kinds of suits."

"Okay," Cooper said, not wanting to tell her he was glad it wouldn't be her. He went to his room, grabbed a few things, and headed out. By the time he made it back to the living room, Adele had her laptop back on her lap and her head was bowed, looking at the screen. He said goodbye and left, still considering if this was the best course of action. Riley might be upset with him for going to the jail alone. Cat probably wouldn't care one way or the other. Adele was right, he needed to get a good look in Randy's eyes.

Nearly an hour later, after going through security, Cooper sat at one of the small green metal tables in the visitors' room. There was a woman and a young child at the table next to him, visiting a man Cooper assumed was the child's father. Another man was a few tables away, visiting a younger man Cooper assumed was his son. All of these prisoners were low security risk, probably brought in on drug or property crimes. He had assumed he'd be speaking to Randy through the glass with a telephone, but the prison guards had ushered him into here.

A moment later, a man with graying short hair and striking blue eyes in a green prison jumpsuit was ushered through the door. He was handcuffed, but his feet weren't shackled. He walked beside the guard casually with the air of a man who'd gone down this path before.

As the guard uncuffed him, Randy looked down at Cooper. "We haven't met before, have we?"

"No," Cooper said, assessing him. He'd seen photos of Randy from the trial. The man in front of him looked like the same man, paler and significantly older but the same. Cooper lifted his chin and spoke with a cool, calm demeanor. "I'm a private investigator who might be working with Cat regarding the podcast. I wanted to meet with you before I commit to taking on the case."

"I see," Randy said as he folded his hands on the table. "What do you want to know?"

"I don't normally take cases involving children, especially kidnapping and probably murder. I wanted to get a look at you and speak to you before I decide what I'm doing."

"Okay." Randy didn't seem to be offended or shaken by Cooper's directness. "Did Cat give you the file to read?"

"I've read it." Cooper cocked an eyebrow. "It didn't tell me much of anything other than you were at the store at the same time as the girls. You briefly interacted with one of them. It seemed to me the cops zeroed in on you right away. You didn't have much of an alibi. Am I missing anything?"

Randy took an audible breath and shook his head. "That about covers it. I feel horrible that something happened to those girls. I'm being straight with you when I tell you my only interaction with them was seeing them come out of that store. One of the girls dropped something and I picked it up. I handed it back to her, she said thanks, and they were on their way. I went into the store, bought the few things I came for and left. That was it. They weren't outside when I left."

It was the same thing his statement had said in the file. "Why did the cops focus on you? If your interaction was so brief, why you? Did you know any of the girls? Had some previous interaction?"

Randy's shoulders slumped forward. "I swear to you, I don't know. I've been asking myself that same question for thirty years. I was in the wrong place at the wrong time. I don't have more of an answer than that."

There was something in the man's defeated tone and the way his eyes remained fixed that gave Cooper the first shred of belief that he was, in fact, innocent. It didn't mean Cooper didn't have more questions. "When was the first time you knew you were a suspect?"

Randy paused for a moment, seeming to recall the memory. "The next morning. I was on my way to work and Det. Lyle Tucker showed up on my doorstep. That night, after I saw them at the store, I heard on the news that they were missing. I hadn't called the police to tell them I saw them at the store. I assumed someone else had, like the shop owner. I was surprised when Tucker showed up at my house, accusing me."

"Is there a reason you didn't call the police yourself and report seeing them?"

Randy chewed on his lip and shifted his eyes away. "I thought someone else would."

He waited to see if Randy would say more, but when he didn't, Cooper leaned in. "I was a detective for a brief time before I became a private investigator. All of that leads me to believe that something you said, or more specifically, didn't say, allowed Det. Tucker to focus on you. If we are going to help you, we need the truth."

Randy leaned back, his thumb thumping on the table. "That's the thing, you can't help me. I lost close to thirty years of my life here. There's nothing you can do. You can't give that back to me. You can't undo the sheer torture of living in prison. Can you?"

Cooper steadied his resolve. "No. I can't give anything back to you that the system took." He started to say something and Randy cut him off.

"If you find their bodies, what's to say the cops and prosecutor won't come after me again? This time they will lock me up for whatever time I have left." There was righteous anger in his tone. Cooper couldn't combat it. Randy was right – that was the risk he was taking. He shrugged. "I appreciate what Cat is trying to do, and I promised her I'd tell my story. I'm not going to help you point the finger at someone else. I'm not going to do to someone what they did to me. Do you understand me?" Randy leaned his head down and stared hard across the table at Cooper. "Do you understand me?"

Cooper was about to say yes but stopped cold. There was something in the man's tone and the way he was locked in on Cooper that sent a shiver down his spine. He played over Randy's words in his head one more time.

I'm not going to do to someone what they did to me.

"I understand," he said finally after a few beats. "Why are you here in the county jail and not in the state prison?"

"There were threats against me," Randy said evenly. "There were threats that I wouldn't make it out of prison alive. Do you know how they treat child offenders in here?"

Cooper had heard the stories. "Who sent the order to move you here?"

"I don't know. The guard came to my cell a few days ago and pulled me out. They brought me here and told me there were threats. They said I'd be safer here. I'm in a cell alone and they have been decent to me."

"Were the threats from other inmates?"

"I don't know. I assume so, but I haven't had any trouble with anyone in a long time. I've been a model inmate. I got a college degree, taught a few of the other guys how to read, and did my time as quietly as I was allowed. I avoided fights even when people came after me. I think I even convinced a few of the guys and the guards that I didn't have anything to do with those missing girls. Then they came and said there were threats and they moved me."

Cooper could see that Randy was confused by it too. "Do you feel safe here?"

"I do," Randy said with a nod.

Cooper hoped the man remained safe for the rest of the time. "Are Cat and Riley interviewing you the day you're released or later?"

"I'm not sure about the plan."

Cooper wasn't sure of it either. He knew Riley was interviewing him for the case and Cat for the podcast. He wasn't going to step on their toes. "I appreciate your time. We will be doing what we can on this case to help find the girls. I'm sure whatever you're willing to share will be helpful."

"I'm going to say what I know – my story from when I saw the girls to when they convicted me. I don't know anything more than that."

"Noted," Cooper said, not sure how much he believed the man.

While the meeting had decreased some of Cooper's anxiety about the case, he wasn't leaving more convinced of the man's innocence.

CHAPTER 4

I showed up at Cat's studio with three specialty coffees and a box of assorted pastries. I had texted Cooper while I was on my way and asked if he was going to stop by our favorite coffee shop. That was usually his job when we had these meetings. He went to the shop a couple of times a day. It was his favorite place downtown. I was offering to be nice, never once thinking that I'd be the one getting everything. I had no problem paying, it was navigating the treats back to the office where I didn't excel. I wasn't the most graceful creature to roam the planet.

When I received his reply that he was going to be late and that I should stop at the shop, I resisted the urge to ask why. We had been partners and friends long enough that I knew if he wanted to tell me something, he'd be out with it. Since he didn't mention it, I didn't press.

If I wasn't suspicious when I got his text, I surely was when I stopped by the shop and the girl behind the counter told me Cooper hadn't been in all morning.

I got to the front door of Cat's office with the treats. I had made it the three blocks through downtown Little Rock to her office without spilling anything. Her door stood in front of me – the last and most daunting challenge. I set the box of treats down on the ground and, as I rose to open it, Cat stood on the other side, waving frantically through the square window at the top. I bent back down to grab the box as she opened the door.

"Riley!" Cat sang, her voice growing louder as she pulled open the door. "Where's Cooper? He's always here early and I haven't heard from him." Cat stepped out of the way, so I could carry everything to the conference room.

"He texted me and told me he'd be late. No explanation though." I put the coffee down and gestured toward her drink – a caramel macchiato with extra foam. "They had the blueberry muffins you like too."

Cat flipped the lid of the box. "Oh, all of it looks so good." She turned her head to me. "Do you know I only allow myself these when Cooper brings them? Otherwise, I'd have gained twenty pounds by now. He's a terrible influence."

I laughed, knowing just how right Cat was. Cooper had a sweet tooth more so than anyone I knew, and he wasn't happy unless he had everyone in on the fun. "I don't know how he doesn't gain weight. He's as fit as he was when I first met him. I'm not even sure he hits the gym all that much."

"I'm naturally fit. I don't need the gym." Cooper chuckled from behind us, drawing our attention. When we were facing him, he saw the curious looks on our faces. "I know you're wondering where I went." He paused for dramatic effect. A move that made me want to shake the information out of him.

"Don't toy with us," I begged, only half-kidding.

Cooper leveled a serious look at me. "You're going to be angry with me."

"Me?" I asked, feigning sweetness. "Why would I be angry with you?"

Cooper reached for his coffee and a chocolate croissant. He took a sizable bite and washed it down with coffee before thanking me. He slumped down in one of the conference room chairs. "Hear me out before you start griping." I assured him I would and Cat did the same. "I went to see Randy Stock."

"What?" I yipped louder than I meant. I held my hand up and acknowledged my promise from moments earlier. "Go on. Explain." I took the chair directly across the table from him and sat. Cat remained standing.

"First, let me say that I knew you'd be angry. I had reservations about this case, and I needed to meet Randy man-to-man to decide what I was going to do."

"You're concerned he's guilty?" Cat asked as she slowly eased herself into a chair. Gone was the lighthearted, jovial demeanor from moments earlier.

"I was," Cooper admitted. "The more I read the case file, the more concerned I got. I understand there is little evidence against him. But the last thing I want to do is exonerate a guilty man."

Cat shook her head furiously. "That's not the angle, Cooper. I told Randy that the only thing I'd be doing is telling his story. I made no promises of helping prove he's innocent after the fact. I told him without question that was not my goal. My only focus is working to find some justice for the girls. They are still missing. We need answers, no matter where they lead. If the evidence shows us that Randy was innocent and not involved, I told him we'd turn everything over to his lawyer so he can sue civilly. But if the evidence pointed back to him, he had to understand that we were going to the police, and there was a chance he could end up back in prison for the rest of his life. His participation is voluntary and no quid pro quo. He was fine with that."

Cooper said he understood. "The whole case doesn't sit right with me. These girls have been missing for nearly three decades. I think we are safe in saying they are deceased. That means someone killed them and got away with it. I don't like cases involving children, and the last thing I want to do is suggest Randy is innocent unless we can prove that. I needed to know what I thought of him before you and Riley got involved and impacted how I felt. I needed to read the situation clean before I started."

"And?" I asked, understanding why Cooper went to see him. I might have done the same thing in his shoes. I hadn't thought as deeply about the case as Cooper had. Cases come and go. I try hard not to invest too much emotional life into them. Between the two of us, Cooper was far more emotional – not that I'd ever tell him that.

"I think he's innocent," Cooper explained, pausing to see if they had any reaction. When they didn't, he went on. "He said he wouldn't do to someone what they did to him. It told me he believes he was set up. And I think he was. He will not do that to someone else. He was clear with me that the only information he'd share is what he knows as fact."

I wouldn't have expected anything else. "I can understand if Randy is innocent that he wouldn't want to point the finger at someone else without any evidence. Did you ask him if he suspected someone?"

"I did and he doesn't. He said there are threats against him. That's why he was moved from the state prison to the county jail."

"Threats?" Cat asked, interrupting him.

Before Cooper could respond, I asked, "Why would they move him? Prisoners get threats all the time, Cooper." It was something we had witnessed before. Never had I known a prisoner to be moved. There had to have been more to the story than that. "Who sent the threats? The families? Someone inside?"

Before Cooper could respond, Cat said, "He's been a model prisoner. I spoke to the warden at the state prison before taking on this case. I wanted to get a better understanding of what Randy has been doing all these years. Was he violent in prison? Was he a model prisoner? I needed to know before I started. By all accounts, he was quiet and engaged. He finished a degree, and he's been teaching and working. Almost no behavior problems other than when he first arrived and was attacked by other prisoners. He fought back. But nothing in years. Who'd threaten him?"

We were staring at Cooper as if he had all the answers.

"Well?" I nudged when Cooper didn't respond.

"I don't know," he admitted. "Randy didn't know. He asked me if I knew what they did to child predators in prison. He said he's being protected in county. Someone has his back."

Nothing about that made any sense to me. By the looks on Cooper's and Cat's faces, they thought the same. I directed my attention to Cat. "Can you call the warden and find out?"

She shook her head. "He barely wanted to speak to me the first time. It took him nearly a month to call me back. I don't think it will do any good."

Luke didn't have much to do with the prisons. I didn't have any contacts at either the big state prison where Randy had been held or the county jail. There was no point focusing on that if we were never going to know. "I guess if we are meant to know the threat, we'll find out. It's good they are willing to keep him safe."

Cooper wasn't going to let it go that easily. "I want to know in exchange for what, though? The why has been bothering me the whole ride here. You know prisons don't do that. There had to be a reason." When I didn't bite and Cat didn't have anything to offer, Cooper shrugged it off.

"Who gave his name to the cops? I don't remember seeing that in the file."

Cat got up and returned with the file. She dropped it on the table with a slap and flipped it open. "It wasn't in the file I gave you. I just found the information in an old news article. Other than the shop owner who had seen Randy there, the detective said a man by the name of Brad Hogan came forward. He was parked down the road from the convenience store. He saw the exchange between Randy and the girls. He told police that Randy stood outside and watched the girls. When they rode off, he went to his truck and headed in the same direction."

"Randy went inside the store after he saw the girls," Cooper countered. "He told me that he went inside, bought the few items he was there for and left. The shop owner confirmed that. He specifically said the girls weren't outside when he came back out. Does the newspaper story indicate Randy never went into the store?"

Cat lowered her eyes back to the article. "That's exactly what it says." She flipped through several pages. "As we know, the shop owner gave a formal statement that said he sold Randy a bag of chips, a mini ham and cheese sub, a bottle of Coke, and a lottery ticket. He said Randy was in the store for about ten minutes, give or take."

"That's a direct conflict," I said, stating the obvious. I couldn't recall if Randy's defense attorney had brought that out during the trial. "I'm more inclined to believe the shop owner. He'd have no reason to lie and say Randy was in the shop when he wasn't."

Cooper agreed with that. "It would be such a weird thing to lie about. It doesn't exonerate Randy and doesn't make him guilty either. It's almost inconsequential other than to impeach this other witness's testimony. Why don't we have a statement in the file from Brad Hogan?"

Cat couldn't answer that. "It wasn't in the police file. He didn't testify at the trial either. It's like the cops took the tip and didn't do anything else with it other than use it to go after Randy."

She left the table and came back with another stack of papers, this one bound with a black coil. We watched as she flipped page after page, read from it and then went back to flipping pages. She read some more, then jabbed her index finger down on it. "Neither the prosecutor nor the defense called Brad Hogan. He's never brought up again, but this article clearly states his name and what he said he told the police. The article doesn't provide a quote from Brad, but the detective mentioned him. Why would Brad lie to the police, and why wouldn't the cops use the statement?"

"The cops must have found something about him not helpful or credible," Cooper offered.

"Maybe to deflect from his guilt," I said. "Brad was there too when the girls came out of the store. What was he doing down the road from the store?"

"An appraisal," Cat responded, reading the information from the article. "He's a real estate appraiser and was about to start his next job."

"Was any of that confirmed by the cops or did they just take his word for it?"

"No. Nothing was confirmed." Cat glanced over at Cooper. "Do you think that's what Randy was hinting at – that he wasn't going to railroad someone else the way Brad did to him?"

"I think that's exactly what he meant."

"We are going to have to find Brad and interview him," I responded, only half paying attention. I had received a couple of texts during our conversation that I had ignored. The most recent text that lit up my phone caught my attention. I reached for my phone and went directly to the text.

"What's wrong, Riley?" Cooper asked.

It took me a moment to scroll through the past texts to make sense of what I was reading. My heart dropped at seeing the words. I raised my head to Cooper, my mouth slightly agape, trying to find the will to speak aloud what I just read. "Two girls are missing in Hillcrest. My friend, Emma, just texted me. She said it's all over the news. Luke just dodged the media and wouldn't give a statement, only that they were in the initial investigation and they had no answers."

Cooper rushed to his feet. "We should head up there and see if we can help search."

Cat and I agreed. As we were getting ready to leave, Cat said softly, "Randy is still in prison. He can't be blamed for this one."

It hadn't even crossed my mind, but Cat was right. If he was out, all eyes would have been on him.

CHAPTER 5

Luke found Christopher Evans hunched over his desk in his office in downtown Little Rock, not far from the courthouse and the police station. Luke had made it past the administrative assistant at the front desk, sidestepped two of the other attorneys in the office who wanted to know why Luke was there, and made his way to Christopher's office undeterred.

He hit his knuckles against the doorjamb. "Christopher Evans," Luke said with a tone of authority. The man raised his head, his eyebrows shooting up. Luke introduced himself and entered the room without being asked. "I'm here about your daughter, Scarlett."

"What about her?" he asked with a dismissive tone. "She's too young to get into police trouble, so what's her pathetic excuse for a mother accusing me of now?"

Luke zeroed in on the man, offended on behalf of Amelia, who said she had already texted him asking if Scarlett was with him. She hadn't received a message back. Luke didn't mince words. "Your daughter is missing, Christopher. Amelia was hoping that she was with you."

"Missing? I don't understand what you mean by *missing*." There was no trace of concern in his tone.

Luke explained the situation, watching him carefully for any change in demeanor or response. The man remained a blank wall. Luke took a few steps toward his desk. "Do you understand what I'm telling you?

Your daughter left school with a friend and never made it back home. Have you heard from her today?"

"No," Christopher said with a dismissive wave of his hand around the mess of papers on his desk. "I have a trial upcoming and I'm deep into it. I saw Scarlett this past weekend."

Luke couldn't imagine not seeing his child every day. "Tell me what's happening here, Christopher. I told you that your daughter is missing. There's a whole city of people out there looking for her and you don't seem concerned at all."

Christopher sat back. "You'll have to forgive me because I don't believe Scarlett is missing. This is another ploy of Amelia's to make me somehow look like a bad father. She knows I have this trial coming up, and she's working to derail me. This is all a game for her."

"I assure you this isn't a game. Amelia is at the school right now. Your daughter is missing with another girl. Their photos are all over the news already. Have you been here all day?"

"All day since I got in at seven this morning. I have barely left my desk."

Luke gestured toward the man's cellphone. "Look for yourself. Scarlett and her friend walked home from school and never made it to the other girl's home. The mother notified the school right away and went in search. They called the police immediately. They notified Amelia at work and she went right to the school. Amelia said she texted you. I am coming from speaking to her. We were hoping that you'd had some contact with your daughter. That you might know something."

Christopher sat there in silence for several beats. He didn't reach for the phone or do anything to confirm what Luke had told him. "She's really missing?"

"I'm sorry to tell you, but yes, your daughter is missing. We have no idea where she might have gone. It's why I'm here asking you."

Luke couldn't get a read on him. "When was the last time you spoke to Scarlett?"

"Last night before bed. She called me through the video chat she has on her iPad. We set that up for her so she could reach me whenever she wanted, and she can reach her mom when she's with me."

"Are there any parental controls on the app? Could someone else videochat with her?"

"Like her friends at school?"

"That or anyone. You know some of these apps can attract the wrong kind of people looking to interact with kids."

Christopher pinched the bridge of his nose. "Are you insinuating I set my daughter up to be taken by a predator?"

Luke could see why it was so hard for Amelia to deal with him. "I didn't suggest any blame. The apps aren't the most straightforward. Kids are on them to talk to their parents and friends, but predators slip in pretending to be kids. It's not about blame. It's about finding Scarlett."

Christopher's back straightened and his face grew red. "I think I'd know if my kid was being groomed by a predator. I don't like the accusation. I think you should leave."

Luke stepped back. "I didn't accuse you of anything. I can't force you to talk to me, but if you know where your daughter might be, I need to know."

"I don't know where she is. If she's missing, that's on Amelia." Christopher stood, shoving his hands in his pockets. "I appreciate you coming to tell me how my ex-wife has failed. It will be helpful in my petition for full custody."

"Are you kidding me?" Luke didn't know what was wrong with this guy. "Your daughter is missing from school. Amelia was at work just like you're at work. She came to the school immediately. This isn't about blame."

"She blamed me. That's why you're here."

Luke couldn't disagree with that, so he sidestepped it. "It's procedure to speak to the parents of the missing child. For all I knew, Scarlett had contacted you and you picked her up."

Christopher stared at him without saying a word.

"Look, file your petition or whatever. You can't get custody over a dead kid." It was a cruel and heartless remark, one Luke hoped wasn't foretelling of the future. "When you get your head out of your backside and you care that your daughter is missing, give me a call." Luke tossed a business card down on the desk and left without looking back.

He stopped at the front desk long enough to show the administrative assistant a photo of Scarlett. "Christopher's daughter is missing. Have you seen her here today?"

The young woman shook her head.

"Has Christopher been here all day?"

She shifted her eyes to the right as if watching for someone to come from the hallway. She chewed on her bottom lip.

"It's a crime to lie to law enforcement. A little girl is missing. If you know something, I suggest you tell me."

"I don't know anything about Scarlett," she said quietly. "Christopher left about eleven and came back around twelve-thirty, angry and frustrated. When I asked him what was wrong, he said nothing was going right today."

"Court?"

"No. He didn't have any court or meetings today. He was supposed to spend the whole day prepping for an upcoming trial. One of the other partners was even looking for him and was annoyed he wasn't in the office. He couldn't be reached by cellphone either during that time."

The man had told Luke he'd been at his desk all day. It was also right in the window that Scarlett went missing. "Do you have any idea where he went during this time?"

"No."

There was something about the way she said it that sparked Luke's interest. "Have there been other times when Christopher has left the office without telling anyone where he's going? Times he's been unreachable?"

She looked to the side again to make sure no one was coming. When she focused back on Luke, she nodded slightly. "It's been an ongoing situation."

"For how long?"

"The last six months." Voices down the hall made her sit straight in the chair. "I can't say anything else."

Luke understood but left his business card in case she wanted to talk further. He encouraged her to call him anytime. Then he left. There would be no point in speaking to the other lawyers while Christopher was still in the office. He'd check their website and call them separately. If Christopher had a track record of going missing during this time of day, it might not have anything to do with Scarlett at all. Yet, he had lied to Luke about it.

Luke got down to the street and called Granger. The phone rang and rang, then went to voicemail. He hung up without leaving a message. Luke could go back to the school but didn't see any point. Since seeing Amelia, he'd been working on the assumption that Scarlett was the target. For all he knew it had been the other little girl, Jenna Herin. That's where the girls were headed after school. To the Herin house. Jenna's mother Gail had been the one to call it into the school and the police station. Even if they had left the school distraught, Luke still needed to speak to them.

Luke headed back up to Hillcrest and arrived at the Herin house as a throng of media were camped out in front. As soon as Luke was out of his SUV, all eyes were on him. Reporters shouted questions as he shielded his eyes from the flashes and made his way up the driveway.

He knocked once on the door. "It's Det. Luke Morgan," he shouted above the din of reporters. He was hoping that someone in the Herin family would hear him and open the door. Luke understood why they'd be avoiding the media spotlight. He waited before he knocked again.

A man peeked out of the closed living room blind and Luke flashed his badge.

A moment later, Scott Herin introduced himself to Luke as he ducked his head low as the cameras focused on him from the street. "I'm trying to stay out of the media until we can make a formal statement," he said as he stepped aside to let Luke enter. "I don't know anything, so what's the point of saying anything to those vultures. They have a photo of the girls and know they are missing. I'm not sure what more they need from me right now."

Luke moved past the small foyer into the living room. A wicker basket of children's toys lay on its side. A throw blanket and pillow took up one end of the couch. It was a room lived in. "Is your wife here?"

Scott gestured toward the ceiling. "She's up there with the two other kids. We have three, our daughter Jenna and then four-year old twin boys. The rest of our family, our siblings, are out searching. When we left the school, they told us to stay here. Is there news?"

Luke shook his head. "I'm sorry. I haven't heard anything. I have spoken to the Evanses. Amelia at the school and Christopher just now at his office. Neither of them has heard from the girls. What can you tell me?"

Scott raked a hand through his thick blond hair. The way that it stuck up in the front made Luke wonder if it was a gesture that he'd been doing for the majority of the day. A gesture of frustration or fear, maybe. "I don't know anything. I'm a communications director at St. Vincent's Hospital. I've been in meetings for most of the day. Gail called me when the girls didn't come home from school. She wondered if she had gotten the days mixed up and the half day was tomorrow. I don't know why she called me. Panic, maybe. I told her to call the school. I didn't think anything at first. Then she called me back in a real panic after she'd been told the girls had left the school about forty minutes prior. It only takes about ten minutes to walk the few blocks, and that's if they are chatting with their friends. I rushed up here as soon as I could. I told her to call 911. I met her at the school, but Gail couldn't take it. She broke down and we came back here."

Luke was glad that at least one of the fathers was on top of it. "Were you at your office all day?"

"All day. I arrived about eight this morning and went from one meeting to the next. Gail was lucky she caught me. Otherwise, she'd have had to leave me a message." Scott offered up the names of co-workers if Luke wanted to check with them. "I know you have to clear the family in cases like this. Whatever you need, my wife and I will provide it."

Luke took the information and would follow up with a call when he was done. Just because he might trust what the man was saying didn't mean he wasn't going to do his job. "Have there been any threats against you or your daughter?"

"No," he responded with a sharp shake of his head. "We don't live the kind of life that anyone would threaten us. We are simple people. My wife has her hands full with the twins. Then Jenna is involved in all sorts of activities. Det. Morgan, our lives are focused on our children. I'm home for dinner every night. I tuck the kids into bed with my wife. Weekends are spent running errands, doing chores around the house, and spending time with the kids. It's a satisfying but uneventful life. I can't imagine anyone targeting us and certainly not Jenna."

That's what Luke had assumed. He asked a few more questions that didn't give any information that could help the search. When he was done, Scott looked toward the door. "I want to be out there searching with everyone. Do you think I can do that?"

Luke looked over at the door with him. "The media is camped out there. I suggest you prepare something to say – a call to action to rally the community to help you find the girls and show a photo of Jenna." Luke looked back at him. Scott would be a real asset with the media. He'd never suggest this to Christopher Evans, who'd come across angry and insincere. Scott, though, was a concerned father who had a career in communications. "Humanize the girls. I'm not saying someone has taken them. But right now, we have to assume the worst. Plead with that person to let them go. Arrange a meeting spot. Do whatever you can do to get through to them. Do you understand?"

"I do," Scott said, chewing on his lower lip.

"I need to speak with Gail," Luke said.

Scott's eyes shifted toward the stairs. "No problem," he said, his tone tight. "I hope that she can speak to you. My wife..." He trailed off, running a hand down his face. "She's troubled. She had a rough childhood. It's complicated." He swallowed hard and started to say more but stopped himself.

It was the first crack in his demeanor that Luke noticed.

CHAPTER 6

I arrived at the school just as Luke was walking down the block towards us. Cooper was as surprised to see him as I was. I wouldn't have thought a homicide detective would have been called in unless there had been a development. My stomach dropped, hoping that there hadn't been.

I didn't know how we could help. But I assumed the more people searching for them, the better.

When Luke saw us, he gestured toward the police line that had been set up as a perimeter around the school. It was clear they weren't there to keep parents and volunteers out but to keep the media at bay.

We reached the barrier and waited for Luke to catch up to us.

"Why are you here, Luke? It's a missing person."

He glanced down at me. "Orders," was all he said before getting us through the barrier.

He walked ahead of us toward the school door. As he pulled it open for me, Luke said, "There's not much I can tell you. Two girls – Jenna Herin and Scarlett Evans – went missing as school let out earlier today. They were supposed to have walked to the Herin house, but the girls never arrived. Gail called her husband to make sure she had the right date for the half-day, then called the school. She took her twins and went outside and called for them. She searched the streets. By then, the girls should have been home. Gail called 911."

Cooper followed Luke. "Have you spoken to the parents?"

Luke stopped in the middle of the school's lobby. "Scarlett is the daughter of Amelia and Christopher Evans. They are in the middle of a nasty divorce. Amelia suggested that Christopher might be the one responsible because he had threatened to take their daughter away from her. I met with him and he's a real piece of work. He struck me as someone who didn't care too much about his child at all, other than how he could use the kid as a pawn to get back at her mother."

"That's motivation for kidnapping," I offered.

Luke didn't disagree. "The admin at the law office said that he's been leaving the office in the middle of the day without telling anyone where he's been going. Christopher left during the time the girls went missing. I didn't bother to go back to his office to interview him about that because I want to know more first before I bring him in for a formal interview, which I'm going to need to do if these girls aren't found soon."

I understood now why Luke looked so pained. "What about the other parents? Did you speak to them?"

"That's where I'm coming from now," Luke explained, turning back to look at the school door. He took a step toward us, closing the distance. He dropped his voice. "I met Scott, the father, first. He was a breath of fresh air compared to meeting with Christopher, who didn't even seem to be taking it seriously. Scott gave me the information I needed, asked how he could best help find his daughter, and his alibi checked out. I called after I got done with them. The thing is, when I asked to speak with Gail, he told me she was troubled. I got the impression he didn't want me to speak to her."

A few things jumped to mind. "Controlling? Domestic violence?"

Luke shook his head. "While I can't rule it out, I don't think so. I spoke to Gail and she was a mess. She could barely keep it together, which is what you expect from a mother whose child is missing. It was more than that, though. She kept saying over and over again that she knew this was going to happen. That her family was cursed. She had the twins with her, so I couldn't get into it. But she didn't have any information that was helpful about her daughter or Scarlett."

"What did she mean that the family is cursed?" I asked, thinking it was an odd thing to say.

Luke rubbed his hand over his head, leaning down to speak directly to me. "Gail's maiden name is Albright. She's Samantha Albright's older sister."

I sucked in a sharp breath as Cooper muttered in disbelief. "It can't be. Did you confirm it?"

"I did," Luke said. "It took me a few minutes to understand what she was saying about her family being cursed. After Gail explained, she kept saying that she knew Randy Stock had taken her child. She said she was sure of it. I explained Randy is still in prison and there was no way it was him. She doesn't believe it. Gail is sure that he got out early or had someone take the girls for him. She's convinced and has been for a long time that once released, he'd be coming after her."

"Why?" Cooper asked, the same look of confusion on his face as mine.

"Gail said right after the girls went missing, someone called the house and was breathing heavily. Later, the calls were more taunting. A man would taunt her about her missing sister. It was the same voice, deep and gravelly, who said he was coming for Gail next. That they'd never find her, just like no one ever found her sister."

I didn't believe it. "Those calls couldn't have been coming from Randy. He was in prison this whole time. He never even got bail. If he were making those calls, someone at the prison would have known. Calls are monitored. You know that, Luke."

Before Luke could respond, Cooper said, "Randy was still in jail when those girls went missing this morning. It was right about the time I was with him at county jail."

"County?" Luke asked sharply. "Why was he at county? He was in state prison last I knew."

Cooper explained about the threats being made against him. "They moved him to county before his release. I've never heard of anything like that happening, no matter the threat."

"No," Luke said, shaking his head furiously. "There's something not right about any of this. There is no way they'd move him because of a threat. That's not what they do, no matter who it is. That can't be what's going on."

Cooper shrugged. "I don't know what to tell you. Randy Stock is sitting in the Pulaski County Regional Detention Facility on West Roosevelt Road. I met with him this morning. He was moved a couple of days ago in anticipation of his release. When I asked why he was moved, Randy said he was told there had been threats made against him and he was moved. He didn't know any more than that. You can call the state prison and see if you can get some answers. I can assure you, Randy didn't take those girls, no matter what's happening within the prison system."

Luke expelled a frustrated breath. "None of that makes a lick of sense."

I touched my husband's arm. "Does it matter right now what's happening with Randy? We know he didn't take the girls, and we also know he couldn't have been the one harassing Gail's family all those years. He wouldn't have been able to make those calls from prison. We know Randy couldn't have taken the girls today or been harassing Gail, so then it's likely Randy didn't kidnap and murder those girls all those years ago."

Luke didn't agree. "That's a leap, Riley. We can't say that for sure."

I changed the subject. "Did you call for dogs to trace the girls' scent?"

"Granger did. They are on the way. We have whole units out

searching. As you know, I've already covered the media and the girls' photos have been on the school's website and plastered all over social media channels. I'm not sure what else we can be doing right now."

"Why are you back at the school?"

"I need to follow up with the principal to see if there were any threats made. I didn't get to speak to her earlier. I was too consumed with the parents."

"What can we do, Luke?" Cooper asked. "Let us be of help. Maybe we can call the parents of the other kids in their class. See if they went to their houses or the kids might know where they went."

"Teachers are already doing that."

Cooper offered a few more suggestions that Luke shot down.

I had one but I wasn't sure he'd go for it. "What do you think about us interviewing Gail? She knows about the podcast. She told Cat she was going to participate."

Luke considered for a moment. "Don't interview her with Cat present. Not given this situation. Interviewing her about her sister is one thing. With her daughter missing, it's a whole different ballgame. She's convinced Randy Stock took her daughter, which we know isn't possible. You might be able to get through to her – at least talk some sense into her."

Luke turned his attention from me to Cooper. "You can assure her that you spoke to Randy this morning and that there is no way he took her daughter. I don't want anything attached to this current case to be on the podcast. I need Cat as far from this as possible. Can you both assure me of that?"

Cooper and I shared a look. Cat was not easily controlled.

"We'll do our best," Cooper said, assuring him as much as possible. "We will go to Gail's now. Cat is in her studio doing research. She didn't want to get involved in this, which is why she isn't here. We were in her studio when we got the news about the girls."

"Good. Keep her out of it." Luke said goodbye but called to us as we walked off, "I'm giving you leeway, but the leash is short."

"What's with him?" Cooper asked me when we were out of earshot.

"He's stressed about the case." I knew that wasn't all that was wrong with him. He had been worried about us digging into the old kidnapping case. He also didn't fully trust Cat, which is not something I wanted to remind Cooper.

Cat had been involved in other cases with law enforcement. Luke had grown to tolerate her and the podcast. He'd even been grateful for it at times. Liking Cat personally didn't expand Luke's trust, which he gave to few people. Cat was Cooper's friend. They had formed a bond early on. I had gotten to know Cat and liked her. I trusted her too. I also understood where Luke was coming from.

As we walked the short distance to Gail's house, it struck me how little time there was for something to have happened to the girls. There was no sign of the girls as we approached the home.

Cooper looked at his watch before we went up the walkway. "That took us less than five minutes and we weren't even walking that fast."

The area was known to be safe. The tree-lined neighborhood was a mix of older homes with quirky design details. They would have walked on sidewalks on narrow suburban streets. Craftsman homes in blues, yellows, and whites dotted the path. Each had its square patch of grass, some with trees in the front yard. A few had fences marking off their property line. Other than the police and the media in the neighborhood, it was quiet.

I had looked for a house in Hillcrest years ago when I was first searching. Had I not found the house in Heights, this would have been my second choice. It had a real neighborhood feel and not one that induced fear or concern about girls walking the few blocks after school.

We made our way up the walkway, dodging the media that had

camped out on the curb. A few reporters who knew us shouted questions, which we ignored. Given our presence, they'd wonder if the family had lost confidence in the police already and called in private investigators. Luke didn't seem bothered by that speculation, so I pushed it from my mind.

As Cooper knocked, someone moved the blinds to the side and looked out the window. Cooper flashed his private investigation badge. "I hope he doesn't think we are media."

The man gave a curt nod and pulled open the front door. "Det. Morgan texted me that he was sending someone down. He didn't explain how you could help."

I introduced us and explained my connection with Luke. "We are investigating the previous disappearance of Samantha Albright, Kathleen Elliott, and Violet Yeaton. When Luke told me that Gail is Samantha Albright's sister, we thought we should speak to you both."

Scott shook his head. "My wife is in no condition for that. She was utterly traumatized by her sister's disappearance. Now with our daughter…" His voice broke and he sucked in a breath. "I have to protect her. She's not well."

"That's why we are here," Cooper said evenly. "I was with Randy Stock this morning at the jail. There's no way he could be involved with your daughter's disappearance. When Luke told us that someone had been harassing your wife on the phone, we knew it couldn't have been Randy. Calls at the prisons are monitored."

Scott stepped back as his hand went to his face, nearly covering his mouth. "I didn't even consider that. What do you think that means?"

When Cooper hesitated, I spoke up. "It means that we aren't sure that Randy Stock is guilty of taking those girls all those decades ago. It means that the person responsible has been out in the community harassing Gail and now with your daughter missing, she might be the key to all of this. We need to speak to her to find out more."

"It's all to find your daughter," Cooper added. "At least let us find out what Gail might know. Even the smallest detail could send us in the right direction."

Scott didn't respond with words. He stepped back and allowed us into the home.

CHAPTER 7

After Scott directed us to the living room, he went upstairs to take care of the twins and sent Gail down to us. She sat on the edge of the couch, her eyes blistering red from crying. Her face was dry, but it had the ruddy complexion of a woman who had cried off all her makeup hours ago.

Gail sat with her hands around a worn gray stuffed rabbit that had seen better days. One of its eyes was missing and a cross stitch of yellow had sewn the eye shut. "This is Jenna's. She has slept with it every night since she was two years old. She called him Wabby. That's how she said rabbit when she was little." Gail sniffed back tears. "I don't know what more I can tell you. I told Det. Morgan everything I know."

"We're here because we have some information," Cooper started, but before he could get much further, Gail asked if it was about her daughter. "Not directly, no. I know that you think Randy Stock is involved with what's happening with your daughter. I was at the jail this morning, meeting with him when Jenna and her friend went missing. He wasn't involved, Gail. There's no way he could have. I was there with him the whole time."

"Then he has someone helping him," Gail said with conviction. "I know he took my sister and now he's taken my daughter."

Cooper looked to me to see if I could say it better than him. I shook my head and gestured for him to continue. I wasn't the one who had sat face-to-face with Randy. I didn't have much to offer. Cooper turned his attention back to her. "I don't think Randy Stock had anything to do with this. I'm not even sure that he's the one who took your sister."

"Then you're an idiot," she said sharply, nearly spitting out the words. "That man has tormented me since I was a little girl. Do you know he called the house the day Samantha went missing and taunted me that I'd be next? He hasn't stopped calling."

I asked, "What did he say on that first call? Be as specific as you can be."

Gail raised her eyes to me. But she didn't utter a word.

I sat down on the couch next to her, studying Gail as she twisted the stuffed rabbit in her trembling fingers. The late afternoon sun slanted through dusty venetian blinds, casting prison-bar shadows across her face. I wanted to reach out and hug her, but I knew I had to keep a professional distance. There was a huge divide between what we knew to be true and Gail's reality.

"Please," I said, my voice filled with urgency. "We want to find Jenna and we need your help to do that. What did the man say when he called you the day your sister went missing?"

She turned her head to look at me. "Say her name. No one ever says her name."

"Samantha. What did the man say the day Samantha went missing?"

I studied Gail as she twisted the rabbit's ear between trembling fingers. "I came home alone after school. I'm older than Samantha and I got out later that day for some reason. I can't recall why now. My mother wasn't home and I had assumed my father was at work. I think they already knew the girls were missing and were talking to the police. They didn't tell me right away. The phone rang, and when I answered…" She squeezed her eyes shut. "He was breathing, this horrible wet sound. Then he whispered, 'Such pretty girls, the

Albright sisters.'"

My stomach clenched. Cooper pulled out the notebook he always carried. His pen scratched across the page.

"Did you tell the police?" I asked.

"Of course I did!" Gail whirled to face me. "It was the next day when the nice detective came that I told him. My parents were angry that I didn't say something sooner. I tried. I swear to you I tried, but everyone was so concerned with Samantha, no one was listening to me."

"I'm sure you did." I couldn't imagine the chaos of that day. It didn't surprise me that Gail got lost in the shuffle. "What did the detective say when you finally spoke to him?"

"By then, they were already looking at Randy Stock. They told me they knew who was doing it and they were going to arrest him and make sure he didn't hurt me or any other little girls."

It was interesting to me that the detective had decided that early on it was Randy. They never even looked for an alternative suspect. "Did you have any audio of his voice saved at that point?"

Gail shook her head. "He had only called once and I answered. There was no audio then."

"Once Randy was arrested, did the detective bring you in so you could compare the voices?"

Gail squinted at me in confusion. "No. That never came up. My parents wouldn't let me go to the trial. I heard him on the news and he didn't sound like the man who called, but people can disguise their voice."

Cooper stopped her. "You said there was no audio then. Did that come later?"

Gail nodded. "As I said, he never stopped calling me. Not even after he was arrested. Not even when he was convicted and sent away to prison. The calls just never stopped."

"How often did he call?" Cooper's pen stilled.

"Often. Sometimes a few in a week. Other times, months might go by. Always that breathing." Gail's hands fluttered to her throat. "It didn't matter where I was or what phone number I had, he always found me. When I got my first cellphone in college. The day I got married. The morning after Jenna was born." Her voice broke. "Last week. The number is blocked."

"That's impossible," Cooper cut in. "Randy has no phone access like that. He certainly can't be calling you from a blocked number. A call from the prison is announced on your end. He can't just call you without you knowing it's coming from the prison."

"Then how does the caller know so much?" Gail demanded. "How did he know I moved here to this house? How did he know Jenna's name?" She snatched her cellphone from the coffee table, jabbing at the screen with shaking fingers. "Listen!"

The speakerphone crackled. Heavy breathing filled the room, followed by a wet chuckle that raised the hair on my arms. A gravelly voice whispered, "The Albright girls are so pretty when they sleep. Do you want to go to sleep like your sister? Come on, Gail. I want you to be mine. Your daughter, too. I'm coming to get you." Then the line went dead. Silence.

Cooper was already on his feet, pacing. "When did you say this call came in?"

"Last week on Thursday. I called the police like I do with every call, but they don't do anything. I can't even get a detective on the phone. There isn't one assigned to Samantha's case. It's closed and they don't care anymore." Gail sank back onto the couch. "He's going to kill Jenna just like he did Samantha."

"We don't know Samantha is dead," I said quietly, not even sure why it came out of my mouth. Of course, the child was dead. "They never found..."

"Because he hid her!" Gail's scream made me flinch. "Like he's hiding Jenna now! You have to stop him, please." She dissolved into harsh, wracking sobs.

I moved closer to her, placing a hand on her shoulder while my mind raced. Stock was still locked up tight – Cooper had confirmed it himself. But these calls. Someone knew details they shouldn't. Someone was torturing this woman, playing on her worst fears. Now her daughter was missing, just like her sister.

"We're going to find Jenna," I promised, squeezing her shoulder. "I need you to think carefully. Is there anyone else who might know these details about your life? Anyone who's been following your story all these years? Any threats back then that you or your sister didn't tell the police?"

Gail shook her head violently. "It's Randy Stock. It has to be him." Fresh tears spilled down her cheeks.

Cooper caught my eye, his expression troubled. We both knew the problems with the original investigation. The lack of any evidence. The shady witness statement. The defense's claims of police coercion that the jury had dismissed.

"We'll look into the calls," Cooper said. "I'll take the numbers from you and track the numbers as well as check Randy's visitor logs. There has to be an explanation."

As I watched Gail rock back and forth, clutching the rabbit like a lifeline, a cold certainty settled in my gut. Either Randy had an accomplice or the system had locked up the wrong man, leaving a child killer on the loose to strike again.

As I sat with the realization, Cooper was faster on the jump to get things done. He asked Gail if he could take a recording of the saved message on her phone.

Gail waved him off to do whatever he needed to do. I reached out to put my hand on her back as she continued to cry. She brushed me off, turning to me with red, soaked eyes. "Find Jenna and find out what happened to my sister. I'm not strong enough to take this. I barely survived my childhood. This man has been tormenting me my whole life."

I found myself struggling for the right words to say. Normally, I was good at offering comfort to those who were victims of crime. This time, whether it was the pain that tinged every part of her being or the fact that I was still in shock by what I'd heard, I couldn't do anything more than offer a promise that I didn't know I could keep.

As we left Gail in the living room, Scott met us in front of the door. "She needs to see a doctor," I told him. "She's been through too much. A doctor can prescribe something to keep her calm, get her to sleep a little. Your wife is tormented and it started long before today."

Scott swallowed hard, looking past me into the living room. "I'll call our primary care doctor to see if he can refer us to someone. What should I do in the meantime?"

"Monitor her phone," Cooper suggested. "She probably won't let you take it from her, but she shouldn't have to listen to any more of the man's calls. They are terrible. I don't know how she's been able to tolerate it this long."

"I've tried to block the calls in the past. A few days go by and he calls with a different number. Most of the numbers are blocked, others show up, but there's no voicemail set up on the other end when I call back. They can't be traced to anything. The cops told me they're burner phones. I don't know how to get them to stop."

"We'll do what we can to get to the bottom of this," Cooper assured him. It fell short of the promise I had made but was more realistic about what we could do.

Once out on the sidewalk, we navigated back through the media. I wanted to shout at them to leave the family alone. I kept my head down and mouth closed as we pushed through them, making it a few blocks away before either of us said anything.

Cooper reached his hand out to stop me. "That was insane in there, Riley. There's no way that's Randy calling her unless he has an accomplice."

"That's what I was thinking too." I still couldn't quite put into words what I was feeling. I stood there on the sidewalk, feeling out of my element. I walked into their house thinking one thing and left thinking something entirely different. "I hadn't been too sure of Randy's innocence when we started this. I was willing to see where this case would take us. I don't see how this can be him. You were with him today. There's no way he'd get that kind of phone access in the prison."

Cooper agreed with me. He blew out a frustrated breath. "I need to get the logs to see who has been visiting him. I also need to figure out why he's been moved and who exactly was threatening him."

"Maybe he knows something," I offered, not sure even then why Stock would be moved. There was just something weird with this case all around.

"Like who took the girls?"

"I don't know. How did Cat end up with this case?"

"She didn't tell me. She just asked that we help her with it. She thought there might be something to investigate, given the girls were never found. Let me call her."

As he went for his phone, I stopped him. "We can ask her that later. We should go interview the other girls' families to see if they have been receiving any strange calls. Then we can meet back at Cat's to discuss what we found."

Cooper squinted his eyes in confusion. "You mean the families of Kathleen Elliott and Violet Yeaton. Are they still around?"

"They are," I responded. "Cat had them all scheduled to be interviewed on the podcast. Kathleen's mother is still living. She was an only child. Violet Yeaton's father is still living in the same house in the Heights."

"I'll take the Yeatons," Cooper offered.

"No. You go handle the prison system and figure out who has been visiting Randy. I'll head over to Kathleen's mother's house. We need to know if they believe Randy Stock was the guy and if they have received any calls from him back then or over the years. If someone is harassing all the families, that's far different than just Gail Albright being targeted. If it's only Gail, then maybe he's someone connected to the family."

Cooper cursed softly. "Do we tell Cat about what we are doing or keep her in the dark? You know how Luke doesn't like her involved in current cases."

I didn't want to make that call. I considered it for a few moments. "I think it's okay to tell her what's developed and let her know that Luke doesn't want anything published on the podcast. I'd leave out everything we just learned about Gail. At least until we find out more. We can't stop Gail from telling Cat about the calls."

"Law enforcement doesn't even care about them."

"Maybe they will now that Gail's daughter is missing. Just call me if you find out anything."

CHAPTER 8

L uke ran down every lead they had, not that there were many. He talked to every teacher the girls were in contact with, the school administration, and even the janitor, who knew far more about the kids than some of the administration. Luke followed up with relatives of the girls and neighbors.

He did everything he knew to do. Now he was standing in the front hall of the school, waiting for the dog to arrive. Granger was working with the teams of volunteers who were combing the city. They had every resource available out there to find the girls. The dog hopefully would give them some clarity about direction, or if the girls were taken by car, which was the working assumption. They had even sent alerts to everyone's cellphones that the girls were missing. They didn't have the vehicle information for a standard Amber Alert, but they provided the information they had. Granger said that the alert immediately brought out a swell of volunteers to help them search. The community was coming together to do anything and everything they could to find the children.

Luke had two articles of clothing – a sweater from Jenna's cubby in her classroom and Scarlett's unlaundered T-shirt that Amelia had brought from the house.

Amelia stood with her back straight and her hands clasped in front of her next to Luke, ready to help in any way she could. Luke didn't know if it was the best idea for her to be there, but he had already cleared her alibi. She had been in the courtroom while her daughter went missing. Luke worried more for her mental health. He didn't know how she could separate those emotions between prosecutor and mother. Luke was waiting for her to fall apart at any moment.

"You don't have to do this, Amelia. I got this. You can go home. Maybe join the other searchers?"

Amelia didn't look at him. "I have to be here. This is where I need to be."

Before Luke could try to convince her, Alex Porter and her dog, Bailey, arrived eager to get started. After a short introduction, Luke handed Alex the clothing and let her do her job without interference. Seconds after sniffing, the dog had his nose to the damp pavement and took off in a flash, pulling Alex behind him.

"The scent is strong," she said as she was pulled ahead of Luke and Amelia.

Luke's boots crunched on the dry leaves as he followed the narrow sidewalk. The low hum of distant traffic was the only sound, muffled by the trees that lined the street. He glanced at Amelia, her face pale, eyes wide and focused. Her gaze fixed on the road ahead.

Ahead of them, Alex kept her eyes on the ground, watching Bailey as he sniffed the pavement and shrubs. The dog was relentless, his nose to the earth, every step purposeful, each sniff a clue. But so far, there was nothing to show for their efforts.

"Come on, Bailey," Alex muttered under her breath. The dog paused, then circled a nearby tree before continuing.

Luke exhaled sharply, frustration creeping up his throat. They continued down the street, the houses silent on either side of them. Bailey's ears flicked, his body taut with tension. They reached an intersection. Luke felt the hair on the back of his neck prickle.

"Stop," Alex said suddenly as they watched Bailey's behavior change.

The dog pulled hard on the leash, darting toward a parked car on the corner. When he reached an area near the curb, the dog moved in a circular motion, still sniffing the pavement, then sat.

Luke moved closer, his eyes scanning the car – an old sedan with chipped paint.

"Do you think…?" Amelia began, her voice breaking on the edge of a question she didn't want to ask.

Alex turned to her. "I'm not sure about the car. I suspect it's just the curb. Either way, the girls stopped here, maybe for a significant amount of time." She waited to see if he'd get back up and continue, but Bailey remained firmly planted. Alex gave him a command, and Bailey got to his four paws and then jutted into the road. He headed in one direction, then turned around to face the opposite end of the street. He sat again.

Alex looked back at Luke and Amelia. "Bailey is indicating that direction. I believe by car or otherwise he would have pulled up the road, following their scent."

Amelia's hand flew to her throat as an audible groan escaped her parted lips. "She was taken in a car. How are we ever going to find her?"

Luke put his hand on her back. "We'll find her. At least now we know they were here and what potential direction they went." He knew it meant little. Whatever car the girls were in headed toward Kavanaugh Boulevard, the main road that ran through Hillcrest. Once there, they could have gone in any direction. For all Luke knew, they were already well out of Little Rock. He wasn't going to voice that to Amelia.

Amelia wiped the tears that had started to form. She raised her chin. "They were only a block away from their destination. You can see the Herin house from here."

Luke turned in the direction she was looking. He hadn't walked this specific block from the school to the Herin house. They were one block over from where he'd been. They were so close.

"What are you thinking about, Luke?" Amelia asked him, rightly sensing the shift in his mood.

Luke didn't want to say. He didn't want to give her anymore cause for worry. "I was just thinking about how close the girls were to getting to their destination. Who knew Scarlett was going home with Jenna today?"

Amelia eyed him suspiciously. She was a prosecutor, after all, and knew how all of this worked. She knew crime as well as he did. "Gail Herin knew the girls were coming to her after school. I can only assume she told her husband. Christopher knew because Scarlett told him the other day. She had initially asked him if he could take time off from work to spend with her on her half day of school. He told her he had a big case coming up. She told him that she was going to her friend Jenna's instead."

"Does he know where the Herins live?"

"Luke, do you think Christopher had something to do with this? You said you spoke to him at his office and he didn't know where Scarlett was. I don't think that if he picked them up from school, he'd let this go on for this long. He's cruel, but he's not insane."

Luke didn't know what he thought. "You're probably right. I'm just considering all the options."

Alex gestured back to the beat-up car parked at the curb. "Given Bailey went out into the road and has indicated a direction, I think we can probably rule out this car. I don't want to make that call."

"Let me handle that," Luke said, taking down the plate number. He'd search for the owner but gave it a cursory glance inside to make sure there was nothing apparent from the outside. Right now, he had no reason to suspect the car was involved in anything. He'd follow up on it to make sure. Luke didn't want to do that with Amelia standing on the spot where her daughter had been taken.

Luke turned to Alex. "Do you think there is any other way you and Bailey can help us?"

"Not unless there's another area where we find a scent. He followed the trail to the endpoint. If you have another area where it picks up, call me and I'll be there." Alex walked off back toward the school with Bailey, leaving Luke and Amelia standing at the curb.

"What do you want to do, Amelia?" Luke asked. "I need to go handle a few things and don't want to just leave you standing here."

"I'm fine," she said with a shake of her head. It was clear she wasn't fine. She wasn't going to admit that to Luke or probably anyone else. She still maintained the demeanor of a tough prosecutor who could handle anything. Luke knew she'd crack at some point. It wasn't going to be now.

She had steely determination written on her features. "I want a few minutes here then I'm going to join the search group. I know some of the assistant prosecutors have left the office to help. I should show my face." Amelia turned her head to look directly at Luke. "Do you know if Gail and Scott are home? I'd like to speak to them."

Luke couldn't stop her from going to the home. He cautioned her about going. "Gail is not as together as you are, Amelia. She's highly emotional given her past. I spoke to Scott and briefly to Gail. I don't know that you'll get much from her."

Amelia didn't seem to understand. "What do you mean by her past?"

Luke realized then his mistake. He hadn't told Amelia about Gail's connection to Randy Stock. He wavered on whether he should tell her or not. In the end, Amelia would find out from the media or another source. It was better to be upfront.

"Gail's maiden name is Albright. She was the older sister of Samantha Albright, who was kidnapped by Randy Stock. I'm not sure—"

"I know that case," Amelia said, cutting him off. "Our office was reviewing it not that long ago. I never made the connection."

"Why?" Luke asked, not hiding the surprise in his tone. "It's a closed case. Stock was convicted of kidnapping. I know he's set to get out of prison soon. I know there's a push to look at murder charges for Randy, but there's just not any evidence of that. Is the case at the prosecutor's office closed?"

"It is closed," she admitted, hedging her tone.

"What aren't you saying?" Luke thought back to what Cooper had told him about Stock being in the county prison. "You know he was moved from state to county."

Amelia squinted her eyes. "That doesn't make any sense. We weren't notified of that. Do you know why?"

"Threats." Luke explained his connection to Cooper. "He was at the prison this morning. A friend of Cooper's, Cat O'Conner with *Rock City Killers*, is about to focus the next podcast series on the case. She asked Cooper and my wife for help on the case. It's why he was visiting Stock this morning. As you know, he has maintained his innocence and the girls' bodies have never been found." Luke's back tightened as he said the words. It was the last thing Amelia should be thinking about. Her expression remained neutral though.

"It doesn't make sense that Randy Stock would be moved."

Even though Luke didn't want to belabor the conversation, Amelia still hadn't answered him. "Why were you looking at the case?"

Amelia took a step closer to Luke. She dropped her voice even though no one was around to hear them. "My office is concerned about a lawsuit. I reviewed the case, Luke. I don't understand how we brought a case against him. If a detective brought me that case today, I'd tell them we have no chance. There is no evidence to tie Stock to the case. One witness who briefly saw him interact with the girls. He was where they were last seen. We have no bodies, no physical evidence to tie him to the girls, and no confession." Amelia held her hands palms up. "Nothing, Luke. It's probably one of the worst investigated cases I've seen in my career."

Luke stepped back as if he'd been punched in the gut. Riley had tried to tell him and he'd pushed back, trusting his fellow detective without really knowing the case. He had been toeing the party line in the department. "What does all that mean?"

"It means if he sues us, we are going to settle," Amelia said matter-of-factly. "There is no way we'd win the case. We have no legal standing. When I reached out to the detective, Lyle Tucker, he assured me he had the right guy. When I pressed him why he thought that, Tucker couldn't come up with a cogent argument. He was just sure it was Randy Stock. He called me a fool for even discussing it."

"Did you know about the podcast?"

Amelia shook her head. "Not specifically. I know the families were concerned about Stock's release and that the girls' bodies had never been found. There was talk about hiring a private investigator to continue the investigation. I didn't know about the podcast or that investigators had been hired."

"They haven't been hired," Luke corrected her. "Riley and Cooper have worked on other cases with Cat and are volunteering their time. I don't know exactly what they planned to do or how much they believed in Stock's innocence. My only understanding is that Cat wanted to bring some awareness to the case because the girls had never been found."

"Is he participating?"

"I don't know. I haven't had much of a chance to speak to either of them about it. I certainly didn't know that your office was concerned that the man was wrongly convicted."

They both grew quiet thinking about the meaning of it all.

"Do you think whoever took those girls could have taken my daughter?" Amelia asked the question they both had been contemplating.

"It's what Gail believes. But she is convinced Randy Stock is the one responsible for her sister. I tried to tell her that he is in prison. I even sent Cooper and Riley over there to speak to her. I don't know if they were able to convince her of it."

"Maybe I should go talk to her then," Amelia said as she stared past Luke. "Isn't that your wife?"

Luke turned in time to see Riley coming right for them. She had a fierce determination in her step and more worrisome was the crease across the bridge of her nose that only appeared when she was afraid.

CHAPTER 9

O
f all the people that could have been standing on a corner in Hillcrest, Luke would have been my last guess. I had last seen him heading into the school. I hadn't officially met the woman next to him. She had the posturing of a detective, but I knew all of his colleagues.

"Luke, what are you doing out here? Any news?" I asked the question as I offered my hand to the woman with him and introduced myself. My hand fell limp in hers when she told me who she was. "I'm so sorry about your daughter. Please know there are a lot of us out here working to find her."

Amelia said she appreciated the sentiment. "I know it might seem strange that I'm here. I just don't know what else to do. Luke said you went to speak to Gail."

There was a question in her tone I wasn't sure I could answer. I looked to Luke for permission to share. He encouraged me to go on. I didn't know how to say what I needed to without trashing the police department. Given that I was standing in front of a detective from the same office and an assistant prosecutor, I was on shaky ground.

Amelia rightly picked up my hesitancy. "Just say whatever you have to say."

Not that I relaxed as I found the words. "Gail has been receiving threatening and harassing phone calls from the man who took her sister. They started the night of the kidnapping and have continued. Law enforcement hasn't taken it seriously."

Luke said he didn't understand. "What do you mean continued? When was the last one?"

I explained what Gail had told me about the calls and the recording I had heard. "Gail believes the man has finally come for her daughter. I'd say that's a credible assessment given what's happened."

Amelia sucked in a sharp breath. She opened her mouth to speak. Her only utterance was a low groan. Luke put his hand around her back to comfort her. "Do you believe he is the one who took the girls?"

"I don't know," I responded, even though I was certain it was. I didn't have any evidence to prove it. There was no point causing Amelia any more distress than needed. "The biggest challenge is convincing Gail that it can't possibly be Randy Stock who took her daughter. Cooper assured her he was with Randy this morning at the jail. We don't believe there is any way he could be making these calls all these years undetected."

Luke agreed that any calls coming out of state prison would have been monitored. Even if the correctional officers had missed one or two calls, they hadn't missed the volume I had described. "Is there any way he's working with someone on the outside? Could he have had a partner in this?"

To my surprise, it was Amelia who said she didn't believe so.

I locked my gaze on her. "Do you believe that Randy Stock is innocent?"

Amelia explained to me that her office had been looking into the legal case against Stock. "I know the public statement coming from my office and the police department is that we would like to go after him for murder. Behind the scenes, I was asked to review the arrest and prosecution on the chance he decided to sue us. His case was never overturned on appeal, so I don't know how far the case would get in the court system. But that said, he'd have a good case. Luke and I were just discussing that when you showed up. Have you met with him?"

"No. Cooper met with him this morning. I've reviewed the trial transcript and, like you, couldn't find the evidence even for an arrest. It sounded to me like the detective got tunnel vision and the community wanted a suspect, even if it meant never finding the girls."

Luke held his hand up to stop me. "I don't think Lyle Tucker intentionally went after the wrong man. I'd agree that he might have gotten tunnel vision, especially if he didn't have any other leads to follow." Amelia agreed with that.

I wasn't so sure. There was no point arguing it there with them when I didn't have anything to back up my argument. I focused on what I did know. "Cooper left to find out who might have visited or been speaking with Randy while he was incarcerated. That should rule in or out the potential that he was working with someone. Cooper is also going to follow up with the police department to understand why no one would even take a report that Gail was being harassed. I heard one of the messages. It was sick. The first call she received she told Det. Tucker and she said he wouldn't even listen to her. He just said Randy was being arrested and the calls would stop. They never stopped."

I knew I was making Luke feel like he was under the microscope. It wouldn't have been his department that turned down looking into the harassing calls. Still, I wanted some acknowledgment from him that things hadn't gone as they should have then or now.

Luke did one better. "Let Cooper know I'll take that off his plate. I'll look into it myself. If Gail was being harassed and now her daughter is missing, then it might very well be a lead in this case."

I appreciated his willingness to do that. It would put him in a position of questioning other officers' decisions. "I am headed to speak to the other families of the victims to see if they had been getting any harassing calls or if it was just Gail." I turned to Amelia. "Were you getting any harassing calls at home or work before today?"

Amelia shook her head. "Nothing. I'm starting to think my daughter was in the wrong place at the wrong time."

I assumed that was probably true. "What are you doing out here?"

Luke gestured toward the car parked on the side of the road. "The dog and his handler brought us to this spot. The dog indicated the car and then went into the road. We assume the girls left by car."

I pointed to the broken-down car sitting in front of us, not typical of the neighborhood. "But not this one?"

"We don't know," Luke said, stepping away from us to answer his ringing phone. I took that moment to focus on Amelia. I didn't know how she was holding it together. "How are you doing?"

Amelia wrapped her arms around her middle, hugging herself. "I have to keep busy. I can't just sit at home and wait. I know how these kinds of investigations go. The volunteer searchers are busy looking. We have every law enforcement agency in the state and neighboring states alerted. The girls' photos are already circulating online and in the national news. There's not much more to be done than what's being done. Being here gives me purpose, makes me feel like I'm doing something."

That I did understand. "Do you have family locally?"

"No," she said with a shake of her head. "My family is in Oregon. I moved here for my ex before we got married. I got a job in the prosecutor's office and have been here since. I want him to co-parent, so I wouldn't dream of taking Scarlett away from him. I have friends who know what's going on. They are all out searching." As Luke finished his call and approached, Amelia turned to him. "Any news?"

"Unfortunately, no. That was my partner. He's calling in for some support to organize the volunteers because we have far more than we know what to do with at the moment. A local church in Hillcrest is offering us space to use as a volunteer command center. I should probably head over there after we deal with this car. I asked for a crime scene team to come up here, but we need to find the owner first. I asked Granger to run the tag. He should be texting me back at…"

As if right on time, his phone chimed in his hand. Luke lowered his head to read the message. "The car is registered to Darlene Harris." Luke raised his head and stated the address. It was just down the block from where we were standing.

Luke turned and walked in the direction of the home. I don't think he anticipated that we were both going to follow right behind him because he stopped and turned to us. He looked as if he were going to tell us to wait. His direction was kinder. "Let me see if they are home. Why don't you wait by the car for the crime scene team? You can let them know I'm running down a lead when they show up. They know not to start anything until we have permission. We have no warrant for the car right now."

I knew he was brushing us off for good reason. He didn't want Amelia to lose it at the person's home. I agreed we could do that for him and retreated a few steps. We stood there near the car, trying to make small talk. I asked questions about Scarlett and allowed Amelia to talk as much or as little as she wanted. When she retreated into silence, I did as well. When she started talking again, I listened. That's about all I could do for her.

Luke came back within a few minutes holding some car keys. "The car's battery is dead and the owner permitted us to search it, not that she believes it has anything to do with the girls. She's been home sick for a few days and hasn't driven it since the battery died. I don't think this is going to yield much."

I stepped past Luke off the curb into the road. "Do you have a working theory?"

"No." Luke glanced down at me. "I assume they went out toward Kavanaugh. Going the other way brings them deeper into the neighborhood."

I asked Amelia what I thought was an obvious question. "Would Scarlett get into a car with a stranger?"

"I'd like to say no. Scarlett is a vocal kid. She stands up for herself and can be difficult at times. She's stubborn and opinionated even at her young age. I guess when you have parents who are both attorneys, some of it will rub off."

"You'd say then she either went willingly with someone she knew or it would take some force." I watched Amelia's face contort at the thought of someone harming her daughter. I couldn't feel bad for asking the question. It was pertinent information.

"She wouldn't go willingly. She knows better than that. We've even practiced responses at home if a stranger tries to approach her." Amelia grew quiet for a moment, letting whatever she was considering settle into her. "The only way I could see her going was if her friend was going and she wanted to protect her. She'd try to talk her out of it but would go so her friend wouldn't go alone." Amelia looked down the road. "They were so close to getting to the house. I don't understand why they'd willingly go with anyone."

I had several questions that I'm sure Luke was working through on his own. They weren't the kinds of questions that I could ask in front of a victim's mother. I wanted to know registered sex offenders in the area, if he canvassed to see if anyone heard the girls yell out. He had only just found this spot, so I was sure he hadn't done any of that yet.

There was one question I could ask. "Luke, you said you assume that if they were taken by car that they'd headed toward Kavanaugh Boulevard. The restaurant at the end of this road has surveillance cameras. It's been burglarized a few times, and the owner set up cameras recently. One of them faces the street. It might have picked up something."

"How do you know they installed them?"

"One night I went in there to pick us up dinner, and he was talking about them. He said the security company cut him a good deal. It's worth a shot." Luke wasn't hesitating about going to get them, he just seemed surprised he hadn't known. What was clear was that he didn't want to take us with him. I could tell that he was starting to feel the weight of having Amelia with him. It would hamper his ability to freely interview people if he had to be careful about the words he used.

If Luke couldn't say it, then I would. I turned to Amelia. "I know you want to do everything you can to find the girls. Do you think you want to come with me to the volunteer center and help organize a few things? I need to go interview those other parents, but I have some time. It sounds like they need some good organizational skills in there. It will make the search more effective."

Whether Amelia got the hint or if she was just tired of being brushed off by Luke, she readily agreed. "I can probably do some good there. Luke, will you call me as soon as you find anything?"

Luke promised her that she'd be his first call. "If you're not for coordinating everything, we can find someone else, Amelia."

She shook her head. "No. I can't sit still. This would be good for me. It will keep me active. Is there a tip phone bank being set up? My office has resources for that, too."

"Let me text my partner, Granger. He can walk you through everything that's been done and not been done so far. He can help you with whatever you need." Luke sent off a text and gave Amelia Granger's phone number in case she needed it. "He said he can meet you there in about thirty minutes."

Amelia turned to me and thanked me. "You don't need to walk me over there. You have enough to do. I appreciate the suggestion." She leaned in, wrapping her arms around me in a warm embrace. I wasn't expecting the sign of affection. I assumed she needed the hug.

As she walked off, Luke waited until she was out of earshot. "That was smart thinking on your part. I'll go look at the surveillance footage after the CSI team arrives."

"You lied when you came back from meeting with Darlene. What is it?"

Luke nodded slowly. "I lied about the battery being dead. Darlene didn't know that her car was back. Her brother, Erik, has had the car. She hasn't seen him but he's unreliable. He's known to go off on a drunken bender, and when he does, he gets violent."

My heart thumped in my chest. "Does he live around here?"

Luke shook his head. "It's not far from here. This is still too close to the school. He's a few blocks away. I have his address and need to go there first. I already texted another detective who was headed there immediately. I was trying to figure out a way to leave Amelia here."

I understood now the panic I had seen on Luke's face. "Go," I said, putting my hand on his arm. "I'll check on Amelia for you later today after I check in with the other parents."

He leaned in to kiss me, then he was gone, running to chase down leads.

CHAPTER 10

For the second time that day, Cooper sat across the table from Randy Stock. The man didn't hide the surprise on his face that Cooper was back again. Cooper had placed a call to the jail to inform them he was coming back to see Randy. Once at the jail, he had asked for a meeting with the warden. He was told that it would be at least an hour before the meeting could take place. Cooper assured them he'd wait for however long it'd take.

Knowing he'd have a much tougher time getting information from the state prison, he had called Adele to see if she had any connections. She had a handful of resources that might prove useful. She wasn't sure, but she'd try.

"I'm surprised to see you back again," Randy said, his expression uncertain.

"I have to ask you something and I need you to be honest with me. Two more girls are missing."

Confusion fell over him. "What do you mean missing?"

"From Hillcrest. This morning, while I was here with you." He purposefully held back the information about Gail and her family connection. "Do you know anything about that?"

"How would I know anything about that?" he asked, his voice rising. "I'm stuck in a cell and don't have any television access. I was with you this morning."

It was an honest reaction. "I need to know if you know anything about it."

Randy shook his head. "Now I'm going to be blamed for something I couldn't possibly have done."

"No one is blaming you." Cooper tried to reassure him while watching his reaction, which only grew in anger.

Randy's hand jutted out in a frustrated gesture. "You're here asking me about it!" The guard shouted at him to settle down. Randy looked over at him then back at Cooper. He closed his eyes and his mouth. He took deep breaths in and out of his nose. Cooper wondered if it was some calming technique he learned in prison.

When Randy opened his eyes, he was like a different person, back to center. With a calm tone and neutral facial expression, he said, "No, I didn't have anything to do with it. Just like I didn't kidnap those girls thirty years ago. I don't know anything about it, so I can't help you."

Cooper knew he had to continue to press him. He mentioned the phone calls Gail received. "I know that you couldn't be involved with the phone calls because the prison is monitoring you. Who has visited you while you've been here?"

"No one."

Cooper rephrased. "I don't just mean here in the county jail. Who has visited you during your total incarceration?"

"My sister in the early days. After a couple of years, I told her to stop. There was no reason for her to continue to visit me. Our parents are dead, and she needed to focus on her family. The friends I had dropped me as soon as I was accused. No one wants to be associated with a man who could kidnap and murder little girls."

Cooper had compassion for him. "During all of these years, you never had visitors or phone calls other than your sister?"

"No one." Randy must have noticed the look on Cooper's face. "Don't feel bad for me. I've learned to live with it. I made some friends inside, kept my head down, and stayed to myself for most of it. I read a lot. More than I ever did on the outside. You know my body may have been imprisoned, but my mind was free to go anywhere. Reading made that possible. Non-fiction helped me learn things I might never have and fiction gave me a life I wasn't experiencing."

This was a man who had made the best possible use of his incarcerated time. He didn't come across like a vengeful killer taunting the victim's family. Of course, most wouldn't. Cooper knew that there could be lots of sides to people – some they showed and some they kept well hidden. "Is there anyone other than your sister that you've had communication with on the outside?"

Randy shook his head.

"What about direct threats?"

Randy gestured toward the prison guard. "Threats are the reason they moved me. They have not, however, shared those threats with me. You'd have to ask the prison warden for that information. I've never received threats from the outside directed at me. In the early days of my incarceration, I spent a lot of time alone because I'm sure you know they don't take too kindly to child predators inside. Someone must have felt bad for me because they made sure I was safe. A fight here or there but nothing like what happens to most child offenders."

It was the second time Randy referenced the prison system keeping him safe. It was abnormal to say the least. "What about after that initial phase in prison? Did you feel unsafe?"

"There's a routine inside. An ebb and flow of danger. I did my best to keep myself out of the way of it. Someone important must have realized I was innocent, or word got around that I wasn't to be messed with because I stayed out of the fray for the majority of my sentence."

Cooper would have to confirm all of this. So far, there was nothing Randy was saying that would be cause for suspecting him of harassing the Herin family. "Before I asked you about the calls, were you aware that someone has been calling Gail Herin and threatening her?"

"Who is Gail Herin? That's not a name I know. Someone from the prosecutor's office?" Randy asked, his voice still even and calm.

Cooper realized then he hadn't mentioned Gail's maiden name. He had used her married name when mentioning the calls. "She used to be Gail Albright."

The name sparked meaning for him. "Samantha Albright, one of the girls. Is she related?"

"Gail is her older sister. I believe the media and the police did a good job of keeping her name out of the media back then. But still, someone called the house the night the girls went missing, threatening Gail that she was next. They have been calling and calling over the years. Even after she was married and moved to a house of her own."

Randy raised his eyes to the ceiling. "Everything in prison is recorded. There's not a call or piece of mail that isn't searched. I know drugs and other contraband get in. I don't think I could be consistently calling and harassing someone without someone taking notice."

That had been Cooper's line of thought. "One of the young girls missing today is Jenna Herin. She is the daughter of Gail Herin."

Randy's mouth fell open and his eyes got wide. "This can't be a coincidence, especially a few days before I'm due to be released."

"I don't think it's a coincidence either. That's why I'm here to make sure that you are in the clear," Cooper assured him. It didn't seem to make Randy feel any more at ease. Cooper wouldn't feel at ease at all if he were in the man's shoes. "Something is going on that none of us understand. Someone on the inside is keeping you safe. These harassing calls to Gail Herin have been happening for thirty years, those girls are still missing, and now two more missing girls. There's a throughline here that I don't understand."

Randy shrugged. "I don't have an answer for you. If I did, I'd tell you.

I couldn't even start to explain what's happening. Clearly, whoever took those girls is still local and is harassing that woman and has now taken her daughter. Do you think he wants credit for what he's done?"

Cooper sat back, not sure what to say. Killers throughout history have wanted credit for their crimes. No other young women went missing after Randy had been arrested. It was something Riley brought up earlier to give credence to the law enforcement investigation – at least no other girls were harmed, she had said. They didn't know about the calls at the time.

"Anything is possible," Cooper finally said. He and Randy spoke for a few more minutes. Cooper tried other ways of trying to get him to admit to making the calls or taking the girls but Randy didn't budge. When he was done, Cooper was satisfied with the man's answers.

"How does it feel to be almost free?"

"I'm not letting myself think about it until I walk outside those prison gates. I feel like anything could go wrong, you know? I don't want to get excited too soon."

Cooper understood that feeling. He had felt that nervous anticipation in other ways. "Is there anyone coming to get you? Do you have a place to stay?"

"Men's halfway house in downtown Little Rock. I have a room all set up and a counselor that I'll speak to. They will help me with my transition back into society." Randy cocked his head to the side and sighed. "As I said, no family except my sister out of state, and I don't want to bother her with this. No friends anymore. If I can manage in here, I can manage out there. The day after my release, I have a meeting with Cat for the podcast. Will you be there?"

"I'll be there," Cooper assured him. Part of him wanted to offer Randy something, some assurance that he had people on the outside who would help him, support him. Cooper knew what it was like not to have family. He had to build his own, but he didn't want to overextend himself or offer something he'd have to walk back later. He chose to remain quiet about that. If the time came, he could rally some people to help. "Take care of yourself. Hopefully, the next time I see you will be at Cat's."

As Cooper got up to leave, Randy called after him. Still seated at the table, he said, "I hope they find those girls. I didn't have anything to do with this. If I could prove it, I would. I'm locked up. If that isn't alibi enough, I don't know what is. Please catch him, so I don't get mixed up in this when I'm on the outside." Randy paused, seeming to consider his words. "That sounded selfish. Of course, I want the girls to be found safe. I just meant…"

"I know what you meant. We are working on it. It's going to be okay." Cooper didn't know that, but he wasn't sure what else to say. The odds were against Randy Stock and they both knew it.

Cooper asked the guard if he could show him to the warden's office. He still hadn't heard if the man had time to meet with him or not. He wasn't going to come back to this godforsaken place again. The guard cautioned him that Warden John Kirby might not have time for Cooper today.

"He's going to have to make time," Cooper said in response, not sure where he was summoning the confidence. The jail was the warden's kingdom for him to rule over. Cooper was just a visitor and could be kicked out and not let back in ever. That wouldn't serve him well now or in the future.

The guard took Cooper out of the visitor's area, down through several locked gates to a hallway with Army green drab walls that were in desperate need of a paint job. The tile floors had long since seen better days. They passed by several wooden doors until they got to the end of the hallway right next to another exit door. Cooper assumed that if something were to go down in the jail, the warden would have an easy exit.

The guard knocked on the door, and a man from behind it shouted for them to come in. He opened the door, "Cooper Deagnan here to see you. He requested a meeting when he came to see an inmate. I know you haven't responded to the meeting, but he's insisting. He's a local private investigator who works closely with the Little Rock Police Department. He was meeting with Randy Stock."

"Stock?" the warden asked, not hiding the curiosity in his tone. "See him in."

The guard stepped back into the hall and told Cooper he just got lucky. He let Cooper pass by and disappeared back down the hall the way they had come in. Cooper steadied himself for the meeting, not quite sure what to expect.

He stepped through the door, pushing it open farther to accommodate him. Kirby sat behind a wooden desk with three monitors in front of him. The older man with sparse, graying hair poked his head above the screens. "How can I help you?"

Cooper walked to the man's desk, explaining his involvement with Randy Stock. "I'm not sure you're aware, but there are two missing little girls in Little Rock right now."

"I heard the news. What's that got to do with Stock? You can't be suggesting he did something from jail."

"No," Cooper said with a tone to indicate that maybe he was. "Gail Herin, maiden name Albright, is the mother of one of the missing girls. She is also the sister of Samantha Albright, one of the girls Randy was accused of kidnapping."

"Convicted," Kirby corrected him. "He was convicted of kidnapping. That's different from accused."

Cooper didn't correct himself. "I need to know if Randy has had any visitors while he was here or made any phone calls."

"Neither."

"You know that without looking?" Cooper didn't know how that was possible.

"I know that without looking because he isn't allowed any visitors while he is here in our custody. There were threats made against him in state prison, which is why he was moved here."

Cooper didn't understand. "I got in to see him here. I'm a visitor?"

The warden made a dismissive gesture with his hand. "You're in the system. An investigator. Stock can speak to cops, lawyers, and the like."

"Were there any of those who came to see him?"

"No."

"What about phone calls?" Cooper pressed.

"No." Warden Kirby's voice grew annoyed. "I told you that man hasn't had contact with the outside world since he was moved here a week ago."

"Tell me about that. It's not common for a prisoner to be moved, even if threats are made. Who called for him to be moved?"

Warden Kirby looked at him as if he had ten heads. "I'm not at liberty to say. Above your pay grade."

"What was the nature of the threats?"

Kirby threw his hands up in dismissal. "I got the call a week ago that Stock was coming here and he was to be protected before his release, so that's what I did. I'm not at liberty to disclose more. You're either going to have to speak to the warden of the state prison or a judge to compel me. Good luck with that," he added with a laugh and a shake of his head.

As Cooper thanked him and turned to leave, the warden called him back. Cooper stopped at the doorway.

"What's your interest in Randy Stock?"

Cooper saw no reason to lie. "I'm involved in a podcast about the missing girls and wanted to know if he did it. I didn't want to be involved in defending a guilty man."

"He's guilty by the eyes of the court and a jury of his peers," Kirby retorted.

"That doesn't mean much in our current criminal justice system." Cooper wasn't going to back track on what he thought to be true. "The case against him was weak, and the community needed a scapegoat to feel safe. The girls were never found."

The warden pursed his lips. After a moment, he asked, "Is there any other reason?"

Cooper looked out into the hall to see if anyone was standing there. When he was sure they were alone, he took a few steps back toward the warden's desk. He explained about the girls missing from that morning and the ongoing phone calls to Gail Herin and her relationship to Samantha.

"The calls never stopped. I didn't think Randy was involved in that, but I had to be sure. You're telling me that he's not in communication with anyone. That no one came by here, and he made no calls. If all that's true, then I'm right and he's not involved."

"Huh," was all the warden said. Then he shrugged. "I guess maybe sometimes we do get innocent ones in here. Maybe that's why he's being protected. As you said, there's no way he made those calls. He couldn't have even orchestrated the calls for someone else to do it."

"Then you see my dilemma."

Just as quickly as the warden had been interested, he wasn't. "Either way, you need to go now."

Cooper thanked him for the time and made his way out of the jail, hoping never to have to return to the dank building.

CHAPTER 11

L uke didn't waste any time getting to the restaurant. It had the perfect view of Kavanaugh Boulevard and Walnut Street. Those coming off Walnut would be forced to turn right or left onto Kavanaugh, with the restaurant parking lot straight ahead. If Luke were lucky, the video might give him not just the make and model of the car but a clear photo of the driver.

Luke walked into the restaurant on a high of what might be found. He flashed his badge to the young kid standing in the front. "I need to see all your surveillance footage. There are two missing girls, and your camera might have caught something."

The kid raised an eyebrow as he finished with a customer. "You have a warrant? I don't think the owner would like me handing that over to the cops."

Luke took a step toward him, the high he had been feeling dissipating quickly. "Did you hear what I said? Two young girls are missing from the school. You might have the only evidence that allows us to find them alive. Time is critical."

The young man with his hair twisted up in a bun on the top of his head ignored Luke. He finished seating a few customers. When he was done, he grabbed for his cellphone, punched in a few numbers and handed the phone over to Luke. "As I said, not my place. Not my rules. Without a warrant, I need my boss to give me the go-ahead. I need this job, man. I feel for you but that's the best I can do."

Luke released a breath in frustration, taking the phone. When the man answered, Luke explained the situation, the critical timing of it. The owner argued that he had no legal right to the footage and that the cops had done little to help him when he had break-ins.

"What do you want in exchange?" Luke finally asked, getting down to the meat of it. It would be a tit-for-tat situation. The police department would have to have some extra policing in the neighborhood for a while to hopefully catch whoever had been breaking in. Luke was fairly certain that there were already significant patrols in the area, but he readily agreed. He didn't care at that point what he needed to do to get the surveillance footage. He knew working his way through the courts to get a warrant would take too long.

Once he got the green light for the footage, he ended the call and handed the phone back to the kid. "Show me to the surveillance feed," Luke said in as commanding a tone as he could muster.

Luke sat in the dimly lit room with his eyes fixed on the flickering screen in front of him. The video feed from the surveillance camera was grainy, but it was all they had. The hum of the overhead fluorescent lights buzzed in the background, an irritating reminder of how long he'd been staring at the screen. His jaw clenched, his fingers tapped nervously on the armrest of the chair.

The date and time were stamped in the top corner of the screen. About an hour into watching, Luke couldn't believe what he was seeing. His breath hitched. The two girls were visible in the corner of the frame. Their backpacks bounced on their shoulders as they walked down the sidewalk, oblivious to the danger.

Luke's eyes locked onto what else was in the frame. A silver sedan – distinctive in its shape, sleek but understated – slowed at the intersection where the two girls were heading. The car idled for a moment, and Luke's gut twisted. The driver slowed to a crawl.

Luke leaned forward, eyes narrowing, his heart thudding in his chest. As the video played on, he could see the car, but the driver was harder to make out. His face was angles, shadowed under the brim of a baseball cap. The man was wearing a long shirt, driving gloves, and nothing of the man's skin was showing.

As the girls neared, Luke's stomach turned as the car pulled forward, stopping just in front of the two girls. The moment hung in the air like a slow-motion nightmare.

The man rolled down the passenger-side window. He said something to Jenna as Scarlett stood behind her friend. The video feed didn't provide audio, but it was clear that he was engaging Jenna, who didn't seem afraid but rather curious. She kept looking back at Scarlett. For a moment, the two girls appeared to argue.

Luke's hand clenched into a fist on the desk. The girls hesitated for just a second, looking at each other, uncertainty clouding Scarlett's expression.

Jenna took a hesitant step forward. Scarlett tugged at her friend's arm, urging her to keep walking. But Jenna hesitated just long enough. Long enough for the man to seize his chance.

In one fluid motion, he was out of the car. He lunged, grabbing Jenna by the wrist with a strength that seemed impossible. Jenna screamed, trying to pull away, but the man was relentless, his grip iron tight. He threw her into the car with force.

Luke's breath caught in his throat.

After getting Jenna in the car, Scarlett started to run, but she wasn't fast enough. The man lunged for her, grabbing her around the waist and scooping her up like she was weightless. He threw her into the back seat with frightening efficiency. Her hands banged against the window in a frantic attempt to escape, but he was already inside, slamming the door shut before speeding off.

Luke slammed his fist onto the desk. The sound echoed throughout the room, the force of it surprising him. His mind was already racing. He could feel the anger bubbling inside him, threatening to consume him.

The video continued to roll, but Luke barely registered it now. His hand shot out to hit the pause button, freezing the frame. He stared at what he thought was the best image of the man, but even then, he couldn't see his face. It was covered by sunglasses, a beard, and a low baseball cap shielding most of his face. His clothing was dark, nondescript, and because of the actions of scooping up the girls, he never quite stood at his full height, which Luke put at average. His weight was average, too. Still, Luke snapped a photo. He'd send it to both families to see if anyone recognized the man.

Luke's frustration and desperation in his chest felt like a fist wrapped tight around his heart. The urgency hit him like a physical blow. He called the police station without hesitation. The ringing in his ear felt like an eternity, but finally, it connected.

His former partner, now captain, answered. His tone was rushed and out of breath.

Luke's sounded the same in his ears as he explained finding the surveillance footage. "We've got a hit. A silver sedan, four-door, license plate DCV192. We need an Amber Alert sent out now."

He didn't wait for a response before hanging up, his finger already calling Det. Granger. As soon as he picked up, Luke blurted the information. "Start running the plate. We need to get eyes out there and over to the address immediately. Those girls are in danger."

"I'm on it," Granger reassured him, hanging up, leaving Luke alone again with his growing anxiety and his thoughts.

Luke stood, his legs a little unsteady, as he moved toward the door. When he reached the front of the restaurant, he barked orders to the young man not to touch the video recording. He didn't care that customers turned to look at him with their eyes wide and some with brows raised, wondering what he was doing.

Luke needed to get a tech from the police department in there to secure the video footage. He didn't want some hotshot young kid tampering with the evidence in the meantime. Luke couldn't go far until they arrived. He hated the idea of being tethered there, but what choice did he have?

Luke called the tech supervisor, asking for one of their staff to come to the restaurant. The man promised Luke someone would be with him within twenty minutes. They were on high alert to act on whatever Luke needed.

He waited in front of the store, pacing, dodging customers as they arrived. All of them watched Luke stew in his stress. He was hamstrung at the moment until either Granger called or the tech arrived.

What kept him going was the thought that there was hopefully enough time to get to the girls before too much harm came to them. He imagined what he'd do to the man once he found him. There was nothing worse for Luke than crimes against children. He could take almost anything else and he'd seen it all. He'd been working homicide – gang homicide, homicides by diabolic serial killers, domestic violence, murders of passion, and revenge. Nothing was ever worse for him than when a child was involved. He knew the detectives who specialized in those kinds of cases. He didn't know how they slept at night. Luke would be haunted by them.

The tech arrived almost at the same time as Granger pulled up in the police SUV with its lights blaring. Luke rushed the tech to the back room of the restaurant. "I need a copy of this recording. The whole thing. Then I need blown-up photos of the abduction and the man, frame by frame. Don't leave anything out. This is all going to be critical evidence. We are going to need to release it to the media at some point. The clearer you can get the images the better."

The tech assured Luke he had it under control.

Luke charged out, satisfied that it would be handled. He found Granger standing on the sidewalk waiting for him. "Do you have the address?"

"Name, address, and rushed warrant. Tyler pushed it through for us. He called a judge and told him he needed it signed immediately and he wasn't going to wait. He wasn't sure if we'd need it or not, but he didn't want to take any chances. The girls are in imminent danger. We have every right to breach his property."

"No, it's good," Luke said, knowing in his gut that if the girls were there, they'd find even more evidence. "Let's take your SUV. Do we have any backup?"

"Already on the way," Granger assured him.

They hadn't been partners long, but Luke couldn't have been happier with the choice. The big man was on top of his game in every regard. Once inside the SUV, Granger flipped the lights and put his foot to the floor, racing through the narrow city streets toward the far west Little Rock address.

The car had barely come to a stop on the rural property when Luke's boots scraped the gravel as he stepped out of the SUV, his hand already hovering over his holstered gun. The house loomed ahead, barely more than a collection of rotting wood and rusted tin. Granger moved beside him, his brow furrowed, eyes scanning the isolated stretch of land.

Granger gave a tight nod and adjusted his jacket. They moved fast, staying low, keeping to the shadows. The rural stretch of land offered little cover. A cold wind whipped through the air, the kind that made the hairs on the back of your neck prickle. The house was dark – no lights, no signs of life – but Luke wasn't buying the calm exterior.

They reached the porch without a sound. Luke gestured for Granger to take the left, as he positioned himself at the door. He crouched and examined the frame, noting the weak spot in the old wood. They didn't have time for subtlety. He gave a quick signal, and Granger stepped back, his breath steady.

The door exploded inward with a single, powerful shove from Luke's shoulder. The old wood splintered with a sickening crack, and the hinges screamed in protest. They flooded into the darkened room.

Luke called out the man's name. "Walter Fields! This is the Little Rock Police Department. Come out with your hands up!" He took a tentative step, then stopped, waiting to hear any noise. It was dead silent. Luke called out the command twice more. There was no one there. Luke gestured to Granger to advance.

Granger had his gun out, sweeping the room with practiced speed. Luke followed, eyes darting around, cataloging every detail. A faded couch sat up against a wall flanked by two end tables. The furniture was old, but the room was tidy.

"Clear," Granger said, his voice tight as he checked the left side of the room.

Luke moved to the right, his eyes trained on the doorway that led to the back of the house. The silence was suffocating.

"Anyone here?" Luke called out, his voice low, hard. No answer. Nothing.

Luke's fingers brushed the edge of a table, pushing a clutter of old papers aside. One of them was a photograph – black-and-white, faded at the edges, but the image was clear enough. A girl. No older than ten. Her eyes were wide with fear.

"Granger," Luke snapped, lifting the photo. "Get over here."

Granger crossed the room in two long strides and glanced at the picture. He swore under his breath.

The tension was building in Luke's chest. If the guy was still here, they were about to find him. Luke would have to temper his anger to let the man live long enough to tell them where the girls were located.

They moved deeper into the house, each step a calculated risk. The floorboards creaked under their weight, and the smell got worse the farther they went.

Granger pushed open a door. "Bedroom," he muttered. A bed with messy sheets was pushed up against a far wall, and a dresser that had seen better days matched the two nightstands that were across from it. But it wasn't the bed or the furniture that caught Luke's attention.

It was the wall.

The wall was covered in photos. Kids of all ages. Mostly young girls. Some of them were smiling – normal kids. Others were staring past the camera.

Luke's eyes froze on a single, vivid photo in the center of the wall. The two girls were standing on a corner near the school. Their heads were bent close to each other, laughing as if they were sharing a secret. The background was of the school. It was fuzzy – hastily snapped – but unmistakable.

"He was watching them," Granger said, his voice tight, as if he could sense the same thing Luke was feeling.

Luke didn't answer. His hand was already on his radio, relaying a quick message to dispatch. The house was too quiet for someone to be hiding for long. "We need to search this place top to bottom."

CHAPTER 12

I parked my car in front of the modest ranch-style house. The house sat in the middle of a quiet suburban street, nestled between two other well-kept homes. The lawn was neat and the hedges trimmed. A small, wrought-iron fence outlined the front yard. The small house and yard had a certain charm often missing from homes in Little Rock these days. Most of the older homes had been torn down to make way for modern monstrosities. Not this one. It had retained its character. It was the kind of place you wouldn't expect to find a mother haunted by decades of grief.

For thirty years, Agnes Elliott had lived with the nightmare of her daughter's disappearance, and now, with Randy Stock about to be released from prison, the old wounds had to have been reopened. I wasn't sure what to expect. I had called ahead to make sure Agnes would be home and to see if she'd even be willing to speak to me.

I approached the front door and rang the bell. It didn't take long before I heard footsteps inside. Agnes, her face lined with age but her eyes alert, answered the door. She was dressed in a faded sweater and slacks, her hands wringing a dish towel.

"Riley," she said softly with warmth in her voice. "Come in."

I stepped inside. The house smelled faintly of lavender and something baking. The walls were adorned with family photos, some black-and-white, some newer, and there were knick-knacks scattered across the shelves. The place was cozy, lived-in, with the kind of familiarity that came with a life spent raising a family.

"Thank you for agreeing to meet with me," I said, glancing around the living room as Agnes motioned for me to sit on the couch.

Agnes settled into the armchair across from me, her hands now folded in her lap. "You said you wanted to speak to me about Kathleen. It's been a long time since someone…" she paused as if trying to find the word. "Official," is what she landed on. She started again. "Not even the cops have wanted to talk to me."

I could see the pain in her eyes. Not quite a fresh wound, but one that never healed. "I can't imagine what it's like never having found her." Agnes thanked me and nodded, acknowledging the ongoing pain. "I'm here because as you might know, Cat O'Conner is starting a podcast about the girls. Since they were never found, and as you said, no one is still looking, she thought she'd bring some awareness to the case."

"And because Randy Stock is about to get out of prison," Agnes filled in what I had avoided saying.

I nodded. "I was going to leave this conversation up to Cat. I know you said you'd participate in the podcast. I'm here because of what I learned today."

Agnes raised an eyebrow. "What is that?"

I explained about the missing girls, which Agnes had seen on the news. She expressed concern and sadness that it seemed to have happened again. "My husband, Det. Luke Morgan, is the lead investigator on the case. In the course of helping him, I spoke with one of the mothers. Gail Herin."

Agnes gestured toward the flat-screen television affixed to the wall. "I saw the father on the news a few minutes before you arrived. They seem like a lovely family."

"They are," I said, echoing her sentiment. I remained focused on her as I delivered the most important piece of the puzzle. "Gail is the older sister of Samantha Albright."

Before I could say more, Agnes lurched forward, shock blanketing her face. "You can't be serious. They didn't say that on the news."

I hadn't seen a recent news update. I wasn't surprised that no one had made the connection. "The last names are different, and Gail is too distraught to speak to the news. The police are still evaluating what this could mean. I'm not even sure what it could mean."

Confusion spread over Agnes's face. "I'm not sure how I can help you with this. I feel terrible for Gail. It's awful what the families have gone through." She paused for a moment as if trying to find the right words. There was a catch in her voice when she spoke again. "Continue to go through. I don't necessarily believe in closure. I think the pain of loss is always with us. We just choose over time how that fits into our lives. It doesn't end. Not knowing what happened and not being able to properly bury my child has been difficult. It's the absence of information that's gut-wrenching. For Gail to be going through that again…it's too much for anyone to bear."

I caught something she said. "You said you're continuing to go through the trauma. I understand that trauma like the loss of a child has no end date. But is there something specific that's triggering it lately? For instance, have you received any bothersome phone calls?"

"The harassing ones? Sick, vile calls toying with me about the fate of my daughter? If so, yes." Agnes leaned forward slightly. "How do you know about them? The police wouldn't take any reports about it. I changed my number a few times. The calls keep coming."

A chill ran down my spine. "Gail has been receiving them, too. I'm here because of that. I needed to know if Gail was being targeted or if it was all the families. When did they start for you?"

Agnes's face tightened. Her eyes were a steely resolve. "They started just after Kathleen disappeared. They have continued for thirty years. Sometimes the man on the other end would be silent. Sometimes, I'd hear breathing. Sometimes, he'd whisper things that only someone who knew me, knew my family, would know. Over the years, I've tried to ignore them. But they always come back."

"Do you have any idea who could be calling? Any number showing up on the call ID?"

"No," she said with a force in her tone. "My husband tried to find out. He hired private investigators to trace the number, but back then, it was coming from various phone booths around the city. Later, the number was blocked or it came back to burner phones. I don't answer, but the voicemails are vile. I tried to save them over the years. Law enforcement didn't care. I stopped saving them."

I didn't want to make her relive it. Still, I needed the information. "If it's not too painful to tell me, what kind of things has he been saying?"

Agnes turned her head to look out the window. "He's told me my daughter is still alive. He's told me what he did to her when he took her and how she begged for me. He said he would come for my other children. At one point, he told me that he was coming for me too." Agnes turned back to look at me. The corners of her eyes were damp. "I honestly believe it's what killed my husband. He had a heart attack a few years ago. He felt powerless. You know that's a common state of being for women. We know what that's like. We can accommodate that. For men, it's too much."

I knew exactly what she was saying. "Is there anything in his voice that sounds familiar to you? Anything that might give me a hint at who he is? An accent? Anything?"

She shook her head. "I can tell you who they aren't coming from." Agnes leaned forward. "It's not Randy Stock. I know I'm supposed to believe that Randy Stock did this, and the newspapers have been reporting that all the families want him prosecuted for murder. They never spoke to me. The detective on the case barely spoke to me. I've never believed Randy was capable of something like this. He couldn't have made those phone calls either."

I was surprised by what she was saying. I tried not to show it. My eyes flicked to her face, trying to gauge her reaction. "What made you so sure?"

She hesitated, staring at the floor. Her voice was quiet when she spoke again, as though she was dredging up an old memory she hadn't visited in years. "We went to school together. High school. He was different back then, but not in the way they've painted him. Randy wasn't a monster. He was shy. Quiet. He never really fit in, but he wasn't violent. Not like they made him out to be."

I leaned in, my curiosity piqued now. "Do you think he was framed?"

"I don't know if he was intentionally framed or if the detective was incompetent. The judicial system screwed up. I understand though. We wanted someone to blame. Someone needed to be held accountable. Did you ever question why I didn't testify at his trial?"

I knew neither Agnes nor her husband had been called as witnesses. I assumed that they didn't know anything to help the prosecution. "I've read the trial transcript. I didn't question it."

Agnes jabbed a finger into her chest. "I wanted to testify for the defense. The defense attorney wouldn't let me. He said I couldn't alibi Randy, so I didn't have anything to offer the defense. I refused to testify for the prosecution, even to speak about my daughter. It was the price I paid for knowing Randy didn't do it. I only knew him from high school and around town. It wasn't enough to help."

"How could you be so sure?"

"Call it a mother's instinct. The person who took my daughter and called and kept calling is a monster. Randy never had that in him." Agnes held a steady gaze with me. "Tell me if I'm wrong, but I assume Randy couldn't be making those calls from state prison. The calls were happening even after he was arrested. That was my first clue that confirmed what I already knew about his character. Now there are other missing girls and Randy is still in prison. What more proof do we need?"

I watched her, my heart heavy with the weight of her words. I could see the years of pain etched into her face – the way she held herself like a cloak, a grief that was too heavy on her shoulders. "Randy's getting out soon. I'm going to do everything I can to make sure the truth comes out. I just need your help."

Agnes's expression softened, her eyes distant once more. She was looking beyond me, somewhere far off in the past. Her voice cracked as she spoke again, barely above a whisper. "I just want to know what happened to my daughter. I want to know who did this to her and the other girls. But most of all, I want to know why. Why would someone do this?"

My throat tightened, and for a moment, I found myself at a loss for words. There was so much more at stake here than a single case. There were lives, lost and broken, and the ghosts of those who had never been found. I needed to find the truth so no more families would be torn apart. She was right – this man was a monster. "We'll get your answers. I promise."

Agnes didn't respond. The look in her eyes told me she was tired of hearing promises that were never kept. She had hope. I could see that much. She was going to hold me to that promise.

Before leaving her home, I listened to a few of the recordings and jotted down a few of the older numbers that she had saved for decades. They wouldn't do me much good. Those phone booths were long gone. Still, something was better than nothing.

Twenty minutes later, I found myself on the porch of Terry Yeaton's house. He was a single father to two grown adult sons now. His wife had passed when their daughter, Violet, was just three years old. Losing both wife and daughter within the span of a few years had to have been devastating. I couldn't imagine the pain that he felt. Terry had been willing to speak to me. He was glad there was new interest in the case as he hoped, like the other families, that the podcast might bring about some answers.

Terry pulled the door, looking older than his years, worn down by grief and unanswered questions, but there was still fire in his eyes.

"You Riley?" he asked, his voice gruff.

"I am. Thanks for agreeing to meet with me."

He nodded, stepping aside to let me in. The inside of the house smelled faintly of old wood.

"Coffee?" he asked as he moved past me into the back kitchen. By the time I followed him in, he was already pulling out two mugs from the cupboard without waiting for my response.

"Sure. Cream and sugar if you have it."

"You drink it like my wife did." Terry grinned, his eyes softening for a moment before hardening again. "I agreed to talk to you because I promised Cat I'd participate in the podcast. I can't keep going through this, so I hope this is it."

I nodded but didn't go as far as to say I understood. I hoped I'd never have to understand grief like he felt. When Terry set the coffee down on the table, he gestured toward the chair. He took the opposite seat, folding his large hands on the table.

"Thirty years," I said softly, looking at him. "I'm sure you think about Violet every day."

"Every day." Terry's voice dropped, the words slow but steady. "There's not a single moment I don't think about where she is, or if she's still alive, or what kind of life she'd be living if this hadn't happened." He rubbed his face, tiredness bleeding through in every line of his skin.

I explained why I was there and that I had been meeting with the other families. I explained Gail's connection to the recent case and her connection to Samantha Albright. Unlike Agnes, Terry had made the connection on his own. "She was a little girl back then. I don't know that I ever met her."

"I'm here about phone calls both Agnes and Gail have been receiving. I need to know if you received any back then when Violet went missing."

Terry's expression darkened. "Real sick stuff." He took a deep breath, his voice thickening with emotion. "They weren't just back then, Riley. The last one I received was about two months ago. He's kept it up. Toying with me."

"Did you try going to the police?" I asked, already knowing the answer.

"Of course I did," Terry said with a hollow chuckle. "They said they caught the guy. Randy Stock, right? They're convinced he's the one. He's been in prison for thirty years. The calls kept coming. They didn't have an answer for *why or how* the calls kept coming. I knew Stock couldn't be making them from prison. If he had been, there'd be a record for that. I called the prison and was assured that no inmate was harassing people on the outside. I was assured that Randy Stock wasn't calling us. I demanded answers from law enforcement and didn't get any. I even tried to visit the man in prison, and he denied the visit. You want to know what I think?"

I leaned forward with my gaze locked on him. "I'm all ears." I was hanging on the man's every word, knowing in my gut he had something important – some detail that would get me to the truth.

CHAPTER 13

Terry pointed at me as he spoke. "I think they got the wrong guy. I know my daughter and those other poor girls are dead. Yet, no one has found their bodies. Stock's been in prison for thirty years, and now he's getting out, and these calls are still coming. It's like the one who really took the girls wants us to know they got the wrong guy."

None of the news reports reflected what Agnes and Terry felt. "Why did you want to visit Randy Stock in prison?"

Terry shifted in his seat, his hands clenching into fists, knuckles white. "I wanted to talk to him face-to-face. I wanted to look into his eyes and see his guilt. I wanted to ask why he was calling me or having someone call me. Most importantly, I wanted my daughter's body."

"And he refused."

"He refused," Terry said with anger brimming in his voice. "If he's innocent, I can't say I blame the man. He already faced me in court when I spoke about my daughter. You know what he did?"

I explained that I had read the transcript. "What did he do?"

"He looked right at me, his head held high. Then I saw his eyes water when I spoke about my daughter. What kind of cold-blooded killer cries like that? It wasn't fake. It was real. That's why I started to think they had the wrong man. Then the calls kept coming, and I was even more convinced."

I let the silence linger for a moment. I wasn't even sure what to ask him.

Terry filled in the silence. "Here's the thing, Riley. There was one phone booth where the calls often came from. That was the only clue I ever had. Thirty years ago, I followed that lead. I wasn't about to let it go, not after what happened to Violet. I stalked that phone booth for weeks, waiting for someone to show up. Then I saw him."

"You saw who?"

Terry's gaze hardened, a deep breath filling his chest as he stared at me like he was seeing something from the past. Something that had never really left him. "I believe I saw the man making those calls. I can't say he's the one who hurt my daughter, but I'm sure he was the one making the calls. I never got a good look at his face. He ran off before I could get to him. But I know that he saw me. He ran. Coward."

"Do you remember what he looked like?"

Terry stood up, shoving his hands in his pockets. His voice softened. "I didn't get a good look at his face. He had a hat on. Everything about him was average. If I had been able to get my hands on him, he'd be dead."

The look of resolve on his face told me he meant what he said. "If you think of anything else, please call me."

Terry walked me out. "I hope they find the two missing girls. I don't want any other family to go through this."

I left wishing that I had more words of comfort to offer him.

A little while later, I found myself back at Cat's studio. There had been no word from Luke even though I had tried to call him. He sent me straight to voicemail. I had stopped at the church to check on the volunteers and to see how Amelia was doing. She had found her purpose in organizing the volunteer efforts. It was a good task for her to sink her teeth into. I wasn't sure how she was doing it. If I had a child who was missing, I don't know how I would respond. I couldn't see myself having the fortitude that Amelia was showing.

I walked through the door, said hello to Cat's assistant, and she pointed me to the back studio, telling me that Cooper had arrived there not long ago. I made my way down the hall as Cooper and Cat's conversation reached me. He was telling her about his visit with Randy.

I entered the room without either of them noticing me.

"There is no way he's making those calls," Cooper said as adamantly as I heard him say anything.

"I agree," I said, finally. They were both glad to see me. Each rushed to ask me questions. "One at a time," I said, not able to hear each of them while they were talking over one another. They stopped and allowed me to sit.

I explained about the meeting with Agnes and Terry. "All of the families have been receiving the calls. Agnes knew Randy back in high school and is convinced that he's not responsible for what happened to her daughter. Terry is on the fence but claims he stalked the phone booth thirty years ago where the calls were coming from. He saw a man but couldn't get a good look at him. The guy ran when he saw Terry. I wish he had more of a description, but he said the man just looked average. Then again, we can't be sure that's who he saw. Maybe the person just got a look at Terry's face and ran out of fear."

Cat asked, "Is he still going to participate in the podcast? That's good information he can share."

I confirmed he would and turned to Cooper. "What did you find out?"

He told us about his meeting with Randy. "The guy hasn't been making the calls. He also hasn't had any visitors or sent any mail to direct anything. The guy is innocent of that much."

Cat put her pen down. "Are you still questioning if he's guilty of kidnapping the girls?"

Cooper didn't even need to think. "No. I'm not questioning it. The system put an innocent man in prison for thirty years for nothing more than being in the wrong place at the wrong time. There is no evidence. I've read that trial transcript back and forth and there's nothing. It was sloppy police work that I can't believe the prosecutor's office allowed to go through. They maligned Randy. I think they desperately wanted someone to be guilty."

I agreed with everything Cooper said, and I hadn't even interviewed the man. "Did you get in touch with the state prison where he was being held?"

Cooper nodded. "They won't send me any records. We don't have the authority for that. They assured me that phone calls are monitored and no prisoner of theirs is harassing anyone."

"What about the reasoning for Randy to have been moved?" Cat asked, going back to jotting down notes. "You both said you thought that was odd."

"Luke thought it was odd too," I said, confirming that it wasn't a normal course of action.

Cooper told us that he asked and no one would tell him. "The bottom line, they keep saying it wasn't their decision, that it came from above and they can't disclose. They aren't telling me who ordered it or why. I don't see any wiggle room for finding out."

We weren't going to know why specifically or what the threat was for the move. We'd have to settle for not knowing. I gestured toward the television in Cat's office. It was affixed to the wall but not on. "Have we heard anything about the current missing girls?"

"No," Cat said, offering to turn on the news. We declined for now. "Do you think the two cases could be connected?"

I raised my eyes to Cooper. He gestured for me to take the question. The reality was I didn't know for sure – couldn't know. "I suspect there is a connection. It doesn't make sense that there wouldn't be. Gail Herin is the connection. He took her sister and now her daughter."

"How old would that make him?" Cat asked with doubt in her voice. "Thirty years have passed between the two incidents."

It wasn't really that long in the life of a killer. The crimes seemed eerily similar to me. "If he were in his twenties or thirties when he took those girls, he'd be in his fifties or sixties today."

"No other crimes in between?"

Cooper said, "Many children are missing all over the United States. The last statistic I read was that a child goes missing every forty seconds. Some figures suggest four hundred and sixty thousand children go missing each year. Some studies show that hundreds of thousands more go missing that are never reported."

Cat's mouth fell open at the sheer number of it. "How is that even possible?"

"Missing doesn't mean abduction." The last time I had read the stats, they were similar to what Cooper explained. "Even when looking at abduction, which ranged anywhere from four to twenty thousand, not all of them are stranger abductions. Most are family-related. Child custody issues and the like. The biggest fear is stranger abduction, but that's a minuscule percentage of overall cases."

"Then he might have been lying dormant all these years," Cat responded, still not sounding sure.

I wouldn't have gone that far. "I don't think he has. It doesn't mean he has to abduct a child to abuse them. The fact is, we don't know because we don't know who is doing this. He could have moved to another state or been in prison for something else. He could have been married, and his family relationship prevented that drive. There are so many factors we don't know what we don't know."

Cat wasn't going to let it go. She pushed. "But you do think the cases are connected?"

"I think they are," Cooper said evenly. I was glad he spoke up. He was better at getting through to Cat than I was at times. "There are too many factors that say they are connected. I firmly believe Randy is innocent, which means that person is still out there. They have been harassing the families all these years and now he has targeted Gail. There's a connection."

Cat shook her head as if finally understanding. "Should I change up the podcast to fit the current situation?"

Cooper turned his head to look at me. I knew what he wanted to say, but he wanted me to be the bad guy. I told Cat I didn't think it was a good idea. "Let Luke and the other detectives handle this. If there is a definitive connection or it comes up in the interview with Gail, then proceed. I wouldn't have it be a focus of the podcast. Too complicated and takes away from your real mission of finding answers for those families."

Cat agreed without a fight that she would keep her original focus. "The one person who still refuses to speak to me is the detective. He hasn't called me back."

Luke had already warned me not to seek out Lyle Tucker. There was no way we were going to be able to avoid doing that. "Cooper, did you know him when you were with the police force?"

"I knew of him. He was close to retirement when I started. The same for Luke. He was not one of the training detectives either, so it's not like either of us shadowed him."

Cat asked, "What was the perception of him? Was he a good detective? Lazy? Did you get any kind of sense of him?"

Cooper considered the question. "It's hard to say with rumors. You know people talk. It's hard to know what's true or not. We were rookies back then."

I knew he was trying to toe the line. "You owe no loyalty to the police department," I reminded him. "We need to know what kind of detective he was. I can get an idea of how poorly this case was investigated. What I think Cat is trying to ask is if his poor performance on this case is indicative of how he was on every case or if there was something special about this one."

Cooper glared at me. I didn't think he ever had trouble saying anything in front of Cat. Maybe, this was one of those rare things he wanted to keep close to the vest. It was all going to come out eventually.

Cat picked up what was happening, and the tension in the room rose. "I'm not going to put something in the podcast you don't want in," she reassured him. "I thought we had gotten past this."

"We have," Cooper said, relenting. "From what I heard, and who knows if it's accurate, Lyle was a great detective when he first joined. Over time, he got lazy. He cut corners and got tunnel vision. It happened in more than a few cases. A couple of the other detectives had to step in from time to time and redirect the investigations."

"Yet no one stepped in when the girls went missing," I said, but there was a question in my statement.

"No," Cooper said with a shake of his head. "That case was nearly a decade before my time. Some detectives thought Lyle had done the job right. That he got the right man behind bars. There was a rumbling of others who didn't think the evidence was there, especially because no sign of the girls was ever found. There was no physical evidence to tie Randy to any of the girls. Nothing at all. Of course, DNA was new back then. It was still in its infancy, not like today. But there were no hairs or clothing. No schoolbooks or anything. There was not an ounce of physical evidence on Randy's person, house, or car to suggest that he had any direct contact with the missing girls. That stopped a lot of detectives in their tracks. A few said there was a rush to judgment. None went as far as to say that Lyle was wrong or even that he didn't get the right guy. No one was brave enough to question him directly or to say Randy shouldn't have gone to prison."

It was as bad as I had suspected. Luke was doing the same thing now – asking me not to push because it would embarrass the whole department. That wasn't how we worked. We had to take the swing. I decided right then that we had to interview him. "Cat's right. We need to get Lyle on the record, and we need to better understand his perspective on the case. I suggest we go in without confrontation to see if he can help us understand the case better. Let him be the expert. Then we can hit him with the hard questions."

"It's going to anger Luke." Cooper was giving me the look he did when he wanted to know if I was willing to go up against my husband. He should have known the answer by now. He shrugged it off. "It's your funeral. I don't have to live in your house."

That part was true. "Luke has bigger things to worry about right now. You call Lyle and set it up."

CHAPTER 14

L uke and his team were working to methodically go through the home. So far, they hadn't found anything belonging to the two missing girls other than the photo of them near the school. There was nothing to indicate that Jenna or Scarlett had been brought back to the house. Still, they searched because they were uncovering a treasure trove of evidence of other crimes.

The last room to be searched was an office in the back of the home. The door had been locked, and it took some time to breach it. As they entered, Granger was already moving, his eyes scanning the shelves and the corners of the room. Luke moved toward a small desk in the far corner. He pulled open the drawer. It was filled with old paperwork, receipts, and more photos. He set them aside and kept searching.

He knocked on the bottom of the drawer and it echoed back. Luke wriggled his fingers around inside, looking for a latch or something to lift the bottom. He finally grabbed a letter opener from the holder on the desk and jammed it down along the side, tugging the false bottom up.

There he found a notebook.

The red cover was worn in places, and the metal spiral had come loose at the bottom, leaving jagged metal edges. Worn and tattered pages peeked out from the cover. Pages that had come loose from the binding.

Luke flipped it open, scanning the pages. On the second page, he found a list. A long list. Names. Addresses. Dates. He was organized. If Luke was looking at what he thought was a list of kidnapped girls, the man's crimes went back decades. This was a pattern that stretched back years, to cities far beyond Little Rock.

"Granger, you need to see this." Luke's voice was low but urgent. Granger crossed the room and leaned over his shoulder, eyes scanning the pages with quick intensity.

He let out a low curse, just as terrified as Luke by what he was seeing. "All those kids. He's been doing this for decades." He stepped back, shaking his head in disgust. He stepped back from the notebook and gestured back toward the room with the photo wall. "Do you recognize any of the kids in those photos?"

"No, not really," Luke said, even though he hadn't taken a good look at it. They were going to need more crime scene techs to take these photos and tag every single one of them. Start uploading them and searching databases for missing children. "We are going to have to cross-reference this with his notebook. There are dates and times when he was in certain cities. Initials too. I don't know the meaning of this."

Granger stared down at the desk. "There has got to be hundreds of kids' photos. Some of them look like professional photos. Do you think he did that for work?"

Luke didn't know. They hadn't found a dark room or cameras or anything that he assumed he would have seen in the home of a professional photographer. Luke couldn't rule out that the man's studio was somewhere else.

He left the room and went back to the bedroom with the wall of photos. It took up an entire wall of the room. Granger was right that some of the photos looked professionally done. None of the children were deceased or being abused in the photos, and none of them were sexual. He studied them carefully, one by one, taking in their faces, their clothing, even how their hair was styled. The photos went back decades. But they did look professionally done and looking individually weren't so frightening. It was a wall of them, and some of the way they were merged in the collage that gave a haunting vibe.

Luke was so focused on the current case that he hadn't even stopped to consider that it might have been Walter Fields who had been responsible for the kidnapping and assumed murder of Samantha Albright, Kathleen Elliott, and Violet Yeaton. He wished he had photos of the three girls with him to know if there was a connection. For all Luke knew, Walter had been snatching kids going back decades.

Luke remained at the wall of photos while activity swirled around him. The crime scene techs were taking evidence, looking for blood and other evidence that unspeakable violence had taken place in the home.

"Luke," Granger called from the other room.

He took one last look at the wall and retreated to the small office. "What's up?" Luke asked as he walked into the room, scanning it for Granger. He didn't see the big man until Granger leaned his head out of the small closet on the far wall. Luke crossed the room with intention. "What did you find?"

Granger stepped fully out of the small closet and let Luke into the crowded space. "Through the clothes. There's a false wall behind there."

Luke did as his partner suggested, the clothes making a metal grinding noise along the rack above his head as he shoved them over more. He moved the wooden makeshift door back, which wanted to swing closed automatically. "How did you find this?" he shouted to his partner as he entered the room that didn't hold anything more than a narrow twin-sized bed. There was a stained set of blue sheets tossed on the bed with what might have been a white blanket. It was so stained and dirty that it appeared grayish.

Granger didn't join Luke in the space. There wouldn't have been room for that. "The clothes were shoved to the side enough that I could see spaces between the boards of the back wall. I knocked on the wall and it was hollow."

There was no light coming into the room other than the light coming through the closet and that was only enough for Luke to see the bed. He couldn't get a good look at the dark wood walls and floor. Luke stepped back out and grabbed Granger's flashlight. He returned to more closely inspect the rest of the space. The walls had scratched marks near the bed as if someone was trying to break through it.

Granger, with his voice raised enough for Luke to hear him, said "Walter was keeping someone back there. See how there's no dust on the floor. The space has been utilized recently."

Luke shined his beam down on the floor to see exactly what Granger had seen. The floors were clear of dirt and dust as if someone had swept it. Luke scanned the flashlight around the room one more time, hoping for some kind of clue but found nothing.

He stepped back into the main part of the office, handing the light back to Granger. "We are going to need the crime scene techs in there, too."

Granger radioed to the team who were working throughout the home. "What's the next step?"

"All we have is the small photo of the man from his driver's license. Did you find any photos of him here in the home?"

"No," Granger said, "Just of the kids. Do you want me to see if any of the crime scene techs have come across anything?"

"Yeah, do that. We need something for the news. He's not going to come back here. I need to research this guy and see what local connections he has. Someone has to know him. How long has he owned this property?"

"Twenty years next month. I didn't get a chance to do any more background research on him. He must work somewhere, know some folks." Granger pointed off in a westerly direction. "There's a house about two miles down the road. We can start there."

"Let's go there now," Luke said, heading out of the room. He didn't have any time to waste. Granger drove them two miles down the road to the next house, a simple Cape Cod-style home with red siding and white shutters on the living room and dormer windows. The vibe of this home had a lighter feel. The grounds were well-kept and the owner had decorated the porch for the fall. Two pumpkins sat on the top step, only one of them carved. Baskets of fall flowers adorned the other steps.

An older woman, about sixty, appeared in the doorway with a brown Labrador by her side. "Can I help you?"

Luke and Granger flashed their badges.

"I'm here about your neighbor, Walter Fields," Luke said, gesturing down the road. "We have some questions about him connected to an ongoing investigation. We'd like your help if you can."

The woman opened the door fully as she told them her name was Minnie Gleason. "You better come in then. This isn't the kind of conversation we should have standing on the porch."

They entered right into her living room from the front door. A staircase was a straight shot up across from the door. There was no formal foyer, and the living room was small and lived-in but well-kept. The kitchen was a straight shot from the living room. Luke didn't think there was a dining room.

"Can I get you something to drink?" Minnie offered but they declined. She relaxed back in her chair. "I'm not sure how much I can help you, but I'll tell you what I know."

Luke asked, "I don't know if you've seen the news. Two young girls are missing from Hillcrest this morning. They had a half-day of school and were abducted on their walk home. We believe Walter might have some information to help us."

"You think Walter took them?" she asked, no trace in her voice either way.

Luke had wanted to ease into it, not knowing the kind of relationship they had. He didn't want to start accusing someone and shut her down before the interview even got started. Luke responded with a question of his own. "Do you know him well?"

"I know him about as well as anyone might know him. Keeps to himself. Doesn't bother anyone as far as I know. There's not a lot of neighbors out here to bother." Minnie's dog propped his front paws on her lap while she rubbed his head. "My husband, Joe, knew him far better than I did. They'd meet at the property line to talk now and then. When Joe passed, Walter came over with a casserole he said his sister made to offer condolences."

"He has a sister?" Granger asked.

Minnie gave a half-hearted shrug. "I don't know her or anything about her. I can't see his property from mine unless I'm standing back there in the field. I'm not out there often. Since Joe passed, I have a company mow for me. I don't walk down that way too much, certainly not in the last few months. I know that he was raised in Missouri and came to Little Rock for work."

Luke offered his condolences. "When did your husband pass?"

"Nine months ago. I only saw Walter that one time when he came to offer his condolences." Minnie continued to pet the dog, who looked up at her lovingly. "Joe didn't like him and he had a good instinct about people. He used to say there was something creepy about Walter. He used to tell me never to answer the door if I was home alone and to never let him in the house."

"Did he ever tell you why?" Luke asked.

"Just said he made some off-color remarks about women that rubbed

Joe the wrong way. He pushed back on it when it happened. Walter would just laugh it off. He told Joe that he didn't have a sense of humor." Minnie smiled at the memory of her husband. "Joe had four sisters and was raised by a single mother after his father passed young. He didn't see anything funny about disrespecting women. I asked him if he thought the man had ever hurt a woman. Joe didn't know, but he wasn't going to take a chance with me home alone. When he told me never to open the door for him, I listened. Even that one time he came with the casserole, I didn't let him in the house. I could tell he was a bit disappointed. Tried to get me to let him in. I told him I had some people here, because I didn't want him to know I was alone. He left and never returned, thankfully."

"What does he do for work?" Granger asked.

Minnie offered a wry laugh. "He works as a photographer. That's what he told Joe anyway. He has a studio downtown. He had invited Joe there a few times, but he declined. I don't know why he'd want to go to the man's studio."

"Have you ever seen him with kids, young girls?"

"I wouldn't know," Minnie said. "As I mentioned, I can't see his house from mine. It's not anything he told Joe about, other than the off-color remarks about women. Good men don't think, don't speak like that. Joe thought about calling the police, but he never had anything credible he could share. It was just off-hand sexual comments. Nothing Joe could prove beyond that, and you can't get arrested for saying stuff. There's a big difference in knowing a man is a letch and being able to prove he did something to break the law."

Luke knew that to be too true. "When was the last time you saw him?"

"Other than when he came to my house? That was the last time I spoke to him."

"What about just seeing him?"

Minnie thought about it for a moment. "Probably a month ago. I was leaving to go to the grocery store and he was coming out of the house. He didn't see me. I certainly didn't honk and wave. I only talked to him that one time over the last year. I think Walter knew Joe didn't like him around because he never came to the house. Just talked to Joe out on the property line."

They talked to Minnie for a few minutes longer, trying to pull any nugget of information from her that she could remember. She didn't have much more to offer. Knowing that Walter was a photographer with a studio downtown had made the trip over worth it.

When they were back outside, Luke stood in her driveway, trying all different kinds of searches to find the studio online. He wasn't successful. "Let me text Cooper and see what he knows about photography studios in the city."

Luke sent off a text as he and Granger discussed their next move.

Not even a full minute later, Cooper texted back, confirming that he'd met Walter Fields once. He gave him the address. It wasn't any more than a few blocks from the police station.

Luke shook his head – the man had been under their nose the whole time.

CHAPTER 15

I arrived at Lyle Tucker's house alone. Cooper had been called away to help Luke investigate a photography studio. Because we were in front of Cat, he hadn't shared exactly what Luke told him, only that there was a photography studio in question. Cooper had met the owner once and offered to show Luke the place.

That meant I was on my own with Lyle.

He lived a short distance from me in the Heights. The house stood at the end of a quiet tree-lined street. Its low-pitched roof and deep overhangs cast long afternoon shadows. A wide front porch wrapped around one side, framed by thick, tapered columns. The wood siding, painted a deep forest green, was impeccably maintained, the white trim crisp against it. A pair of dormer windows peeked from the second floor, their small panes reflecting the light filtering through the trees lining the street.

A concrete walkway, edged with neatly trimmed hedges, led up to the steps. An old-fashioned porch swing swayed slightly in the breeze. The front door was solid oak and heavy.

I rapped twice and waited. After a moment, the door creaked open, revealing a man well into his seventies, his posture still straight despite the years.

"Riley?" Lyle asked and I confirmed. He welcomed me in without any trace of the animosity I was expecting, given we were questioning his investigative work.

The foyer was modest but warm. A Persian rug stretched across the hardwood floor, its deep reds and blues complementing the wainscoted walls. To my left, a narrow hallway led further into the house, and to my right, an arched entryway opened into the living room.

The space felt perfectly curated, as if someone had been looking at an image from an architectural magazine. It was nothing like I had anticipated for a man of his age living alone. A stone fireplace dominated one wall, its mantle lined with framed black-and-white photographs. Heavy oak bookshelves flanked it, stuffed with hardcovers whose spines showed decades of use. A leather armchair sat near the hearth, a folded newspaper resting on its arm.

Lyle gestured toward the couch. "Have a seat. You came here to talk to me about Randy Stock. How can I help you?"

I eased back into the couch and crossed my legs. "What do you remember about the investigation?"

Lyle kicked his legs out in front of him and sank back into his chair. He folded his hands across his midsection. "I was the first one on the scene. I got a call that girls were missing, and the last place they were seen was that store. I went directly there. You know, back then they didn't have a lot of cameras in place, not like they do now. There wasn't a lot for me to go on. The man who owned the store told me he saw the girls come in, buy some candy and drinks, and head back out to their bikes. The girls were in the store occasionally. He didn't think anything of it, knew them by name, and told them to enjoy the sunshine."

"He didn't see anyone bothering them in the store?"

Lyle shook his head. "No. It was routine. The girls came in, grabbed their snacks, paid, and left. Randy Stock was there at the same time. He was standing outside the store when the girls went out. I assume he saw an opportunity – young girls, alone, on their bikes like that. He went into the store, got what he needed, and by the time he came back out, the girls were gone. We suspect he drove around until he found them, kidnapped them…" his voice trailed off.

Lyle had no idea where the girls had been taken or what had happened to them after they were taken. "Who was it that pointed you in Randy's direction?"

Lyle squinted his eyes at me. "I'd have to see the file because I don't remember the man's name. He was there at the store at the same time as Randy and the girls. He said Randy held the door open for the girls but didn't go into the shop. He followed them."

"Right, but that was disputed by the shop owner," I reminded him. "Randy went into the store."

Lyle shrugged it off. "Didn't matter. We still had a witness who saw Randy following the girls. That was all that mattered."

"There is no witness statement in the file, and that man never testified in court." I reminded Lyle that the man's name was Brad Hogan. "Where can I find him? I searched, and his name doesn't come up anywhere."

"Too many years ago," Lyle said off-handedly.

I was starting to wonder if Brad Hogan was even real. "Since we know Randy went into the stores, was there any witness who said Randy was asking anyone where the girls went?"

"No," Lyle said with a shake of his head. "He got in his truck and headed off down the road."

Nothing in any of Randy's interactions would have made me think he'd kidnap the girls. I told Lyle as much. "I'm not seeing how, other than being there, that he'd get on your radar, let alone be the prime suspect. Other than this Brad Hogan, who seems to have disappeared from the records."

Lyle smirked and nodded. "This is why I was a detective and you're just a private investigator. I have the special training to know when someone's behavior is suspicious."

I let his insult slide. It sat in my chest like an undigested pepper, giving me heartburn. "That aside, what beyond Randy being at the store made you go after him?"

Lyle didn't have an answer. "Asked and answered. Let's move on. What else do you want to know?"

I couldn't push too hard or he'd kick me out. I shifted. "What evidence was there once you got to Randy's house that made you think he had taken the girls? Did you find any trace of them in his home?"

Lyle tsked. "You think he was going to leave evidence for me to find right out there in the open?"

My lower back was starting to itch. It was a sure sign that my temper was rising. I countered his question with one of my own. "How was he when you went to the house?"

"He was calm, cool, and collected. Of course, he didn't understand why I was there. I let him incriminate himself first and admit to being at the store. I went in there acting like he was a witness. After he confirmed for me that he saw the girls there, even held the door open for them, that's when I knew I had him. I brought him right down to the police station for further questioning, then got the warrant to search his home. He never went back to his house. He was in police custody from that moment forward."

I wasn't going to let this point go. "What evidence did you have to get the warrant? My understanding is Randy denied his involvement." Lyle sat there silent. "Do you believe the girls are deceased?"

Lyle shrugged as if it didn't matter to him. "We have to assume so. I don't understand why this is being dragged out into the public now."

"Randy is about to be released from prison and the girls were never found," I reminded him. "What do you think about that?"

Lyle pursed his lips and shrugged. "I don't know what you want me to say. We did our best to find those girls, but we couldn't. Randy wouldn't tell us. People go missing all the time and are never found. It's one of those unfortunate facts of life. As per Stock getting out of prison, he should be spending the rest of his life there. I don't sentence people though. I did my civic duty."

I imagined myself punching him square in the face. The smugness was too much for me to stomach. He wasn't even pretending to care about the girls. "What would you say if I told you that the families of the missing girls have received phone calls over the years from someone toying with them, harassing them about the girls. We know Randy didn't make those calls."

"I heard rumors about that."

"They were more than rumors. I spoke to each of the families. Gail told you about the call on the day her sister went missing. The other families called law enforcement and nothing has been done."

"I've been retired a long time. All I can say is if they thought it was credible, they'd have done something with it by now."

I couldn't believe that he was still sitting there defending himself and his investigation, if I could even call it that. He went after someone who was simply seen with the girls for a brief moment. It was something that each of us did countless times a day – held the door for someone leaving a shop while we were walking in. How many of those people just passing by in life had I encountered that day alone…ten…twenty… who knew?

We did it so frequently in our day-to-day lives that it took something out of the ordinary for us to even notice. I couldn't recall the face of one person that I had encountered in the last three days in such a way. To think that's all it took to be a suspect for murder was terrifying. The system had convicted him, so the community was as much to blame as the detective sitting in front of me.

"What's this podcast about?" he asked, snapping me out of the spiral in my head.

It took me a second to collect myself. "The missing girls primarily. Cat is hoping to shine some light on the case and maybe spark some recollections. She's done a great service on some other cold cases."

"This isn't a cold case," he said, interrupting, his tone tinged with anger.

I knew he was getting heated. "The girls are still gone. Someone is still calling and harassing those families. The man who was convicted is about to get out of prison. There are questions if the right man was brought to justice." His eyes flamed with anger. "Look, you can get angry all you like. I'm telling you the facts as they stand. If Randy was guilty, as you said he was, then he spent thirty years in prison for the crime. If we find the girls' bodies and it was murder, then Randy is looking at going back in. Wouldn't you want to see that happen?"

I'd have assumed he would have said yes. Instead, Lyle didn't respond, just stared at me across the room.

"Either way, we need the truth to come out. We need to find out what really happened to those girls. Even with Randy Stock convicted, we still don't have answers."

Lyle rose from his chair and I followed. I took it as a sign that the interview was over. We stood only a few feet from each other in the living room. He looked down at me. "You think you're going to be the one to figure it out?"

"I don't know," I said honestly. I was cocky enough to think that Cooper and I could solve the thirty-year-old case, but I wasn't going to admit that. "I guarantee you we are going to do the very best we can for those families."

"Do you think I didn't do my best?"

He was baiting me. I wasn't going to bite. "That's not for me to say. You're the only one who has to live with those decisions." That wasn't technically true – Randy and the families had to live with it too. "I'll see myself out."

Lyle didn't say another word to me and he didn't follow me to the door. Bubbling rage sat in my chest. I wasn't going to confront him further. I didn't want to shoot down any chance Cat had that he might still participate in the podcast, not that I thought he'd have much of value to say other than highlighting how Randy had been railroaded by a lazy detective. I also didn't want to press my luck that it would get back to Luke.

By the time I hit the street and stood at the edge of my SUV, I knew what I wanted to do next. I'd speak to Lyle's partner, Mary White. She had been one of the only female detectives at the time in the Little Rock Police Department's homicide unit. She had only been Lyle's partner for a year before this case. After, she asked to be transferred.

She was not called to testify at the trial. Because she had not testified and her name wasn't on any of the reports, Cat wasn't going to call her for the podcast. I thought that had been a mistake.

I had already looked up Mary's address and found she didn't live that far from me. She had a three-bedroom two-bath home on Longwood in Cammack Village, a small enclave adjacent to the Heights. I honestly didn't know where the Heights ended and Cammack Village began.

I drove over and parked at the curb in front of the tan-sided home with wide porch stairs that went to the small front porch and wooden door. Mary had a wreath of flowers affixed to the front and a basket of flowers sitting on the steps. The home looked like it had been well-kept.

I knew nothing about the woman, couldn't find anything online about her. I was walking into this blind. Before I even made it to the first step, the wooden door pulled open, and a petite woman with a coif of grayish blonde hair peered out at me. "Can I help you?" she asked me as she stood in socked feet.

I smiled to let her know I was friendly and introduced myself. "I realize you might not want to participate in the podcast, but I was hoping you'd at least speak to me off the record. I have some serious concerns about the investigation into Randy Stock."

Mary's face relaxed in a relief I wasn't expecting. "Come on in. It's been thirty years I've been holding this in. I think it's finally time to share it."

I didn't waste a second jogging up the steps and into her home.

CHAPTER 16

ooper met Luke in front of the Walter Fields photography studio two blocks from his loft. Luke hadn't gone into too much detail about why he wanted the information. Cooper could only assume that it had to do with the investigation.

Luke had told Cooper to scope out the place and see if Walter was there. Cooper arrived and found the place dark and the door locked. The sign on the door indicated the studio should have been open. It was only moments later that Luke and Granger arrived, followed by several more uniformed cops. They sectioned off the short side street and hit the ground running.

Luke rushed him. "Is he here?"

Cooper shook his head, noting the tension in his friend's voice. "What's going on? The place is dark. I don't think Walter is around today. Sign says he should be, but he's not."

Luke approached the building and peered into the dark front window. "No signs of life," he said to Granger. He turned back to Cooper. "What do you know about Walter?"

Cooper tried to recall the time he'd met the man. "You know I'm always looking to upgrade my surveillance cameras. I ran into Walter at the coffee shop down the road, and he was talking to the girl behind the counter about a new camera he had purchased for his studio. I struck up a conversation with him while we were waiting. He told me

"

he also sells some equipment here at the studio. I came down to see what he had. I bought a long lens from him to attach to my camera. It was cheaper than going through my usual dealer."

Granger nodded his head toward the door. "You've been inside?"

"Just once," Cooper said, explaining the layout of the shop. "He said he's been doing a lot more nature work. People don't want photos inside a studio anymore. They wanted to be out in nature – you know, weddings, professional shots, engagements – that sort of thing. He told me he uses the studio mostly for headshots. There is a dark room in the back."

"He doesn't use digital?" Luke asked.

"He does, but he also has been in this studio for more than forty years. He's had the dark room since he set up the studio, and he said he sometimes still uses film."

"I didn't think anyone was doing that anymore," Granger said with a shrug.

"I don't know. The man had some quirks and seemed to like what he liked," Cooper said, still not sure what was going on.

Luke pointed to the floors above the studio. "What about up there?"

"Walter told me those are apartments. He doesn't own the building."

"Any other interaction with him?" Luke asked, still glancing up at the three floors above the studio. They had a warrant for the building, but tenants might complicate it. "What's your take on him?"

"He seemed like a guy into photography," Cooper said casually, not sure what they were driving at. "I assume he's done something wrong if you're here at the studio."

Luke finally lowered his head and focused his attention on Cooper. "His car was seen on a surveillance video taking Jenna Herin and Scarlett Evans. A man was seen getting out of his car and grabbing the girls off the street and putting them in his car. We went to his house out in West Little Rock. Walter has a room full of photos of kids on the wall."

"There is also a small room with a bed behind a closet wall," Granger added. "It looks like he was keeping someone in there."

Cooper muttered a curse as he exhaled. Walter had seemed like an odd guy to him, but he never would have guessed that. "I never saw anything to indicate that in the studio. He didn't have photos up and he didn't give any indication that he was..." Cooper failed to find the right word.

The heaviness settled over them all.

"Do you have a warrant?" Cooper asked, finally.

Granger held up the paperwork. "We want to take this guy in as soon as we find those girls. We aren't doing anything that could compromise the investigation."

Cooper nodded. "What do you need from me?"

"Do you know how to reach Walter?" Luke asked. He pulled up a photo and showed it to Cooper. "That's from the surveillance. Do you recognize him?"

Cooper bent his head toward the phone. All the grainy photo showed was a man reaching out to grab a little girl. The man's face was obscured by his hat and sunglasses. "He didn't have a beard when I met him. I can't tell if it's him or not."

"The families couldn't identify him from the photo either," Luke lamented. He asked again about how to reach Walter.

"I have his business card back at the loft," Cooper explained. "There was a phone number and email on there. I can go get it. If I'm remembering correctly, it was a cellphone number too and not a landline."

"Go get that," Luke told him. "Try to call him and get him to talk if you can. See if he's willing to meet. Don't let on that you know about anything going on. He's not at the house and he's not here. Do you know of other property he might have?"

"No," Cooper said emphatically. "As I said, I had two conversations with the man. The one at the coffee shop and the other when I bought the lens. I haven't been into the shop again. I don't know him other than in passing."

Luke said he understood. "If you find his number, call him. Try to get him to meet today. Push for it, if you have to. We need eyes on him."

Cooper jogged back to his loft, knowing time was critical. He took the elevator up to his floor and hurried down the hallway. He went directly to his desk, where he thought he'd kept the contact information for Walter. The hum of the downtown cityscape filtered through the open window.

He leaned over his desk, scanning the contents of his files, his mind wandering back to the two times Cooper had been face-to-face with Walter. He tried to remember how the man made him feel. Was there any hesitancy on his part to engage with Walter? Did he find him creepy or anything set him on edge? There was nothing Cooper could come up with. The interactions had been brief and to the point. Even the barista at the coffee shop had been friendly with Walter.

Cooper reached for the small stack of business cards that sat next to his lamp. There it was. Walter's business card. He studied the number for a moment before punching it into his phone, the small device feeling strangely heavy in his hand. He knew he had to approach this with caution – make it sound casual but with an urgency to meet. Cooper wondered if Walter would know something was up. He had never called the man before, and if he had just kidnapped two girls, it might be obvious. Walter knew what Cooper did for a living.

The phone rang twice before it clicked into a voicemail message.

"Walter," Cooper said, his voice steady. "This is Cooper. You probably don't remember me, but I'm a private investigator. I had a few questions about some of the camera equipment you use. I went by your shop, but you weren't there. Nothing urgent, but call me back when you can. I'd like to meet."

He ended the call and tossed the phone onto the desk, his fingers tapping impatiently on the edge of the wooden surface. Cooper felt like he struck the right tone. Nothing too pressing, nothing that would scare him off.

Not even a minute passed before the phone buzzed in his hand. It was Walter's number.

"Cooper," A man's voice crackled over the line, distant and detached, "I got your message."

"Thanks for calling me back," Cooper replied, keeping his tone casual. He was having trouble remembering Walter's voice. But something in his tone was different. "As I said in the message, I was hoping we could meet."

A brief pause, then the sound of someone breathing on the other end.

"Where?" Walter asked, his voice now a little more guarded.

Panic filled Cooper's chest. He hadn't thought that Walter was going to be willing to meet. He assumed the man either wouldn't answer or would have told him no. Luke hadn't suggested a place for them to go. He suggested the studio first, but Walter nixed that.

"Mugs in the Heights," Cooper suggested, choosing something casual that Luke would know well. There was enough room for law enforcement to surround the place. "Do you know it?"

"I know it," Walter said quickly. "Give me an hour."

Before Cooper could respond, the line went dead. He stared at the phone, unsure whether to feel more relieved or more suspicious. Cooper immediately punched in Luke's number. It rang twice.

"Luke, he said we could meet in an hour. I chose Mugs in the Heights. I figured it was good neutral territory and both you and Granger know the area well." They both lived in the Heights. "But there was something about his voice. It was different."

"Stress, probably," Luke said with renewed optimism in his voice. "Granger and I will get a team up there and out of sight. When are you heading up?"

"Soon," Cooper said. "I want to get in there and get seated before he arrives."

"Take a table by the window." They made a few more plans for the meeting then Luke ended the call.

He grabbed his coat as the weatherman had called for rain later in the day. He slung it over his shoulder as he made his way to the elevator. The building's lobby was empty when he stepped out into the parking structure, the chill of the afternoon air hitting him like a slap. He tugged the coat on, pulled his collar up, and walked briskly toward his car, trying to shake the sense that something was off. It had been too easy to convince Walter to meet. Even Luke had sounded surprised.

Cooper found a place to park just outside of Mugs at the curb. He didn't see Luke or any police presence. Then again, he assumed he wouldn't. They'd be well hidden.

The bell above the door chimed as he entered, the soft murmur of conversation and the scent of coffee filling his senses. Cooper scanned the room for a moment, but there was no sign of Walter. Just a few regulars tucked into corners with their laptops, their faces buried in their screens.

He ordered a coffee and took a seat by the window, trying to look casual as he checked his watch. He still had a few minutes before the hour was up. Cooper played in his head how it would go, what he should say. He'd worked with Luke before and trusted him. The time ticked by, passing the hour with no Walter. It moved onto the half-hour and Cooper continued to wait. Maybe the guy had changed his mind.

Cooper was about to reach for his phone when the front door chimed. He looked up in time to see a young girl walk in looking for someone. Her hair obscured the side of her face. She stood at the door for a moment. Cooper assumed she was looking for her mom or friends. It wasn't uncommon to see groups of kids in Mugs after school, even young girls like her. It was that kind of neighborhood.

Cooper lowered his eyes and reached for his phone.

"Are you Cooper?" a quiet voice, almost fragile, asked.

Cooper raised his head, recognition immediately sinking in now that he could fully see her face. "Scarlett." He leapt from the table, coming around to her, shielding her small body from the window. "What are you doing here? Are you okay?"

He helped her into the chair and knelt by her side.

She looked at him wide-eyed. "He told me to ask you for help. He said you knew my mom."

The weight of her words hung in the air. Cooper's mind raced, trying to piece it all together, what had happened. Walter returned one of the girls but not the other.

CHAPTER 17

Luke sat in his black SUV parked across from the small coffee shop, strumming his fingers against the steering wheel. His eyes never wavered from the shop's entrance. Luke had left another team to work on the search of Walter's studio. He had been surprised that the man was so readily available and willing to meet Cooper. While Luke had made the request, he had doubted that Walter would agree. Luke hadn't even considered that the man would have answered his phone.

From Luke's vantage point, he could see Cooper sitting at a window seat in the shop. He had specifically asked him to sit by the window. Luke turned his head slightly, eyes scanning the street. His attention drifted toward a shadow crossing the road near the corner. The figure was small, slender – too small to be an adult, too purposeful to be a lost child. He squinted.

It was a girl.

She was walking quickly, her eyes scanning the street as she passed the row of shops on Kavanaugh Boulevard.

At first, Luke didn't think much of it. He and Riley lived in this neighborhood. Kids roamed it freely without too much worry of anything happening – well, that was before today's kidnapping. Now he was sure parents would have their eyes on their children at all times. He watched the young girl head straight towards the coffee shop, stop briefly at the window, turn her head to look in and then reach for the door.

She struggled to tug it open. That's when Luke got a good look at her side profile. Luke leaned forward, looking out his side window to get a better look, but she disappeared into the shop. His phone chimed. Luke glanced down to see a message from Granger, who was sitting on the opposite end of the street where the girl had come from.

"Is that Scarlett?"

Luke texted back just as quickly. "I don't know."

Luke couldn't ignore the burning instinct in his gut that told him it was the young missing girl. His breath caught in his chest as he made a quick decision. If it wasn't her, he was blowing their cover. It was her. Walter had purposefully sent her in. It meant that he had been there, somewhere close, and they had missed him.

Luke sent a quick text off to Granger. "I'm going in. Search the area for Walter's car."

Luke pushed open the SUV door and moved with urgency across the street to the shop. His mind was working fast, piecing together fragments of memories of the photos of the girls he had looked at more than once, and that were now plastered all over the media. The dark hair. Her slender frame. The clothes she was wearing when she went missing.

By the time Luke pulled open the door at Mugs, he knew it was her.

Scarlett sat in a chair facing away from the door with Cooper crouched beside her. Luke scanned her over quickly – she wasn't dirty, she didn't seem injured, and she wasn't crying or expressing fear. She seemed stunned and confused but otherwise safe.

"Scarlett," he said, touching Cooper on the back to let him know he was there. Cooper rose from his crouched position and moved back to the other side of the table. The young girl looked up at him with wide eyes. "I'm Det. Luke Morgan. I know your mom. We've all been looking for you. Are you okay?"

"He told me that you'd be here. He said I could go home with you. That you were someone I could trust."

Luke bent down to be at her level. "Who told you that?" He wanted to reach out and wrap the kid in his arms. He didn't know what kind of trauma she'd been through. He kept his distance, respecting her boundaries. The noise and swirl of the coffee shop wasn't a place for an interview. "Can you tell me what happened? We can go somewhere else to talk."

It was only at the mention of being moved somewhere that the young girl's eyes welled with tears. She blinked rapidly and called out for her mom. Through soft sobs, she cried, "I want to see my mom. Where is my mom? He said I could see my mom."

Luke knew that no matter how much he wanted information out of her right now, that wasn't going to be best for Scarlett. "Okay, we can see your mom." Luke stood up fully and reached for the phone in his pocket. He fired off a text to Granger that it was Scarlett and to keep searching for Walter, that he must be close.

He stepped away from the table to call Amelia. She answered almost immediately. "We found Scarlett and she's safe," he started, not wanting to drag it out. "We are at Mugs." Amelia said that she was rushing there right now. "I need to question her, Amelia. I need to know about Walter and Jenna. It was only Scarlett who showed up here." Luke hesitated, not sure how to say he didn't know if her daughter had been abused in any way. Amelia finished the sentence for him. She was a prosecutor. She wasn't unaware of the risk her daughter faced.

"I'll wait outside until you question her," Amelia said, assuring Luke he needed to do whatever he could. "If I show up there now, you won't get a word out of her."

Luke didn't know how Amelia could remain so reserved and professional. He knew he was asking more of her than he should ask of any parent. He didn't know that if it had been asked of him, he'd have been able to respond the same way. Luke thanked her and ended the call.

Luke returned to the table with a smile on his face. "Your mom is heading here now. She's working at a volunteer place that we set up to help find you. Do you mind if I sit where Cooper is and we can talk until she gets here?"

Cooper rose from the chair before Scarlett could say yes. He jerked his head toward the door, indicating he was going to head out. Luke was glad that he didn't have to ask him. Before leaving, Cooper said, "Scarlett, I'm so glad you walked in here and found me. We are happy you're safe."

Luke wanted to offer her something to drink. He hesitated, knowing that they might need to take swabs. As he sat, he took in the condition of the young girl. She seemed so tiny against the chair and table. "Can you tell me about what happened this morning?"

Scarlett looked up at him with big brown eyes. "Jenna and I were walking home from school when that man told us he was there to pick us up from school. He said that Jenna's mom said he could take us to the park. We were just going down to Allsop Park. That's right down the road. I didn't want to go. My mom told me to never go with people I don't know. I'm not supposed to go with anyone she does know either, not unless he has the code. You don't have the code. That's why I can't go anywhere with you."

Luke smiled despite himself. "What's the code for?"

"It's a special thing I have with my parents. It lets me know that it's a safe thing to do. Mom said that we needed that even with her friends." Scarlett raised her thin shoulders in a shrug. "You know my mom works with bad people. Criminals. She said we had to be safe. That's why when that man said he knew Jenna's mom and I asked him for the code, he didn't know what I was talking about, so I knew he wasn't safe. We have another code too when I'm not feeling safe. Like if I'm at a friend's house and I want to go home. When I call my mom, I just say my code and she knows I want to come home. That way I don't have to say what's really going on. She'll just know."

"That's smart of you," Luke said, meaning it. He'd need to remember that trick to teach other people who had kids. "What happened when you told Jenna you didn't want to go with him?"

"Jenna didn't get to say anything. He got louder and said that he was a friend of Jenna's mom and that he'd just been to Jenna's house. He told us she asked him to pick us up. That she had to go to Kroger and she wasn't going to be back for an hour. I still didn't want to go. I asked him if I could call my mom and he said no. That's when I wanted to run. I didn't feel good – like had a bad feeling in my body."

"Your instinct?"

"What's that?"

"Sometimes our body tells us when things aren't safe. It's that bad feeling you described." Luke touched his stomach. "I get that feeling in my stomach sometimes. When I know danger is there even when I can't see it."

Scarlett nodded her head. "That's what it was like. I don't know why I didn't want to go with him. I just didn't. He grabbed Jenna and put her in the car. I was kind of frozen, then I tried to run. He grabbed me and threw me in the backseat. I tried to yell. That's when he showed me the gun."

"He had a gun?"

"Yeah, inside the car," Scarlett said, furrowing her brow. "Don't ask me about it because I don't know anything about guns. I knew I had to be quiet. He was getting angry and he didn't seem like someone I should make angry."

"What happened then?"

"We drove around for a long time. I asked him if we were going to the park. We passed right by it. That's when I got worried. He said we were going to get ice cream first. Jenna was talking to him, asking questions about how he knew her mom."

"What did he say?"

"He knew her from a long time ago. When they were kids, they were friends. Except," Scarlett paused and looked out the window. When she looked back at Luke, confusion had fallen over her face. "He looked a lot older than Jenna's mom, so I couldn't figure out how he was friends with her from when she was younger. I asked if he was her teacher, and he told me no. Then he told me to shut up. He was nice to Jenna, but he wasn't nice to me."

Luke was beginning to suspect that Jenna had been the real target of the kidnapping. "Did you go anywhere or did you just drive around?"

"Mostly drove around. I thought he was going to take us to his house or something. We didn't go anywhere. Just drove and drove."

"What about downtown? Did you go into downtown Little Rock?"

Scarlett nodded. "He pointed out what he said was his studio. He didn't stop. I thought maybe if we stopped, I might get a chance to run, even if he had a gun. He didn't stop, just kept driving and driving."

"You didn't stop anywhere?"

"Nowhere," Scarlett confirmed. "There was no chance for me to escape. He acted like he wasn't sure what he wanted to do."

"Did he seem angry or worried?"

Scarlett considered it. "I don't think angry. He was nice to us the whole time. That didn't stop me from being scared of him. He was still a stranger even if he was nice."

Luke was gentle with the question when he asked, "He didn't hurt you?"

"No," she said with a hard shake of her head. "I sat in the backseat thinking about how to get away from him. He didn't hit me or yell or anything."

"What about Jenna? Did you see him do anything to her?"

"No. He was being nice to her."

Luke was glad to hear that. He had the sinking feeling that it wasn't going to last long. "How come he let you go?"

"I told him I wanted to go home. When he didn't respond, I said that my mom would be looking for me. That she was a prosecutor and that she would have all the cops out looking for me if I didn't get back soon."

Luke knew that could have gotten her killed. "Did he have the car radio on? There were lots of news announcements that you were missing. Did he hear them?"

"No. He and Jenna were talking."

"What were they talking about?"

"School. Her friends. Her mom a little bit."

That caught Luke's attention. "What did he say about Jenna's mom?"

"Jenna asked him if they were friends because she had never met him before. When he said again that he knew her when they were younger, Jenna was asking questions about what her mom was like in school. She said that something bad had happened to her mom's sister, so now she was overprotective."

The irony of that wasn't lost on Luke. She had a right to be overprotective. But possibly by keeping the leash so tight, Jenna was set up to rebel. "Did he say anything about the sister or ask what happened to her?"

"He said he knew all about what happened to Samantha."

Luke lurched forward at the mention of the victim's name. "He said the name Samantha?"

"Yeah," she said, looking up at him with round eyes. "A few minutes later, his phone rang. When he hung up, he told me that he was going to drop me off at a coffee shop, so I could go home to my mom."

Luke assumed that call had come from Cooper. "What about Jenna?

Did he say what was going to happen to her?"

Scarlett sniffled and tears formed in her eyes. "He wouldn't let her go. She wanted to come with me and he said that they were going on a special trip. That he knew of a special place she'd want to see."

Luke's heart started to race. "Did he say where they were going?"

"No." Scarlett sat back and wiped a tear away with the back of her hand. "I want to see my mom."

Luke glanced out the window of the coffee shop to see Amelia standing near the edge of the curb. "Your mom's here," he said, his voice tight. "I'm so glad you came back. We are going to do everything we can to find Jenna."

Luke could only hope he'd be able to fulfill that promise.

CHAPTER 18

Mary insisted on making us some tea before we sat down to talk. It seemed she was eager to get her story out. She slid a plate of homemade chocolate chip cookies my way. "Eat up. You look peckish."

"I don't think anyone has ever told me I look peckish in my entire life." I pulled back the foil and took out two cookies still warm to the touch. I took a bite and savored the taste. "These are excellent."

"Thank you," she said over her shoulder as she carried the cups and steaming teapot to the table. Mary offered me cream and sugar as she took a seat across from me. "Why are you looking into the old case?"

As I poured hot water over the tea bag, I explained what we were doing and that I had just come from interviewing her former partner. "I am sure he lied to me. He was evasive, and when I pressed him about his evidence against Randy, it was slight, if non-existent."

"There's nothing there. There never has been," Mary confirmed. She dropped some sugar into her cup. "Lyle and I worked together for a few years. He wasn't that far from retirement. I was midway in my career. When we got the call that the girls were missing, Lyle groaned and said that it was the kind of case that would haunt the rest of his career if it wasn't solved. We had no idea at the time what had happened. He was already making a snap judgment that the girls would never be found."

"Did that seem odd to you?"

"Incredibly odd. I wanted to know what he was talking about. Why was he speculating so soon? He brushed me off and said these kinds of cases had a reputation for going bad quickly if we didn't get a lead in the first twenty-four hours." Mary raised her arms in a shrug. "He was right in some ways. Missing persons cases can go cold quickly. We've all seen that happen. I just didn't understand the immediate speculation when we knew so little."

That was odd to me too. The girls might have just been late coming home. "What was he like once you were on the case?"

Mary took a sip of her tea. "After we got out of the police station, when we were in the car on the way to the store where the girls were last seen, I questioned him. I asked how he could make such a statement. For all we knew, a parent had taken them. That's the most common kind of kidnapping. Lyle said there was no way a parent had taken all three kids. He had me there. I had to admit that." Mary grew quiet as she sipped her tea again. She held the cup in front of her. "That wasn't my point. My point was that until we started investigating, we had no idea what happened. No detective should make assumptions that early on. He was full of speculation. That a predator had taken them. He said they were probably already dead. We had no evidence of anything yet. It was all so odd."

I agreed with Mary about that. I had to check my assumptions and bias when we started a case. In the early discussions Cooper and I had about cases, we sometimes gave each other a moment to air those assumptions to get them out of the way.

"Those early assumptions didn't stop there, did they?" I asked.

"No," Mary admitted. "As soon as the owner of the store confirmed that Randy Stock had been seen briefly speaking with the girls, all bets were off. He told me straight out that he knew Randy Stock had taken them. We were only an hour into the case."

"What about Brad Hogan? The witness who said he saw Randy follow the girls? In the newspaper account, he said he never saw Randy go inside the store. That was contradicted by the owner of the shop."

Mary nodded. "I never interviewed Brad Hogan. Lyle never let me speak to him, and he took no formal report. He wasn't called to testify either. It's an odd thing. The reporter never spoke to Brad either. A bit of a mystery if you ask me."

"Is there a reason he didn't come to the trial?"

"He wasn't on the witness list. As far as I know, Lyle was the only one who spoke to him. Between you and me, I'm not sure he exists."

I hated to ask an obvious question. "Do you think Lyle could have made up the witness to bolster him going after Randy?"

"That's exactly what I thought at the time."

"What did Lyle say about him? How did Brad come forward?"

"While I was talking to the shop owner, Lyle went outside. He said he spoke to a guy in a truck. He was gone by the time I got out there. But the man's account didn't square with the fact that Randy most definitely went into that store."

As suspected, that didn't show guilt to me. "Randy was still in the store when the girls left. I believe that was confirmed by others. Then he said he went straight home."

"That's where we found him early the next morning before work," Mary confirmed. "He didn't live more than two miles down the road. There was no evidence in his home. He allowed us to search." There was a hesitation in her voice and she paused.

"Was there something that made you suspicious of him?"

Mary admitted, "He denied seeing the girls at first. Lyle told him that they were missing from the store. Randy said he hadn't seen them. When we pressed, he admitted that he had, and he didn't know why he lied. I think he lied because Lyle was scary, hovering over him and already accusing him. It was a stupid lie to tell the cops. I understand the reasoning. There was no evidence to suggest that Randy was involved." She paused and took a breath. "Lyle did say something strange to me while we were searching the house. He said it was too bad we didn't have anything from the girls because he would have dropped it in there. He knew they had the right guy, but there was no evidence. They needed evidence."

"Framed him?" I asked, not sure I heard her.

Mary nodded. "I was disgusted. I told my supervisor about that later and Lyle denied it. He said I was a hysterical woman who shouldn't be working cases with missing children. That my mother instinct clouded my judgment. Pure sexism."

I couldn't imagine how hard early police work was for women. There were only two women detectives in the detective bureau today. It was still a boy's club. "Is there anyone else you investigated?"

Mary shook her head. "There were search parties out looking for the girls in the early days. We brought in dogs that followed their scent from the store down to where the bikes were found. We believe they were taken by vehicle after that. After a few weeks, we also had search parties looking for remains around that area. It was like the girls vanished into thin air. On their bikes one minute and gone the next. There has never been any sign of them."

"That's not necessarily true."

"What do you mean?"

"The phone calls," I reminded her. "That is evidence. Someone called Gail Albright. She was Samantha Albright's sister. They called the night Samantha went missing, taunting her. The calls have never stopped for her or the other families. Gail's daughter is missing right now. Gail believes it's the same man who took her sister."

Mary sucked in a breath. "I knew girls were missing from Hillcrest. I didn't connect it back to that case. I remember Gail when she was young. She was so fragile then. Hard to reach and within herself. I was the one tasked with interviewing her. She mentioned the phone call. I started to look into it, but even her parents didn't know if it was true or a way to garner some of the attention that we were paying to her sister. There was a rivalry, her parents said. They didn't seem to believe her about the phone call. I didn't know what to do with it. I didn't realize that her daughter was one of the girls missing. That's concerning. Who is the other girl?"

"Scarlett Evans. She's the daughter of Amelia Evans, who is a prosecutor, and Christopher Evans, who is a prominent defense attorney. My husband, Det. Luke Morgan, has been out searching. There is a whole team of people. Gail believes the same man who took her sister now took her daughter." I paused and waited to see if Mary had anything to say to that. When she didn't, I went on. "Gail believes that it was Randy who took her sister. She believes the cops got it right. Mostly, I think she believes it because she desperately needs to believe there was some justice for her sister. Of course, we already ruled out that Randy could be making those calls from the prison."

Mary stared off past me in an expression that was hard to read. Finally, after a few moments, almost too softly to hear, she said, "I had no idea that the calls had continued. You're right that Randy couldn't be making them."

My phone buzzed in my pocket. It vibrated until the call went to voicemail and then started buzzing again. It buzzed two more rounds before I had to excuse myself and answer it. Whoever was calling wasn't going to stop. It was Cooper. The news he had was both comforting and confounding. It gave more credence to what Gail said – that her daughter had been the target.

Mary could tell that the news I was getting was important. She glanced in my direction with eyebrows raised.

When I ended the call, I explained everything Cooper had told me.

"He said Luke will be making a statement to the media soon. They believe the primary target was Jenna Herin, Gail's daughter. They have identified the man who has the girls. They have not been able to locate him."

"Do you have a name?" Mary asked with interest.

Cooper didn't tell me if I could release the details or not. I had no idea if Luke was going to release the name to the public during his press conference. I had to make a judgment call. "Walter Fields," I said hesitantly. "I'm not sure I should be telling you that. Does the name mean anything?"

"He has a photography business downtown. He was arrested for peeping during the nineties. I remember the case because he targeted one woman in the Heights, and she called the cops at least fifty times before we were able to catch him. We didn't know his name then and only had a basic description. It took a long time and a lot of surveillance hours to track him down."

"I'm surprised the police department was willing to spend the hours to catch him." That wasn't a knock on the police department. They were overworked, and a peeping case was low as a priority.

Mary gestured toward me. "I can see your wheels spinning. To be honest with you, had the victim not called us so much, the case would have gone nowhere. She insisted and had some connections to a state senator. She had the pull and the money to make a big stink. You know how that goes. Unfortunately, some victims get more resources."

"When was Fields arrested?"

Mary knew exactly what I meant. "You're thinking he might have been the one responsible?"

"It's not me who is thinking this. It was my partner. They found photos of young kids plastered on the walls of his home and a bunker of sorts behind a closet wall. There are questions about who these kids are and what he was doing."

Mary digested that information without giving anything away on her face. "I didn't pick that up about him. He was a peeping tom, and he might have even gone on to sexually assaulting grown women. I never got the vibe or, frankly, the evidence that he was into children. He didn't exhibit any of the signs."

"He could have kept that hidden," I suggested.

"Anything is possible," she admitted. She sat with her features tight. "Walter Fields can't be the guy who took those girls back then. He was in jail for that peeping case when the three girls went missing. I know that for a fact. The first thing I did when I got back to the office was search where all the criminals who had committed sex offenses were. Fields was sitting in the county jail. A few of the others I suspected right away were either no longer in the region or in jail. I didn't have much to counter Lyle's theory about Randy Stock, other than there was no evidence against the man. They never did find evidence, even the trial was thin."

"Prosecutors like to win. I don't understand why they'd go forward with the case. I saw the trial transcript and it was the thinnest case against someone I've ever seen."

Mary sighed. "It was Lyle who convinced the prosecutor. I remember sitting in those early meetings. The prosecutor's office wasn't happy with the lack of evidence and how quickly Randy had been arrested. They argued that there was no way Lyle even had enough information to arrest, let alone to go to trial. He told them he'd make the case for them. That by the time they went to trial, the girls' bodies would be found and there'd be enough evidence. It never happened. It was a closed case. I asked to be transferred to another partner after that. It wasn't even a few years after that that I left the police department altogether. I didn't like how things were done."

I commiserated with Mary about that. It was a hard career path for women, especially then. "Do you have any theory about what happened to the girls?"

"I'm sure they are deceased," Mary said with a trace of sadness in her voice. "Unfortunately, because Lyle focused on Randy, we lost critical time in the case early on. The searchers never turned up much. It's hard to say how the case would have turned out if we had followed the evidence rather than Lyle's feelings."

"Do you think he had a vendetta against Randy?"

"I don't think it was personal to Randy. He was an easy target. But only Lyle knows why he did what he did."

"He's not talking," I said, frustrated. I asked Mary a few more questions, thanked her, and left her house feeling far more frustrated with the case than when I entered.

CHAPTER 19

That evening, when Luke was still going hard in the field, I found Cat and Cooper sitting at the conference table in the studio. There was a wrapped sandwich, a bag of chips, and a cold soda for me. "I assumed you'd be hungry. I don't think you ate all day," Cooper said by way of explanation. "I was going to have dinner with Adele, but she's not feeling well. She's in bed already."

"Is she okay?"

"She said probably the flu."

I made a mental note to check on her later. While I dug into the food, I filled them in on my meetings with Lyle and Mary.

"Lyle now refuses to do the podcast," Cat said, interrupting me. "Based on what you're telling me, it doesn't sound like it's much of a loss. I can't believe he went after Randy like that with little to no evidence."

I had been thinking about that and wondering what I was missing. "Do you have anything in your research about any prior relationship between Randy and Lyle? Were they strangers to each other? Mary confirmed there was no evidence against Randy, and she confirmed that the prosecutor's office thought the same. It sounded like Lyle convinced them to go forward with the case and he'd turn up evidence later."

"That's not how it works," Cooper said with a disgusted grunt. "Total miscarriage of justice."

"It also ensured that the girls were never found. They were so focused on Randy that no one was out there trying to uncover what happened to those girls."

"There were still searches going on," Cat reminded me. "There were still people who were trying to find them."

"Didn't most of the searches stop once Randy was arrested?" I couldn't remember what I had read in the file.

"There were a lot fewer once people suspected the girls were deceased. That's how it is with every missing person's case. There is a swell of people volunteering in the early days and it tapers off."

I knew that to be true. "No other evidence that you came across?"

Cat held her finger up to ask me to wait. She got up from the table and came back with a file that she slid across the table to me. "I went through all the files I could access early on, back when I was trying to figure out if there was even enough to do a podcast. Two school friends saw them that day. One of the girls was at the store with her mom when the girls were still outside. She talked with them briefly, and they asked her if she wanted to go to the park with them. The girl's mother said that they had to get home. The other friend, a boy from their class, was riding his bike down the same road the girls were on and passed by them. He told the police that the girls were going to a nearby park."

That was the first time I heard about the park. "The bikes were on the side of the road."

"Right," Cat said. "They never made it to the park as far as we know."

"What about the dogs?" I asked, recalling what Mary had told me. "The scent stopped in the street. It meant the girls got into a car."

Cat pulled the file back that I hadn't opened, flipping the cover and going through pages until she found what she wanted. "The dogs were out there two days later. It had rained significantly the day before and the dogs seemed confused about where the girls had gone. One kept pulling farther down the road, and the other indicated that the girls must have gotten into a car. There was no consensus."

I shook my head in frustration. "That doesn't tell us anything. We need to assume the girls were taken where their bikes were left."

"I agree with that," Cooper said as he leaned over my shoulder to read the file. "What park were they going to? Did the witness say?"

"Taylor Park," Cat responded.

It was a secluded, small park just beyond the Hillcrest neighborhood. There were swings and a jungle gym. It was the kind of place where parents with young children went. You have to walk down a dirt trail then take a quick left on the path through the trees. The park opens up from there. There aren't that many people outside of those in the neighborhood who even know it's there.

Cat asked, "How far was it from the store?"

"Not even a mile." I grabbed a sheet of paper and marked an X where the store was, then drew a line down the road where they were last seen. "Over here, just off that road, is a side street with a few homes. From there, you duck into the woods on the dirt path. All in all, it's probably less than half a mile from the store to the park."

Cat cursed softly. "To think that in that short a distance, three girls could vanish forever. Can you drive into the park?"

"No. If you're thinking Randy drove into the park and watched the girls before snatching them, that didn't happen. There's not even anywhere to park near the dirt inlet. It's a suburban neighborhood without much street parking. The girls wouldn't have left their bikes on the road to go to that park. But that's not where the bikes were found."

"Can you show me that park? If the girls were headed there, I want to include it in the podcast," Cat asked.

"It's dark out," I reminded her. "I don't know that we will see much."

"It's okay. It will give me a setting to use in the podcast." She asked us to wait while she grabbed her camera and her handheld recorder. "I might as well get some footage while we are there. It will help me set the stage for the podcast."

We piled in my SUV and headed toward Hillcrest. As I had explained, I needed to park two streets over. We walked the rest of the way. I was grateful that the streets were more well-lit than I had expected.

The narrow side street, tucked away behind a row of houses, sat facing the woods. Halfway down the block, if someone was looking carefully enough, the trees parted to reveal a barely visible dirt path. I only knew about the place because Luke told me he had played there as a kid. One afternoon, not long after we first started dating, he brought me to the park.

"This is secluded," Cat commented as we stepped off the pavement. "I wouldn't have known this was here even if I drove past it."

The path was barely wide enough for a single person. Low-hanging branches brushed against my sides and the top of my head as I entered. Cooper had to duck his head low not to be wacked in the face. The rough terrain marked a sharp contrast with the clean, manicured streets just a few yards away. The light from the street only carried us so far.

The farther down the path you went, the quieter and darker it became. The steady hum of suburban life – car engines, the laughter of children – faded until it was nothing more than a muffled echo. The air was thick as if the trees, and the earth itself, were holding their breath. A strange stillness clung to the place, unnatural, like it was holding something back.

Eventually, the path opened up, revealing the park. There were two large streetlights on either end of the park, offering eerie illumination. The swings creaked in the breeze. The playset – a simple structure of metal and splintering wood – stood alone and lifeless. I was sure the mood lightened when it was full of parents and children. Now, it felt abandoned to the wilderness creeping at its edges.

Around the play equipment, the woods pressed in from all sides. Tall, thick trees crowded the perimeter, their trunks gnarled and twisted like the fingers of some ancient hand reaching out to grasp anything that ventured too close. The forest beyond the park was dense, a wall of green so deep it looked as though it could swallow a person whole if they stepped too far into it. I wasn't sure if the city ever trimmed the trees or took care of the tangled underbrush.

The wind rustled through the leaves, but the sound was hollow. No other roads led into the park. The only way in or out was that narrow, hidden path. It felt different today than when I had been here with Luke. We were jovial then, laughing and smiling at one another, feeling the newness of our relationship. Today, I could feel the distance between the park and the rest of the world.

Every step I took crunched against the ground beneath my feet, the crunching almost too loud in the thick silence of the park. The place was vast, too quiet, as if nature itself had taken a breath and held it. The air had a heaviness to it the closer I made my way past the swings and sand pit. It was a sort of lingering unease that wrapped around me and made me second-guess the decision. I turned my head to see if Cat and Cooper were nearby.

Cooper walked slightly behind me. He was using the light on his phone as a flashlight. His usual confident stride slowed as he kept his eyes on the ground as if grid-searching, even though thirty years later, any evidence that might have been here was long gone.

Cat was scanning the area with that keen, almost obsessive look she always wore when she was recording. She spoke quietly into her phone she was using for both video and audio. She wasn't loud enough for me to hear. Her voice was no more than a murmur.

Cooper's brow furrowed. "I don't know where the woods lead. I assume to houses. We aren't going to get through the thickets dressed like this. We'd need something to help hack our way through. Why are we here? We know the girls were taken from the street."

I nodded. We were both humoring Cat.

"Give me a few minutes and we can go," she said, rightly sensing that Cooper and I felt this was a waste of time.

With nothing better to do than wait, I felt a sudden urge to cross the playground to the other side. It was almost as if there was a rope tied around my waist pulling me across. Curiosity or maybe boredom got the better of me.

I could see why the girls were headed here that day. The park was the perfect place to play on an afternoon off from school. The girls could swing for hours or push themselves on the metal merry-go-rounds that were nearly rusted in place now. I imagined back in the nineties it was a lot of fun and also a place for injury. We had one in a park near where I grew up. The metal scalded the back of my legs on a hot summer afternoon. We loved it though. I'd lie on it and stare up at the clouds as a friend pushed me round and round. The boys would take turns pushing it to see who fell off first.

I was so lost in memories of childhood that I didn't hear Cat call out. She yelled Cooper's name, then mine. Cooper turned to her. I followed. "Do you see that?" She was pointing directly across the park at the thickets between the trees in the direction I was walking.

I didn't see anything even with the brightness of the streetlight above. "What is it?"

Cat froze, her phone lifting in a subtle gesture that barely caught my attention at first. "Let me zoom in." She adjusted the camera and her eyes widened in fear. "Oh my…" she didn't finish. The words were caught in her throat. She raised her head to Cooper. "Come look at this."

Cooper retreated to her and glanced down at the phone. As soon as he saw whatever Cat had seen, a curse escaped his lips.

My pulse quickened. "What is it?" I asked, heading back to where they stood.

"I'm not sure exactly," she said, her voice barely more than a breath. "I thought I saw something. A figure in the underbrush. It's like…" She trailed off, looking down at her phone, then off across the park.

Cooper didn't hesitate. He took a step forward, eyes narrowing. "I'll check it out," he said, not waiting for a response.

He didn't need to say more. Cooper didn't like to wait when something felt off. I understood that impulse – I shared it. My gut twisted, a warning coming from the part of me that had been doing this job far too long.

Cat and I followed right behind him, trying to keep up as he closed the distance to the woods. The wind picked up, biting through my jacket, and the air seemed to thicken with every step we took.

I moved with purpose. Once I reached the tree line, I saw what they were seeing.

It was a body.

My stomach dropped, and the hairs on the back of my neck stood up, tingling with a sudden rush of dread. Cooper broke through the brush, kneeling beside the man. He cursed louder now.

Cat and I stepped forward together, closing the distance. I took one look at the man's face and felt my heart lurch in my chest.

He was dead – no question about it. His skin was deathly pale, and his eyes were wide open, staring blankly at the sky, devoid of life.

But that wasn't what made my stomach twist.

It was the fact that I knew him. We all did.

His face had been splashed all over the news for the last hour.

Walter Fields.

CHAPTER 20

Luke stood at the edge of the park, eyes scanning the familiar landscape. He had played in this park as a kid, hung out and had gotten drunk with his friends for the first time when he was in high school, and had brought Riley here on their second date.

Now it was the site of a murder Luke didn't understand.

The ground beneath his boots crunched with every step as he moved deeper to the other side of the park. His mind raced through the possible scenarios, though none of them made much sense.

Riley's voice broke the silence as he got closer. "Luke, are you okay?"

He didn't look at her at first, his gaze fixed ahead. Then he turned slightly, acknowledging her presence. "Confused, but fine," he admitted, the words tasting foreign in his mouth. It was a lie. But he didn't want to admit the truth to Riley – that he was feeling overwhelmed and like he was failing.

Everything seemed to be one step ahead, just out of reach. The case that started this morning seemed like it had started months ago. He felt like he had aged a decade in just a few hours. The night would hamper further search efforts, and Jenna was still out there. That was his main focus.

Riley fell in stride next to him, not pushing him to elaborate more. It's one of the reasons their relationship worked so well. They were cut of the same cloth and she knew him better than anyone except for maybe Cooper, who had known him longer, who was standing near the edge of the park with Cat.

"I hope you're not recording any of this," Luke cautioned her as he approached, seeing her phone in her hand.

Cat shook her head, used to his sharpness when it came to active crime scenes. "We were getting footage related to the case from years ago when I spotted him. I was taking a close-up of the woods and I saw something strange. Cooper said he'd check it out and that's when he found him. I stopped recording then. I don't have any footage of the body. I wouldn't."

Luke acknowledged it. Turning to Cooper, he asked, "What did you find?"

Cooper pointed toward the body. "After Cat pointed it out, I saw the shoes off in the distance. I couldn't see much more than that. It was hard to make out, but then I got a closer look."

"You didn't touch him?" Luke asked, even though he knew Cooper hadn't.

"No. I had to disturb the scene enough to get up there and take a look. I climbed up that little incline and saw that it was Walter Fields. As soon as we found the body, we called you."

"One shot to the head?" Luke asked, confirming what Cooper had told him earlier. "I have a crime scene team up at the main road. I told them I wanted a look first before they came down."

Cooper said he understood. "One shot straight through the forehead. I don't believe he was killed here. Looked like the body was dumped. There isn't any blood. I assume if he was killed here, there'd be some signs of a struggle or something. His car isn't here. It doesn't look like suicide either. There's no gun around."

Luke absorbed the information and walked the rest of the way toward the tree line. As they neared the edge of the woods, Luke spotted it – just a glimpse at first. A body, crumpled and awkwardly twisted, was partially concealed by the underbrush. The man's clothing was torn, his face half-hidden by a patch of wet leaves.

Careful not to disturb the scene any more than it had been, Luke moved toward the body and peered down. The recognition hit him like a sledgehammer. "Walter Fields," he muttered under his breath.

Cooper stepped forward. "Even though I had only met him a couple of times, I knew it was him. I don't understand it. How can he be with Jenna and dead at the same time?"

Luke nodded grimly. That's exactly what he had been thinking. "I don't know. Unless it wasn't Walter in his car this morning. After we found his wall of photos and the room in the closet, we assumed it was Walter. We should have had a photo to show Scarlett for confirmation, but she was so fragile, I wanted her to go to the hospital to get checked out. There is a child psychologist she was going to speak to. It didn't even occur to me to show her a photo of Walter. I had been sure it was him. It was a poor assumption on my part."

Luke surveyed the area. There were no clear signs of struggle. No drag marks through the leaves either. It meant someone was strong enough to have carried Walter's body. Luke crouched down beside him, his eyes scanning over every inch of the man's form.

He studied the body. What he was seeing didn't add up. He knew from the condition of the body that he had been killed some time ago. "It doesn't make sense," Luke muttered under his breath.

Riley called to him, "If he wasn't the one who took the girls, then it means he was probably killed before the girls were even taken."

"Probably." Luke's mind was racing. "Why leave him in the woods like this? He could have been left in his house or where he was shot."

Cooper already had a theory worked out. "I assume the kidnapper wanted you to think Walter Fields was behind the kidnapping. If you were looking for him, you weren't going to be searching for anyone else. I don't think the killer ever meant for us to find the body. There was a witness who said the three original missing girls were headed to the park and Cat wanted some footage for the podcast. It was blind luck that we found him."

Luke knew Cooper was right. The whole thing had to have been a distraction, a ruse to keep the police focused on the wrong suspect.

Luke stepped back from the body, tugged off his gloves, and reached for his phone. He sent a quick text off to Granger with the photo of Walter that had been running on the news. Luke needed Granger to show it to Scarlett.

He could feel Riley's gaze on him, the quiet weight of her worry hanging in the air. When he was done with Granger, he glanced back at her. "I'll be fine," he said again.

"You're beating yourself up for assuming this whole time that it was Walter. There's no way you could have known, Luke. We all assumed it was him. Why would you think otherwise?"

"I know. Still…" Luke didn't finish his thought, silently wishing he could will his brain not to blame himself. There was no one else to blame. He had seen the license plate on the car, found that wall of photos and the secured room in the man's house, and came to the wrong conclusion.

Cooper agreed with Riley.

Luke's boots sank slightly into the wet earth as he took a step back, his mind working at lightning speed. As if on cue, his phone chimed. He looked down at the screen and saw the text from Granger. It was a simple enough message.

No. Walter isn't the one who took the girls. Scarlett doesn't recognize him.

Even though it shouldn't have been a surprise to Luke, it was still like a punch in the gut. He texted back: *Get Scarlett in front of an artist. We need an image of the person who took her.*

Granger texted back that he was on it.

Cooper scanned the area. "I didn't search too much before. Anything around him? Tracks, footprints, anything?" He carefully moved from the body to the area around it.

Luke frowned, squinting at the surrounding area. "Not that I can see. The crime scene techs are on their way as is the medical examiner. I want to know exactly how long Walter has been dead."

The wind picked up slightly, rustling the branches above them, sending a cold shiver down his spine. A sense of unease settled deep in his gut. He could feel it, the weight of the unknown pressing down on him.

He turned toward Riley and Cooper. "Anyone feel like taking a walk with me? I want to cut through these woods and see where this goes. There must be a neighborhood or something on the other side of these woods. I've never gone this way."

"Sure," Riley said, turning back to Cat. "Do you want to come?"

Cat glanced back at the entrance to the park, where officers and crime scene techs were beginning to file in. "I'll wait here for you. This way we don't have too many people trampling over potential evidence."

Luke was glad that Cat wasn't going to tag along through the woods. As they started their walk, he asked Riley to stand on his right and Cooper to stay on his left as they cut through the woods, grid searching as best they could. The plan was to follow the woods until they couldn't go any farther. Each of them had a flashlight to navigate. The moon was full overhead, giving them enough light for the task. It would be better in daylight, but Luke didn't want to wait.

The trees pressed close as Luke pushed forward, his boots crunching softly against the damp underbrush. His breath was measured and even as their lights bounced off the ground and nearby trees. They walked for more than a quarter of a mile by the estimation on Luke's watch, seeing nothing but woods. The landscape remained unchanged from the park. It didn't get any denser and it didn't thin out either.

Luke wasn't sure what that meant.

"We should be closer to something by now," Riley spoke up, her voice low, but still tinged with frustration. She moved alongside Luke, eyes scanning the perimeter of the thick trees.

"Let's give it a few more yards," Luke started to say as his eye caught something – an anomaly in the landscape. The trees ahead and the brush beneath their feet thinned. He could make out something through the trees. A construction site, maybe.

He motioned for Riley and Cooper to follow him.

They crossed the threshold into a clearing, and Luke could feel the weight shift in the air. A low growl of distant wind stirred the branches overhead.

"This way," Luke said and pushed forward, the sound of his boots no longer muffled by the underbrush. Something was unnerving about this place. A steep incline lay ahead, and Luke's eyes flicked upward. Beyond the thick veil of trees, he saw the faint outline of rooftops and heard the distant hum of traffic.

His gaze was glued to the path ahead. The incline grew steeper and the terrain narrowed.

"Cooper. Riley," Luke said sharply. There was a gap in the line of trees now, and with it, a clear path. The air smelled different, fresher.

They were out of the woods. A cul-de-sac, just a few feet ahead.

"What neighborhood is this?" Riley asked as a few small, unassuming homes came into view. Each one seemed indistinguishable from the other, with neat lawns and flower boxes.

Everything was too normal and quiet.

Luke wasn't sure. He was a bit disoriented, trying to figure out the landscape he should have known so well. He grew up on this side of town. Over the last few years, there had been so much construction, far too much growth that even streets he knew well were unrecognizable.

Cooper scanned the houses. "This cul-de-sac is the perfect place for someone to pull over and park. It's dark. There's no streetlight right here. Someone could pull up along the curb, cut the lights, and be off into the woods in less than a minute. Maybe someone in those houses knows something."

Luke nodded. "Let's check it out. Spread out. Start with the house on the far side."

They moved cautiously, stepping off the beaten path toward the nearest house. There was a faint glow of light from a window in the corner of the house. Luke knocked once on the door, then again, firmer this time. The silence lingered too long, and just as Luke was about to turn away, the door creaked open.

A man, late fifties, with graying hair, peered at him with a wary expression. His eyes darted over the three of them. "Do you know what time it is? What do you want?" the man asked, his voice rough.

"Sorry to bother you," Luke began, flashing his badge quickly. "We just cut through the woods. On the other side is Taylor Park. We just discovered a body of a man there and we are trying to figure out how he got there."

The man blinked, clearly taken aback. "A body?"

Luke confirmed. "Have you seen any unusual cars parked here?"

The man nodded, his fingers gripping the door tighter as he started to close it. "I did see a car there two nights ago. It stayed there for about half an hour and then drove off. I couldn't see who was in it or the make or model. We get kids up here parking sometimes, looking for a little privacy. They don't hurt anyone."

Luke asked him a few more questions that didn't give him much more. When the man went back inside and closed the door, Luke turned to Riley and Cooper. "Let's continue canvassing these houses. I'm hoping someone saw the car and can provide more details. It aligns with how long I think Walter has been dead."

CHAPTER 21

Cooper showed up at his loft dog tired from the day. The last thing he and Riley did before calling it for the night was walk the neighborhood to see if anyone else saw the man sitting in his car at the edge of the woods that night. A few neighbors did, but the person was a ghost. No one remembered what he looked like or the car – other than a nondescript four-door sedan in either black or dark blue. One person even suggested gray. When pressed about how they knew it was a man, people were stumped. One guy just said he didn't know but that the outline and the shadow in the car seemed bigger than a woman. That's all they had to go on.

Luke had gone back to the scene to speak to the medical examiner and the crime scene techs. He encouraged Riley to go home to get some sleep and asked Cooper to make sure she got there. They were both worried about Luke. He had been running from one thing to the next all day.

On the way back, they stopped off to see Cat, who had called herself a rideshare back to her studio while they were canvassing the houses. She seemed a bit melancholy to Cooper. He tried to get her to talk, but she assured him she was fine just tired. Cooper wondered if she was just frustrated that the recent kidnappings were complicating her cold case.

"What's on your mind, babe?" Adele asked as she slid off her silk blue robe and slid into bed next to him. "You look like you're a million miles away."

"Are you feeling better?"

Adele shrugged. "It comes and goes. I'll be fine. Tell me what's going on."

Cooper snuggled her into him and dropped a kiss on her forehead. "I was thinking about Cat. I am starting to wonder if the case back then is connected to the cases now. If so, it leaves Cat in an impossible situation with the podcast. She's already put a lot of work into it. She promised Luke she'd never tackle an open case."

"Then don't. Follow the leads and if it intersects with the current case, that's just how it goes. You all might be able to better help Luke that way."

Cooper sighed. "I feel helpless. I can't do much for Luke. I'm not able to find much for Cat for the podcast. I can't do anything to locate Jenna."

Adele took his hand in hers. "This is the way it always goes. You all are too hard on yourselves. I know a child is missing. I know how heartbreaking that can be. I also know there's only so much you can do." Adele spoke from experience. Her sister had been missing for several years before her body was found. It was the case where Cooper and Adele met for the first time. She knew the feeling that Gail was going through.

Cooper knew Adele would have some insight. "What can we do for Gail? Riley tried to speak to her and she didn't have much to say. She's convinced Randy Stock took her sister, has been the one harassing her, and now took her daughter. I don't believe Randy is involved at all. All signs point to the fact that the lead detective rushed to judgment. He's in prison and has no access to kidnap the girls this morning. I saw him in prison with my own eyes. I also spoke to the warden and Randy hasn't been harassing anyone. I don't know how to convince her."

"Then don't try," Adele said. "Don't dismiss her feelings. Whatever her feelings are, they are valid. Work to understand why she feels that way. Why is she holding onto that even in the face of logic? It's probably because if she doesn't hold onto the fact that it's Randy, she has to face the notion that the real kidnapper got away with it for all these years. It's far scarier to know that he's out there, harassing her, and could have taken her at any time. Now he's possibly taken her daughter. That unknown must be terrifying. At least with Randy in prison, Gail might feel some justice and some safety."

"I didn't think about it that way. I was so focused on wanting to convince her it wasn't Randy."

"That doesn't serve any purpose. She's going to believe whatever she believes until you bring her someone else." Adele reached over and put some lotion on her hands. She rubbed it up and down her arms. "Let the poor woman believe whatever helps her sleep at night – for now, until you can prove to her otherwise."

Cooper hadn't thought about it that way. He put his finger under Adele's chin, turning her head to him and planted a smacking kiss on her lips. "I don't know how I ever survived without you. You've been so focused on my moping that I didn't even ask about your case today."

"It went okay," she said with a shrug. "He took a plea for one to three years in prison. It was a basic robbery charge, but he had priors. I thought I might be able to beat it. If I didn't, he was looking at a much longer sentence. He told me we weren't going to beat it. I had to believe him. I suspect there was more he wasn't telling me."

"Is that common with your clients?" Cooper wasn't sure he liked that Adele worked with some rough offenders sometimes. She was careful about the cases she took as a criminal defense attorney. Knowing she went to the office and worked with some of the worst out there didn't always sit well with him.

"Some," she responded as she yawned. "It takes a while to gain their trust. People are not quick to disclose all the bad. It's not that I need to know they are innocent. I need to know what complications will come up in court. If I know before going in, I can work to mitigate it or cut a deal. I get frustrated when they don't tell me and I'm blindsided."

Cooper felt the same in his work. He leaned over and turned out the light, sinking lower in bed with Adele still in his arms. He fell asleep thinking about Randy's defense attorney and what complications he had faced in the trial. Cooper wasn't sure if there were many, given the little real evidence presented. He'd find the man's name tomorrow and call him.

They said goodnight. Adele rolled over on her side, leaving Cooper to stare at the ceiling until his eyes finally closed.

He wasn't sure how long he'd been asleep when a buzzing on the nightstand woke Cooper from a sound sleep. He slapped at it, bringing the glowing screen of his cellphone to his face. The unknown number went to voicemail and immediately called again.

"Hello," Cooper said through a gravelly sleep-filled voice. "Hello. Are you there?" He pushed himself upright.

"We need to meet," the man on the other end of the phone said. "Now."

Cooper looked at the clock next to where the phone had been. 3:47 a.m. "Who is this?"

"I know who killed those girls thirty years ago. I have evidence."

"What do you mean you have evidence?" Cooper rubbed the sleep from his eyes and glanced over at Adele. She was snoring softly and would be no matter what he did. She was such a sound sleeper that unless Cooper yelled at the top of his voice or shook her, she wouldn't wake. Even her alarm was set at such a volume Cooper had once joked that she was preparing to wake the dead.

"Not over the phone. I need to make sure I can trust you. Be there or else I'll disappear."

"Why not just go to the cops?"

"I don't trust them. After what I have to tell you, you won't either." The man gave Cooper an address where he wanted to meet in twenty minutes. "Come alone."

The call ended as abruptly as it started.

Cooper put his bare feet to the floor and debated whether he should call Luke. In the end, he chose to let his friend sleep. He had enough on his plate. He certainly wasn't going to drag Riley out of bed, and he wasn't going to ask Cat to be his backup. He'd go it alone.

He went to his closet, pulled on clothes, grabbed the keys off the counter, slid his feet into boots at the door and headed for his SUV in the parking garage.

Cooper paused at the entrance of Murray Park, a small stretch of greenery that ran along the Arkansas River, its dark trees huddled close together. The wind kicked up, rustling the leaves in a way that seemed almost anxious.

He checked his phone again. No calls or texts.

Cooper stood at the edge of the park, staring into the dark, the streetlights giving off just enough light to show a winding path that went directly to the river. His gut twisted. He shouldn't be out here alone. There were too many unknowns. Too many risks. But a lead was a lead, and it was impossible to ignore.

He walked toward the park where the man had asked to meet. Cooper's senses were sharp. The ground was soft beneath his feet, and the distant sound of water lapping against the river's edge was strangely calming, if only for a moment.

Then, he saw him.

A figure standing just beyond the reach of the streetlight, half in shadow, half in the dim glow of a distant lamp. The man was tall, wearing a long coat, and though the night was cool, the collar was turned up, hiding the lower half of his face. Cooper's heart thudded in his chest. He didn't like how the man hadn't made any move to approach, hadn't even acknowledged him with a gesture.

"Cooper?" The man's voice was low, almost lost in the rustle of the leaves. His breath came out in a thin mist, and his hands were tucked deep in his pockets.

"That's me." Cooper tried to steady his voice, but his throat felt dry. He stepped forward, keeping his eyes on the figure, making sure to stay alert, to read every nuance of the man's body language. He was rigid and cloaked in the shadows.

"Did you come alone?" the man asked with an edge to his voice. The way he spoke was unsettling – slow, deliberate, like he was measuring each word. When Cooper confirmed he was indeed alone, the man continued. "You need to listen carefully. Randy Stock didn't do it. I know that for a fact."

Cooper's mind raced. "How do you know this?" His voice was barely above a whisper. He couldn't afford to show too much interest and couldn't afford to give the man any advantage. He wanted to ask his name and push for details. Cooper had the sense that if he did, the man would run.

The figure shifted slightly, but didn't move closer. His voice dropped lower, a thin thread of tension in it now. "I was a different man back then."

"Okay," Cooper said slowly. "I don't care what you did. I don't even care that you took thirty years to come forward. I understand how hard this can be. If you know something, I need to know, so I can make sure justice is served."

The man said he understood. Some of the tension left his voice. "Thirty years ago, there was a cop who arrested me for drugs. I got into drugs in high school, dropped out, and got on a bad path. I was homeless for a while and running the streets. I got picked up by the cops often. The last time I remember clearly. I hadn't gotten high that day. I was out of supply and panhandling on the street. The cop who picked me up insisted I had drugs on me. When he reached for me, he slipped a bag of coke into my pocket. That wasn't even my high of choice. But it was enough of a ruse to bring me in."

Cooper had known cops to do things like that. There weren't many he knew when he was on the force, but they gave all cops a bad name. "Do you remember if the girls were already missing at this time?"

"They were because everyone on the street was talking about it. They were worried some of the heat might come down in the wrong place, even though they had already picked up Randy Stock. No one believed it. Not because they knew Randy, but it was too fast, especially because they didn't get the girls back. Do you know what I mean?"

Cooper knew exactly what he meant. "I understand you. The girls were missing and people were talking. A cop planted drugs on you and brought you in. Did you have a lot of interaction with the cop?"

"He was known to plant evidence on people like me. We all knew to be wary of him." The man sighed as if remembering the time. "I got thrown into the back of his squad car and that's when I saw it." The man reached into his coat and pulled out a small, weathered object, holding it out toward Cooper.

For a moment, Cooper didn't understand. It was just a sneaker. A small pink sneaker, worn and faded with age, but unmistakable. "What's that?"

"A sneaker."

"I know that. What's the meaning of it?" Cooper was staring at the object, trying to place where he might have seen it before. It took him a few seconds to put it together. He'd seen a similar sneaker in one of the old, faded posters of the missing girls. He couldn't recall now which girl's sneaker it was, but he was sure he'd seen it before. "You're saying this was in the cop's car?"

The man nodded once, his eyes hidden in the darkness. "Kind of wedged under one of the floormats. It was kind of sticking out enough that I noticed the bump and kicked it with my foot to reveal the sneaker. I had a feeling right away that maybe it was important. Who'd arrest a kid that young, you know?"

Cooper looked at the sneaker again, his mind racing. This was a bombshell – a twist that could unravel everything. "I don't understand how you got it out of the car."

"I didn't," the man admitted. "I had a friend on the inside who was getting out as I was getting in. I tucked the sneaker back up under the mat as best I could. Then I clocked the car number on my way out. My friend broke into the car later that night and got it for me."

"Why?" Cooper asked, wondering about the man's motive. "Why risk it for kids you don't know?"

The man snorted. "I didn't do it for the girls. I assumed they were already dead. If that cop was the one who took them, I wanted to get him in trouble. I wanted him gone. It was revenge. But by the time I could do anything about it, the public was convinced that it was Randy Stock. If all of a sudden, I show up with one of the girls' sneakers, I figured they'd try to pin it on me. They'd say I was working with Randy, who I didn't even know. I saw what they did to him and I didn't want them to do it to me, too."

"What's the cop's name? What's your name? You have to give me something to go on if you expect me to do something with it."

"You don't need to know that." His voice had changed, colder now. "You figure out the rest."

Cooper stood there, still holding the sneaker, his mind spinning. The man turned abruptly, stepping away into the darkness of the park, melting into the trees like a ghost.

For a moment, Cooper didn't move. He just stood there, the weight of the sneaker in his hand.

CHAPTER 22

I woke the next morning still groggy from the night before. Luke came home late. He slept for a few hours before he was back out on the case. I tried through sleepy chatter to convince him he needed more rest. He wouldn't relent and told me he had to get down to the morgue to see the medical examiner about Walter Fields's body. Luke was hoping there'd be word about how long the man had been dead.

I woke around seven, made some coffee, and went into my home office to see what I could get done before meeting with Cat and Cooper later in the morning. There wasn't much I could do to help Luke with his case and things had ground to a halt with ours. I had just started a deep dive on some social media searching when the knock came from downstairs.

Three quick raps. I'd know the sound of Cooper knocking from anywhere, the weight of it and the rhythm. I wasn't expecting to see him. I was already on my feet, pushing myself away from the cluttered desk.

I swung the door open, and he stood there – the scent of sweet croissants and coffee clinging to him. In one hand the treats, but in his other hand, he cradled something carefully. It was wrapped in a plastic bag.

I blinked. "What is that?" I asked as I moved out of the way to let him in.

Cooper handed me the coffee carrier with a bag balanced in the middle. I carried it to the kitchen as he followed behind me. "What if I told you this sneaker was the key to everything?" He didn't wait for a response before setting it down on the kitchen table.

I pulled plates out of a cabinet and carried them to the table, sliding one in front of me and the other to Cooper. I tugged the coffees out of the carrier and unwrapped the folded-over bag to find warm croissants – chocolate for Cooper and a decadent cookie-dough croissant for me.

Cooper pulled gloves from his pocket and snapped them on. Once it was out of the plastic, I was surprised to be met with a child's sneaker – a little girl's sneaker, to be specific. It looked worn down, the sole half detached, and the color so faded it looked more gray than pink. A chill ran up my spine. "What is that?"

"Last night," Cooper began, his eyes locking onto mine, "I got a call from someone who wanted to meet down at Murray Park. Before you lecture me about going alone, I wasn't going to bring Adele. I wasn't going to put you at risk either."

He had anticipated what I was going to say. I pulled out the chair and sat. There was no point lecturing him. "Did you call Luke?"

Cooper shook his head. "I wanted him to get some sleep. I assume he's already gone."

"He left at six. I don't know how he's still standing. He's running on only a few hours of sleep." I didn't want to talk about Luke. He was as stubborn as Cooper when in the middle of a case. I gestured toward the sneaker. "You got a call from someone and met them in the dead of night at Murray Park. I assume he's the one who gave you the sneaker. What's his name?"

"He wouldn't tell me," Cooper admitted. "I wanted the information more than I wanted a name. His face was in the shadows, but I would recognize him again if I saw him. His story was compelling, Riley. I believed him."

"What did he tell you?"

"He was arrested for drugs shortly after the girls went missing. He said the cop who busted him was always giving them a hard time, planting evidence on them. He admitted that he did drugs, but he made it sound like the cop was always trying to set them up."

I eyed him suspiciously. I had heard more than one criminal complain that they'd been set up. "You believe him?"

"I don't think how he ended up in the back of the squad car matters as much as what he found once he was inside." Cooper looked down at the sneaker.

"No," I said with a trace of disbelief in my voice. "He found that sneaker just lying in the back of the car?"

"He said it was tucked up under the mat. He saw the lump and had to work the mat with his foot to free it. Once he saw it there, he knew there was something not right about it. Why would a kid that young be in the back of a cop car?" Cooper recounted the man's story about how he left it there, passed word to a friend getting out of prison, who then broke into the car and got the sneaker back before anyone noticed it.

I wanted to be careful how I responded to this because it was clear to me that Cooper bought into the story. "I don't think we can speculate. Do we know for sure that the sneaker belongs to one of the girls?"

Cooper pulled out his phone, scrolled through photos, and handed it to me. "That photo is a little fuzzy. Look closely and tell me what you see."

I peered down at the image. It was fuzzy, cloudy, almost. The photo was thirty years old and it was a digital copy of a printed photo. Even with all of that, the sneaker was clear as day. "It looks like the sneaker," I admitted. "Whose sneaker is it?"

"Kathleen Elliott. There was a missing poster of the girls that had run in the newspaper. I was able to get an image of it online. I snapped this photo and blew it up. Sure enough, there was the sneaker. It's identical, Riley. I was skeptical too until I saw this. See the little bead on the shoelace? It's the same one."

That's where my focus had been. I was sure there were countless sneakers of the same color and style at the time. Very few people would have had the same hot pink and white bead at the end of the shoelaces. It was something that Kathleen had put there herself. I remember doing something similar as a kid. "What do you think this means? Do we know for sure she was wearing these sneakers when she went missing? That's going to be critical to find out."

Cooper took his phone back and pulled up another image. This one was of written text. He read from it a description of what the girls were each wearing on the day they went missing. Kathleen Elliot had on blue shorts with a pink and white shirt and pink sneakers that her mother said she was never without. She had worn them down to the soles, her mother had commented. They were her favorites.

Cooper put the phone down and reached for the sneaker showing the worn soles. "This is hers. I'm sure of it."

There was little I could say to deny it. "What do you think this means?"

"I think those girls got picked up in a cop car." Cooper put the sneaker on top of the bag and sat back. "That's something that always bothered me about this case. There were three of them. The speculation was that the guy had a gun and that scared them into going with him. Still, three girls, Riley. One of them could have made a run for it."

"They were scared and probably wanted to protect their friends."

Cooper shook his head. "I don't buy it. A stranger approaches you, even with a gun. You've got a bike. You can take off."

"Little girls, Cooper. These were little girls. You're thinking from a grown man's perspective. That said, I do understand what you're saying. If a cop pulled up to them in a cop car and told them they needed to come with him – no matter the story he concocted, the girls would go. Heck, I'd probably go if a cop told me he was taking me to you or Luke because something bad happened to you." It was the perfect ruse to use on them.

"The problem," Cooper said with a sigh, "is that I don't know the guy's name who gave this to me and don't have the cop's name either. There is no way I can track this down."

I considered what he said and wasn't sure he was right. "We know when the girls went missing. That sneaker didn't sit in the back of that cop car for long and we know a friend of his got out of prison on the day he went in. There couldn't have been that many people let out of the jail within those few days. Back then, there wasn't a county jail. It was a city jail."

"Who has the records? Do you think they are still around?"

"There's only one way to find out." It meant we were going to have to start with the Little Rock Police Department to see what kind of city jail records they kept. If not, we'd have to move on to city or county records. Starting with the police would be our easiest route. "I bet Tyler will give us access if we ask nicely." Tyler had warmed to me over time. It had been rocky at the start. The last couple of cases, he had even told Luke to let me be involved if he thought it would help. "Let's go talk to him and see what records he can access."

I didn't expect to find Luke sitting at his desk in the police station. I had assumed he'd be out in the field or at the medical examiner's office. His face brightened when he saw us walk in.

"What are you doing here?" he asked as Cooper and I went to his desk. His tone was friendly, almost happy to see us. "It's been a rough morning."

Cooper leaned on the edge of his desk. "What did you find out?"

"Walter Fields had been dead nearly forty-eight hours when we found him last night. There was no way he was the one who took those girls. I assume whoever took those girls killed him, stole his car, and made it look like he took them."

That was reasonable enough for me. "Do you have any leads on who that could be?"

"No," Luke said, shaking his head. "The other challenge is that Scarlett told me he said his name was Walter. She didn't say that at the beginning, but she told the child psychologist at the hospital. She didn't recognize him from the photo. There's just a ton of conflicting information."

It was to be expected with a child. "What did they find at the hospital?"

"That was at least good news. By all accounts, she was not abused. Traumatized by the kidnapping and being held. Whoever took her didn't hit her or sexually abuse her – that we can confirm anyway. The children's advocacy center is designed for that sort of thing, to interview kids about that kind of abuse. Scarlett denied that anything more happened than what she said. The expert who interviewed her believed that to be true. In the absence of any other evidence or until Scarlett says something different, we have to believe what she says."

I could hear the resignation in Luke's voice. "Can't you go back to the woman who interviewed her and address the issues of Walter Fields? Maybe the person who took her told her to lie or said his name was Walter to confuse us. If she didn't recognize him in the photo and we know he's been dead for forty-eight hours, it can't be him. What about the sketch artist rendering?"

Luke shook his head. "She couldn't do it. She kept changing the details. I don't want to put her through more, Riley. She's been through enough."

"You have to," I said evenly. The truth was Scarlett was the only one who saw the man who took her and her friend. No one else was going to know that information. "I know you don't want to, Luke. I know it might traumatize her more. If you have any shot of getting Jenna back, Scarlett has to tell us what she knows."

"I know," Luke said through a stifled yawn. He gestured toward the bag in Cooper's hand. "I didn't ask why you were here. What's that?"

"Potential evidence." Cooper opened the bag so Luke could see inside. "I know you're bogged down with this case and aren't too keen on us digging around in the kidnappings from thirty years ago, but I had a source call me last night to meet. He told me a wild story and gave me this little girl's sneaker." Cooper relayed the rest of the details. I watched as my husband's eyes got wide, he frowned, and shook his head.

"There must be some other explanation for this other than a cop was involved. I just can't believe that."

"I know. I'm having a hard time too," I said, agreeing with him. "The man wasn't willing to tell Cooper his name or the cop's name. He didn't share any details, but he's been holding onto that sneaker for thirty years. We don't have a lot to go on otherwise."

"Why not come forward sooner?"

"That was the same question I had." I turned to Cooper to let him explain it.

"He said the cop set him up with the drug charge. The cop was known to plant evidence. The guy last night didn't know what kind of retribution he'd face if he came forward with it." Cooper closed the bag with the sneaker. "There was also the logistics to contend with. He was being arrested and didn't figure the sneaker would be there for long. By the time he got out and had the sneaker in his possession, the community and the cops were convinced it was Randy Stock. He didn't think anyone would believe him. Worse, he thought they might suspect him of being involved."

Luke asked, "If you don't have the guy's name or the cop's name, what are you doing here? No one is going to take that seriously. You're not going to be able to get evidence off it now."

"You're right on all counts," I conceded. "There's one thing left to explore. The guy told Cooper that a friend just getting out of jail was able to break into the cop car and retrieve the sneaker. We were hoping there might be some records of who was getting out of the city jail around that time."

Luke shrugged but didn't look convinced. "There might be records. You can talk to Tyler about it, which is who I assume you're here to see." He paused and pointed to the bag. "Have either of you stopped to consider that the man who gave you that might have been the one who took the girls? He could just be toying with you, enjoying watching you chase your tail."

I said yes at the same time as Cooper. "We discussed it but kept coming back to the same conclusion. No matter what, we have to authenticate the story. Are you suggesting you believe Randy Stock might be innocent?"

In Luke's tired state, it took him a moment to realize that, yes, that's exactly what he was suggesting. "Do what you have to do. As you said, there's only one way to know for sure. Track down the guy who got out of prison and see if that story tracks." He pointed to the sneaker. "There might be DNA from the guy holding it for thirty years and from Kathleen Elliott. Let's bring it down to the lab. If the guy was arrested, his details will be on file."

I couldn't agree with Luke fast enough – this was all working according to plan.

CHAPTER 23

Hours later, I came to realize the task I had committed myself to. None of the old jail records had been digitized. I think it's why Tyler was okay with giving us the access. He thought it was a fool's errand. Like Luke, he didn't believe the story about the man with the sneaker. He didn't believe it was connected to the missing girls all those years ago. On the off chance it was, Tyler thought like Luke – maybe *that guy* was the real suspect now toying with investigators as everyone worried about the impending release of Randy Stock.

Tyler's theory didn't make any sense to me. No one had been charged with the murder of the three girls because there had been no tangible evidence that they were dead. Other than a few sightings, no one knew anything. If the man who had reached out to Cooper was the real kidnapper and the girls were dead, he could still be charged. Why implicate himself now? It was too risky. But I also wondered why the man had come forward now after so much time had passed.

Cooper speculated it was the man's guilt that drove him or maybe he had seen the news and suspected the same kidnapper was at play. Either way, Cooper wasn't questioning the man's motive. He was just happy to have some evidence. He had other cases to handle, so I volunteered to head to the basement of the county courthouse to dig through the old jail records. Tyler had called over and greased the wheels for me to get the access I needed. I was excited until I was led to the basement and through a series of dank, winding hallways to what felt like a tomb.

It was the smell that hit me before anything else – the musty, stale air that hung in the damp records room, thick like mildew, suffocating on its history. The man who had walked me down there had flipped on the too dim overhead light, gestured toward a small table in the middle of the room, and wished me luck before retreating.

The room wasn't much bigger than a broom closet, but the shelves stretched all around the walls, suffocating me in their closeness. Each row of files felt like it had been placed there without much care, stacked in no particular order, piles of paperwork spilling onto the floor, forgotten boxes tucked into corners. The records had been left to decay, long forgotten by anyone who cared.

The chill forced me to keep my coat on. I pulled it tighter around my shoulders, but it didn't do much to block out the cold that cut through the old brick walls. The courthouse was cold this time of year, especially in the back corners where no one bothered to turn on the heat.

I sat hunched over the rickety wooden table. The legs wobbled beneath me as I sifted through the endless piles of yellowed manila files. The light from the single overhead bulb flickered intermittently, casting more shadows than illumination, making it harder to see the small print on the aging papers. I'd been at this for hours, my fingers were sore from turning the brittle pages of one file after another, trying to find something – anything – that matched the thin details I had.

I didn't have a name or age or any details about the ghost I was hunting in the files. All I knew was that he was released from the Little Rock city jail either the afternoon after the disappearance or a few days later. I didn't even know what crime he committed or what he looked like. I was fumbling around in the dark, hoping to trip over the information.

He was likely arrested for something minor – nothing serious enough to keep him behind bars for long. It could have been anything like public intoxication, loitering, disorderly conduct, or even a minor drug offense.

I sifted through the mountain of records, each file more worn than the last, each one more frustrating. The paper crackled under my fingertips, like it could crumble at any moment. The stacks were precariously perched one on top of the other, high on shelves that groaned under the weight. They were at least organized by order of date. Only I didn't know if it was a processing date, entrance date or exit. There seemed to be no rhyme or reason for that based on the few files I opened.

With each file I went through, if there was even a hint that it might be the guy, I put it aside.

My fingers stiffened from the chill. The cold settled deep into my bones, and the room, with its damp, suffocating atmosphere, was more oppressive than anything I'd been forced to sit in for a long time. The deeper I got into the files, the more it felt like the walls were closing in on me, taunting me almost. My eyes blurred with the monotony of it all, but I kept at it, hoping that eventually, I'd hit on something that made sense.

About three hours into the search, details resonated, and a name caught my attention. Billy Murphy. I paused, squinting at a file in front of me. Petty larceny. Got out the day after the kidnapping. It noted in the record that he briefly spoke to an incoming prisoner and the guard needed to separate them. I leaned in, feeling my pulse quicken. This could be it.

I made quick work of reviewing the entire file. My eyes scanned over the document, hoping to find the name of the incoming prisoner who had been in conversation with Billy. That wasn't indicated anywhere in the file. I don't even know why it had been noted at all. But someone had written it down and it was the one piece of evidence I couldn't ignore.

This had to be the person. None of the others fit in age.

I reached for my notepad and pulled the blank page toward me. I had figured I would have a lot more in the way of notes to take – more suspects and information to track. I hadn't found anything that remotely fit the information Cooper's source had mentioned. The men knew each other, so it was a solid guess that they might be around the same age.

Billy fit that description. Even where he had been arrested fit where the source said he had spent some time. It was the same part of town. I was sure down deep in my gut that Billy Murphy was the one. I took as much information from the file as I could – name, age, date of birth, hair and eye color, height, and last known address. There was nothing about the man's family or where he was being released to indicated in the report.

Nevertheless, it gave me a starting point.

I pulled out my phone, hoping to connect with the database Cooper and I use on cases. I tried once and then again to connect to the internet. The screen remained black, trying to bring up the website. I tossed my phone down and gathered all the files back, putting them in a neat pile on the shelf, neater than when I found them.

I gathered my things and tore out of the basement of the courthouse, nearly bumping into someone in the main hallway. Once I breached the doors and the fresh air hit me, I stood right on the steps of the building and called Cooper.

"I found something," I said as soon as he answered. I gave Cooper a rundown of the information. "I didn't have enough cell service to search the database. It's also too small on the phone. Can you do it?"

"Give me five minutes and meet me back at my loft."

I made my way over there as quickly as I could. I knocked once on the door, nudged it open, and found Cooper hunched over his laptop. "Any news from the lab about the sneaker?"

He didn't even look up at me. "Not so far. They said it was going to be a while, if they are able to find anything at all. For all we know, the guy who gave it to me wiped the prints from it. The tech told me the sneaker was in poor condition from age and wear. But he said it had a faint smell of a cleaning product."

"Like a disinfectant?"

Cooper nodded. "I didn't notice it. He said it was faint."

"I didn't notice it either. Of course, I wasn't smelling it." I tossed my bag on the couch and tugged my notebook from it. "I think the man's name is Billy Murphy." I went over all the other details.

Cooper got up from the couch with his laptop and gestured for me to follow him back to his home office. He had set up two workstations, one for him and one for Adele. They had talked about moving to a bigger space, but both liked living downtown. I pulled Adele's chair from her desk up to Cooper's and gave him the information again as he typed it into the database.

Cooper leaned forward as he read the information. "William David Murphy lives in downtown Little Rock in the SOMA neighborhood. He owns a house on Center Street."

"Does it say what he does for work?"

"No. It won't give me that. There's no other arrest record for him since the one you found. Looks like the guy might have turned his life around." Cooper looked over at me. "Should we pay him a visit?"

I checked my watch, not that I had anything else pending. "The sooner we can put this situation to bed, the better. Either he confirms the story or tells us that it never happened and we are back to square one."

I turned off the main road and into a quieter part of the SOMA neighborhood. The streets were narrow, lined with trees whose branches reached across like old, tired arms. The houses wore their age with pride. The houses had weathered brick, worn-down shutters, and porches that sagged under the weight of time. I pulled up to a bungalow near the end of the block. It looked like it had been here for decades, a solid structure but fading in the Arkansas heat.

The house had that old-world charm. The blue paint looked like it was fairly new, and a porch swing swayed in the light breeze on the wide front porch on its chain, empty and still. A few windows let in the midday sun, casting lazy shadows across the front. The lawn was well kept and the concrete of the driveway looked newer than the surrounding houses. The whole place had a quiet, unassuming presence. The Ford truck sitting in the driveway indicated that someone was probably home.

Cooper beat me to the porch. He knocked once, waited, and then rapped his knuckles against the wood twice more. After a few moments, a man in his late fifties opened the door, peering out at us with suspicion in his eyes. "Can I help you two?"

"Billy Murphy?" Cooper asked. The man corrected him that it was William now and that no one had called him Billy in a long time. "Understood. We'd like to speak to you about something that happened thirty years ago."

The man started to close the door, but I reached for it before he could. "Please. This isn't about anything you might have done. What you remember might help us find a missing girl."

William pinched the bridge of his nose. "I don't know how I can help you."

Cooper explained how he received a late-night call to meet a stranger in the park, where he was given the sneaker. He pulled his phone out and showed the man a photo of the sneaker in question. "This is important. Factors link the crime from thirty years ago to the missing girl today. I'm sure you've seen the recent case on the news."

William nodded and peered over and looked at the photo, recognition apparent in his eyes. "How do the two cases connect?"

"Gail Albright Herin, Jenna's mom, is Samantha Albright's sister. She's been getting harassing phone calls for the past thirty years. Then her daughter goes missing in the same way."

"That's a weird coincidence. She's an unlucky woman."

"No," Cooper said with force. "It's not unlucky. It's too much of a coincidence. There's a connection and you're the only one right now who might be able to help us."

William gestured toward the phone. "Did the person who gave you the sneaker give you his name?"

Cooper shook his head. "He wouldn't give me your name either."

William opened the door again, looking between us. "How did you find me?"

I explained about the court records. "It was by sheer luck that someone wrote in the report that you were speaking to someone you knew and they had to separate you. Otherwise, I might not have known it was you."

"Lucky me," he scoffed, then sighed deeply. "Come on in. I've been keeping these secrets for thirty years. That might be long enough."

I didn't know what he was about to tell me, but I knew whatever he had to say was going to be important.

CHAPTER 24

Luke sat in the conference room in the police station going over every bit of evidence. Tyler and Granger bounced questions off him and they discussed the many possibilities. Even after two hours of throwing everything against the wall, nothing stuck.

"We are going to have to go back to Walter Fields's house and tear it apart again," Luke said, the frustration in his voice evident. The Arkansas State Police and several search teams were hard at work trying to locate Jenna. It would do no good to have Luke and Granger in the field too. They needed to do the work on the back end to figure out who took her and Scarlett. They were waiting for a call from the child psychologist who was speaking to Scarlett to see if she'd be more forthcoming about the man who took her. There was a lot riding on what a young girl could remember – too much to make Luke comfortable.

"We already tore it apart, Luke," Granger reminded him. "There has to be some connection between the man who killed him and Walter."

"His files at the shop," Tyler suggested. "Have you gone through them?"

Luke confirmed that there weren't any paper files. There was only a computer that had a passcode they hadn't been able to crack. "It's down with a forensics team. We are hoping they can find a way in. We went through the photos. There's nothing that stands out at the shop.

There's no client list or anything. It wasn't in his house either. I have to assume that's in the computer. I'm hoping the forensics team can get into the computer to tell us more about Walter's online activity."

Tyler was satisfied with that. "What is he? A pedophile? A run-of-the-mill pervert?"

Luke looked to Granger. It was something they had been discussing all day. "The truth is, we don't know. None of the photos would be considered pornographic. There was nothing in the photos that we could even use to arrest him. But that's not to say that something wasn't haunting about the images."

"Unsettling," Granger added. "The forensics team started going through them. No one has been identified yet. If Walter was snatching kids and keeping them in there, I'd think we'd have a lot more missing kids."

Luke and Tyler agreed with that.

"No forensics from the room?" Tyler asked.

"Still being processed," Luke said. "The room was stripped bare for the most part. There wasn't dust, so it looked like someone had either been in there recently or had cleaned it. We can't say for certain that anyone was kept in there, but someone was in that room recently."

Granger countered, "With Fields taken out of the equation, I think all bets are off. I can't even say for certain that he's the one who put those photos up on the wall. It might have all been staged for our benefit. Whoever took the girls had to know that as soon as we got the license plate off that car, we were going to the house. It seems like someone went a long way to set up Walter Fields for the kidnapping."

A nagging thought had been in the back of Luke's mind since finding Fields's body. "What if the person who did this expected us to believe that Fields had killed himself, being distraught over what he had done. I know the gun wasn't there, but I don't think anyone expected us to find the body that soon. By the time anyone did find him, a gun by his side could have been long gone. If we hadn't found him for months, we might not even be able to tell the cause of death. The kidnapping was pinned on him then he's dead. The natural assumption is that he killed himself for what he did."

Luke knew Granger was on the same train of thought when he added, "The same way Randy Stock went to prison right away before those girls could be found. Before the case even really had a chance to be investigated."

Tyler waved him off. "We don't want to go down that road. You're starting to sound like Riley and Cooper."

"What if they aren't wrong?" Granger asked, glancing over at Luke. "The similarities are there. The cases are connected, whether we want to acknowledge it or not. There's no way it's a coincidence that Gail Herin's sister went missing, never to be found, and now her daughter."

Luke recalled what Riley had told him about the ongoing harassing phone calls. He looked directly at Tyler. "I have to agree with Granger. I know you don't want us going off on a wild goose chase. Normally, I'd be right there with you. Gail has been receiving harassing phone calls, threatening calls, practically her whole life. The other families did as well."

Tyler sat back and folded his arms across his chest. He had the look of consideration in his eyes. At least, he wasn't dismissing them outright. "When was the last call Gail received and what was the context?"

"Not even a week ago. Threats to her daughter," Granger told him. "Once I heard that she told Riley and Cooper about the calls, I followed up and asked about the nature of the last one. I figured it might be important."

"I should have done that," Luke admitted, praising his partner. He had to admit that he didn't want to dredge up the past and put a spotlight on another detective's case because he knew it hadn't been handled well. There was no point tarnishing the department over one detective's actions thirty years ago. Luke had been holding onto the hope that the right man had been arrested, tried, and convicted. Luke expelled a breath, frustrated with his shortsightedness. "I should have considered that the two cases were connected right away. That one's on me, Tyler."

"No," Tyler responded with force. "There is no way you could have known the cases were connected. You were following the leads as you got them. You did the right thing, Luke."

That may be, but it wasn't what Luke was feeling. "Where do we go from here? We aren't going to know until the forensics come back. We know approximately when Fields was murdered, but we don't know where and by whom. We don't know who took Jenna, but I think it's safe to say it's probably the same person who killed Fields, and there's some connection to Gail Herin."

"Start with Herin," Tyler said. "Go back if you have to and find the connection. If the calls are still coming and it's the same person who was threatening her all those years ago, then there's a connection. He's getting the information about her moving and change of phone number somehow. Go talk to the Herin family and monitor the phone calls. Have her record them and maybe we can get a trace on it."

As Luke started to respond, his cellphone buzzed on his hip. He glanced down to see a text from an officer downstairs who was sitting with Scarlett and her mother, Amelia. "The Evanses are here," he said. "I need to go speak with them." Luke was up from the chair and out the door before Granger or Tyler could stop him, not that either one would.

Luke practically ran through the detective's bullpen and down the stairs to the lobby. He found Amelia and Scarlett sitting on the benches waiting for him. Amelia stood as soon as she saw him. "He threatened her if she told the truth. He said that if Scarlett didn't identify Walter

Fields that he was going to kill Jenna and then come back for her. He instructed her on what to say, Luke. He told her to tell the police his name was Walter. He didn't consider that she might be shown a photograph. She doesn't know anything more."

Amelia was speaking like an attorney. He bent a knee to be on Scarlett's level. "You are so brave for coming back in here to speak to me."

Scarlett nodded her little head, her eyes wide with fear. "I don't know if Walter is his name. That's what he told me to call him. He also told me not to talk to the police."

"He told you not to talk to the police?"

Scarlett took a breath, her body rising and falling with it. "The man told me that I'd have to talk to the police later, not right away. I was kind of surprised that you were there."

Luke realized then he had made a critical error. He shouldn't have tried to interview her right in that café. He had been so surprised to see her that he lacked judgment. "That was my fault. I should have brought you down to the police station where you'd be more comfortable. I know all of this was probably really confusing for you. You did a great job."

Scarlett reached her hand out for Amelia. She was not going anywhere without her mother. Luke couldn't blame her. He guided them upstairs into one of the smaller conference rooms. He asked if they'd like anything to drink or some snacks and both declined. Luke told Amelia that he was going to hit the recording equipment if it was okay with her. She readily agreed.

Once Luke sat down at the table, he softened his face, trying to seem less like a detective and more friendly. He asked her about school and what she had for breakfast. He asked about her favorite sports and her friends. As Scarlett got more comfortable and a lot chattier, he slowly changed the topic to the morning she was taken. By then, she had warmed up to him.

"Jenna told me she felt like she knew him," Scarlett said, then went on unprompted by Luke. "She said it was his voice that sounded like someone her mom knew. He called sometimes and left messages on her mom's phone. Jenna said she had heard him and he didn't say nice things. She didn't tell me what he said, just that he sometimes wasn't nice to her mom. Jenna said she wasn't supposed to know about the calls, but she had been standing on the stairs listening once when her parents didn't know she was there. Is she going to get in trouble for that?"

"No, not at all," Luke assured her, thinking back to what Riley and Cooper told him about the calls. It certainly lined up. "Did the man ever say his name on the calls that Jenna heard or when you were in the car?"

"I don't know about all the calls. Jenna said she only heard two. In the car, he said we could call him Walter. He was going to be our friend as long as we behaved ourselves and did what he told us to do."

"Did he ever tell you his last name?"

Scarlett looked up at her mom, who encouraged her to tell the truth. She focused back on Luke. "I found a book of photos in the backseat that had the name Walter Fields on it. I asked him if the book was his but he didn't answer me."

"Did he tell you anything else about his life?"

Scarlett shrugged. "He was kind of talking low. It was hard to hear him in the back seat. He seemed angry at Jenna's mom, but it didn't make any sense to me." She turned and looked up at Amelia. "He was talking like you do when you're cooking. Like nobody is listening to you."

"I do that," Amelia admitted with a little smile. She glanced up at Luke. "Mostly, I'm practicing for court."

Luke admitted he did the same sometimes. "Did he say anything else?"

"Not really. After a while, he told me that he was taking me back home. Right after he got that phone call. I thought he was taking me back home, but he said we were going someplace else and not to talk to the cops. But to tell you that his name was Walter. That's why it was confusing and I didn't tell you right away. Don't talk to the cops but tell the cops his name. That didn't make any sense to me. I didn't want to get Jenna in any more trouble."

"What happened when he dropped you off?"

"He pulled over and got out of the car. He came to the back door, opened it, and let me out. He reminded me not to talk to the cops or he was going to hurt Jenna and come back and take me from my mom."

Luke held back the curse forming on his lips. "Did Jenna say anything?"

"No. She looked really scared. I think she was okay as long as I was there with her. But she was going to be alone with him. I asked him if Jenna could come with me and he said no." Scarlett's eyes started to water and she brushed a tear away. "I was trying to keep her safe."

Luke reassured her that she did the right thing and he understood why she was trying to protect Jenna. "Is there anything about the man you think I should know?"

Scarlett chewed on her lower lip and remained quiet for several moments. Then her eyes got wide. "I remember something. There was a badge, like a policeman's badge in the middle of the two seats. When I tried to ask him about it, he told me that I asked too many questions. I wasn't sure if it was real or fake, like on TV."

Luke exchanged a look with Amelia. It was clear this was the first time she was hearing this.

Could a cop have taken Jenna?

The question was on both of their lips.

CHAPTER 25

William Murphy's house was warm and inviting in stark contrast to the man's mood. The place was neat with the faint smell of sugar. He gestured toward a small table pushed up against the wall. "Sit. My wife made some cookies. Do you want some?"

Cooper and I declined.

He dropped the plate on the table anyway. "You'd better at least have one. If I tell Martha we had company and no one tried the cookies, she's going to be real sore with me. I'm not in the mood to listen to her today." He waited until we both reached under the tinfoil and pulled a cookie out.

I took a few bites before finishing it off. "Thank you. Make sure to tell her that it's the best oatmeal raisin cookie I've had."

William finally sat. "That will make her day. Now, before I tell you what I know, help me understand how you know the cases are related. It's got to be more than Gail."

I explained about the phone calls Gail and the other families had been receiving. "We don't have a lot to say that the cases are connected, but it's circumstantial. The calls and Gail tie it together. We know it wasn't Randy Stock. We checked the prison records."

"Yeah," William confirmed. "You don't get telephone access like that inside. Even when you do, there are a bunch of people standing around and they monitor the calls. I can tell you as someone who was on the inside, it doesn't work like that unless it changed drastically."

Cooper told him it hadn't. "We believe there wasn't justice served for those three little girls and now Jenna is still out there with that man. We are doing everything we can to try to find her."

"How'd you find out about the sneaker?" William asked again.

Cooper admitted, "As I said, the man didn't give me his name. He called me in the middle of the night and asked me for a meet. When we met in Murray Park, he handed over the sneaker. He wouldn't tell me his name or even your name. He said he'd been holding onto it for thirty years and it was time to give it to someone who might be able to do something with it. He saw the report about the missing girls and thought it might help." Cooper paused to see if William would say anything. When he didn't, Cooper went on. "I had to ask him how he got it. That's when he said a friend who was getting out of jail broke into the cop car."

"Now, wait just a moment. I wouldn't call him a friend, and I wouldn't call it breaking in."

"I'm not looking to bust you for something you might or might not have done decades ago. Someone asked you to get the sneaker. Let's say the cop car door was open. You opened it and found it."

"Well, that's what happened. I went back after hours and found the car by the number and the doors were unlocked. The sneaker was right there under the mat, like I was told. I grabbed it and kept it at home until he got out of jail. I handed it over. That was it and now my good deed is coming back to bite me all these years later."

It was obvious he was still wary of police involvement. "I promise you that you're not in any trouble. You've done nothing wrong. We just need to make sure that the guy's story is real. If you're telling us that you pulled this sneaker out of a cop car, we believe you. Do you have any idea whose car it was?"

William shook his head. "There were a lot of cops back then on the street hassling us. It seemed like no matter what we did, the cops were shaking us down. I don't remember anyone's name and certainly don't remember whose car it was. That was my last stint with breaking the law. I got out, got a suspended sentence and probation and got my life clean. I had been doing some drugs back then. When I got out, I went to rehab and straightened up my act. I got a job, met my wife, and have been an upstanding member of the community since then."

I could tell there was still shame from his previous life. "There is no judgment from us. All we care about is finding out which cop had the sneaker. Are you sure you pulled it from the back of the cop car? You remember clearly?"

William chuckled. "I said I was doing some drugs, but I wasn't that messed up. I was in the process of getting sober. Going to rehab was part of my sentence. I was sober getting out of jail and I was sober when I retrieved that sneaker. I swear on my life that I pulled that sneaker out of the back of the cop car." William thought for a few minutes then gave us the exact date too. "I remember because the next morning was my mother's birthday. I left for rehab after having breakfast with her."

That was definitive enough for me. "Can you tell us the name of the man you gave the sneaker to?"

William wavered, looking between Cooper and me. "I'm not sure I want to do that. He didn't give you his name for a reason. I appreciate him not giving you my name."

I leaned forward on the table. "If you remembered the name of the cop, we wouldn't have to go to this guy. There is a young girl's life on the line. Not to mention that Randy Stock lost thirty years of his life for a crime he didn't commit." When that still didn't persuade him, I took a gut shot. "Do you have children?"

William nodded. "I have a daughter and three sons."

"What if this were your daughter who went missing and was never found? How would you feel having to live with never knowing what happened to her? That's what those three families are going through right now." I paused, letting that sink in. "Thirty years of birthdays, holidays. You just don't know what happened to her. You can't even lay your child to rest. I'd rather know my child was deceased than have to live never knowing what happened. At least, that's a little closure. You might be able to provide that. If we get the name of the cop and solve this case, we might know what happened to those girls. Think about the relief you could give those families."

William raised his eyes to Cooper. "Is she being serious?"

Cooper nodded. "I know the case is old. I'm not sure what we can do with it or if the cop is even still alive. Those families have a right to know what happened to their children and there is still a child missing right now. We have to do everything we can." Cooper pointed to the photo of the sneaker. "There is no good reason why this child's sneaker was in the back of the cop car. We need to find out why it was there."

William considered our words for a few moments. "Pat Jenkins. I haven't seen him since I handed over that sneaker. I don't know where he lives or what he does for work. He could still be a criminal for all I know. I'm not vouching for the man."

"No one is asking you to do that. He is his own man," I assured him. I glanced over at Cooper. We had the information we needed. I stood to leave, extending my hand to William. He grasped it in his. "We appreciate the help as will the families."

As William stood, he said, "I sure hope they find that little girl that's missing right now. The same for those girls all those years ago. It was a terrible story back then. I remember how it tore up this city. Stories fade over time. That's good and bad depending on which side you're on."

We left William's house with our spirits buoyed that we might be on our way to finding out the cop who had the sneaker. "He confirmed the story. That's got to count for something," I said with a trace of hope in my voice.

Cooper stared back at the house before getting in his truck. As he slid into the driver's seat, I was already buckling my seatbelt. "I just can't help but feel that if they had come forward sooner that none of this would have had to happen."

I had allowed myself thoughts like that on previous cases. I'd get bogged down in the what might have been. It was never a good road to take. "We can't change any of that now. All we can do is take the information and put it to use in the best way possible."

While I started my SUV, Cooper searched and found Pat's most recent address listed in North Little Rock just over the river, past the downtown Argenta neighborhood over on Pike.

"The neighborhood isn't the best," I commented, even though it didn't matter. We were going.

The streets, the deeper we got into North Little Rock, past the Argenta neighborhood, were cracked like old skin, flaking beneath the tires of my SUV. Pike Avenue blurred past in a patchwork of broken windows, graffitied brick, and chain-link fences.

"Do you think he's going to talk?" I asked, watching a stray dog limp across the road like it had nowhere better to be.

"He sought me out," Cooper said. "I got the sense that he might have wanted to say more. The reality is he probably doesn't want to get involved."

I had seen many cases like that go unsolved – people kept their secrets.

I pulled up to the sagging white house between a boarded-up liquor store and a small gray cinderblock home that looked like most of the home was sitting on the outside front yard. A dog was curled up in a brown leather sofa that had seen better days. Pat's house looked like it was trying to fall in on itself. Shingles hung loose on the roof, and a plastic tarp flapped uselessly over one side like a Band-Aid.

I cut the engine and reached for the door. Cooper stopped me. "You sure you don't want to wait here?" It was a game we played often. He knew that if he put me in a dangerous situation, Luke would lose it on him. While Luke had long since accepted my work – something we had gone rounds on for far too long – he still counted on Cooper to keep me safe.

I nodded. "Where you go, I go. Plus, if we double-team him, he might not be so willing to slam the door in our face."

We stepped out to the road at the side of the curb. A teenager on a bike watched us from the corner, one foot resting on the curb, his eyes narrowing like he'd already made us for cops. We weren't, but I wasn't sure that made us any safer.

Cooper knocked twice on the wooden door, firm and slow. Any harder, it might have caved the whole thing in. A long moment passed. Then the door creaked open.

Pat Jenkins had carved lines deep into his face and gray hair. He wore a stretched-out T-shirt and a pair of sweatpants with a cigarette burn near the knee.

"You found me," he said, voice gravelly and worn. "Imagine that. I give you evidence and instead of focusing on that, you waste time tracking me down. That's what's wrong with the whole system. You're focused on the wrong thing."

Neither Cooper nor I responded to that. Cooper put his foot up to move toward entering the house. Pat didn't make a move to let us in.

"You came to me," Cooper reminded him. "I need to ask you some questions now. Questions you weren't willing to answer the night we met. We can do this here the easy way, or I can send the cops over. You get to pick."

Pat's eyes narrowed. "That wouldn't be good for anybody."

He stepped back and let us in without another word.

194

CHAPTER 26

The living room was a disaster. A tower of old newspapers slouched in the corner. The coffee table was cluttered with ashtrays, beer cans, and a cracked photo frame showing two boys standing in front of a rusted truck. A sour smell lingered in the air – sweat, smoke, and something older.

We sat on a sunken couch. Pat perched on a milk crate across from us, lit a cigarette with shaking fingers, and blew the smoke toward the ceiling fan that clicked every third rotation like it was trying to keep count of its last few days.

"So," he said. "You wanna know about that night."

"Start from the beginning," I said. "The night you got picked up."

He stared at me a beat too long. His eyes were cloudy but not without sharpness, like the rusted edge of a blade still capable of cutting.

"I was nineteen, dumb, and looking for trouble. Got picked up for boosting a stereo out of a Chevy down by the river. Stupid, I know. They threw me in the back of a cruiser and that was it for me that night."

"What cruiser?" Cooper asked.

"2073. That was the number," Pat said. "I was cuffed, so I didn't have much ability to move around. That's when I spotted the bump under the mat. I nearly asked what was back here. Decided to keep my mouth shut. I didn't want more trouble than I already had."

I leaned forward. "The sneaker?"

He nodded. "Yeah. I toed the mat as best I could and it poked out enough for me to see what it was. Little girl's sneaker in the back of a cop car. What do you suppose that was about? I had a really bad feeling right away. I don't know why, but I immediately thought of those little girls I saw on the news that were missing."

"Did the cop notice that you saw it?"

Pat shook his head. "He wasn't paying any attention to me. Just talking to his partner." He took a long drag from his cigarette.

"Did you get a name?" I asked.

Pat shook his head. "If I knew his name back then, it's long gone now. I remember his face. Thin and pale. One of those mean-looking guys who didn't need to raise his voice to scare you."

He stubbed the cigarette out on a greasy plate and leaned back, exhaling slowly. "They dropped the charges on me a week later. Never explained why. Maybe someone found out the cop put the coke on me. Never heard another word about that sneaker. Maybe he didn't know it was back there, or maybe he was afraid when it was stolen out of his car. What was he going to say – I kidnapped a little girl and some crook stole the evidence on me?" Pat chuckled. "I didn't know who to give it to. If the cops were dirty, who was I gonna trust? No one was going to believe me."

"I believe you. Did you ever see that cop again?" I asked.

Pat nodded slowly. "Saw him two more times. Once in a gas station. He was out of uniform, buying a coffee. He looked right at me like he remembered, too. The second time was in a bar on Broadway. He was drunk, talking to a guy about how 'some messes stay buried.' That's what he said. Like he was proud of it. Then he was gone. I never saw him again."

"You never got a name? Not even on your arrest report?" Cooper asked again.

"They dropped the charges. They weren't giving me paperwork and I wasn't asking for it."

The fan clicked overhead. Outside, a siren wailed in the distance.

"You think he's still alive?" I asked.

Pat shrugged. "I don't know. But if he is – he's still dangerous."

Cooper met my eyes. "Then we'd better find him."

"Good luck with that," Pat said with a sarcastic laugh. "You think, even if you find him, the police are going to care? They are going to protect their own."

I shook my head. "My husband is a detective. I can convince him. He's listened to us before on cases."

"I know who your husband is." Pat surprised us with that. "I've listened to that true crime podcast. That's how I knew to give the sneaker to Cooper. Even so, they protect their own. I'm telling you that. Let me guess, you've already spoken to that detective who went after Randy."

The way Pat said the man's name spiked up the tiny hairs on the back of my neck. "Do you know Randy?"

"Not personally. I knew people back then who knew him. They told me there was no way he could have done that. That's why I held onto the sneaker."

It galled me that Pat hadn't come forward sooner. Cooper must have been feeling the same, given the snarl on his face.

"Why didn't you say anything then, Pat?" Cooper asked, tension filling his tone. "You might have been able to prevent a miscarriage of justice."

Pat shook his head. "You're not hearing what I'm saying. That cop who took me down was dirty. Everyone on the streets knew that. He was dealing the drugs he took from dealers. There was no way anyone was going to believe me. I was a criminal with a long history. I served my time. If I came forward, they would have pinned it on me. I had the sneaker. You think anyone was going to believe me? The first thing they would have done was let Randy go and come after me. I wasn't going to be locked away forever for something I didn't do. I'm sorry for what happened to Randy. I am. Prison is a terrible place to be. I wasn't trading my life for his. And prison was going to be the best outcome. That cop might have killed me had I told his secret."

I couldn't help but think that he was right. Pat would have been even more vulnerable than Randy. I let him know that we understood. "We already took the sneaker to the cops without telling them where it came from. We might have to mention your name."

Pat sat for several moments, his mouth set in a firm line of contemplation. "I don't like this and I don't have to trust you. You're leaving me with no choice. I haven't been in the system in a long time. I don't plan on going back. I'll do what I have to do for those girls. That's why I kept that sneaker for all these years. I was hoping for the moment when I could do the right thing. It presented itself. I guess there's no point backing out now."

"I think that's the bravest thing you could do," Cooper said, commending him for it. He stood and I followed. Pat remained perched on the milk crate. "We don't have anything else unless you do."

Pat craned his neck to look up at Cooper. "Do you think you'll be able to find the cop's name?"

"If he's still alive." Cooper glanced over at me. "Riley was able to find information going back thirty years on an arrest. We might be able to pull your record, too. That should give us the name of the arresting officer."

Pat rose then with a nod. "If you think you're able to find it and you get me a name, I might recognize it. I can't promise that I do. If I can help you more, I will." He brushed his hands down his pants. "Maybe it's time I did what was right."

I thanked him for that. "My husband will do what is right. He's never failed me when it comes to being on the right side of things. I can assure you that he's going to appreciate that you helped us and that you kept that sneaker."

Pat didn't look convinced. "I just don't want any blowback on me. I saw what happened to Randy."

I tried to reassure him as much as I could as we headed out the door. I couldn't see any world where Luke or other detectives would come after Pat for holding onto the sneaker.

When we got back out to the SUV, I paused in the road. "What do we do now?"

Cooper opened the door and gestured for me to get inside. "You'll have to go back to those old records and see who arrested Pat. At least we have a date to work from or a close enough approximation."

I knew finding the arresting officer wasn't going to be a problem. If the record was still there, I'd find it. "We need to go see Agnes Elliott to see if she recognizes the sneaker. If we believe this sneaker is her daughter, Kathleen's, then we need to take it to her for confirmation."

Cooper glanced over at me with a raised eyebrow. "It's being processed. You're not going to be able to take it to her. I snapped a photo of it that I can give you. That will have to be enough."

I appreciated that we at least had that. "If we can get Agnes to confirm it's her daughter's, then we have one more piece of the puzzle."

Cooper didn't disagree. "What do we say when she asks where we got it?"

"We tell her the truth," I explained. "We have to know for sure that Kathleen was wearing the sneaker the day she went missing and that there was no reason for her to ever be in the back of a police car. I want to rule out every other possibility."

"Let's go then."

I called Agnes on the way to make sure she was home. She was surprised to hear from me so soon but assured me that she was there and would be for the rest of the afternoon.

Agnes let us into her house. There was mild interest on her face, but she was a mother who had promises made and broken before. "You sounded anxious on the phone, Riley. What can I help you with now? Did you find something?"

There was no easy way to cushion this blow. "Cooper and I found something. We need you to see it."

Agnes smiled and chuckled lightly to herself. "That's vague. I'll help if I can."

Cooper pulled up the photo on his phone and turned it around to face her. "Do you recognize this?"

Agnes's hand trembled as she took the phone from him. "My daughter's sneaker," she said as tears welled in her eyes. "Where did you get this?"

"Are you sure?" Cooper asked quietly. "We are trying to confirm that it's Kathleen's."

"She never went anywhere without these sneakers. They were her favorites. I tried so many times to get her to wear something else to school. She wouldn't hear of it. Did you look at the tongue of the sneaker?"

"What do you mean?"

Agnes handed the phone back to Cooper. "I wrote Kathleen's name on the inside tongue of each sneaker. Other girls had similar sneakers. I wanted to make sure she didn't lose them at sleepovers. She adored them and she'd be crushed without them. Kathleen could be careless sometimes. Right after she got them, she came home only wearing one of them and a similar pink sneaker of her friend's. I don't know how she didn't notice. I laughed over it, but she was in tears. I had to call up the other mom and exchange them. After that, I wrote her name in them. If those are Kathleen's, her name will be on the underside of the tongue about as far back as I could write it. She begged me not to write it where anyone could see it." There was a faint smile on the woman's face, probably recalling the conversation with her daughter.

Cooper punched in a phone number, got routed to the crime scene lab and asked the tech to check the tongue of the sneaker. His face remained tight as he waited and listened to the response. He hung up and nodded. "The name is there. It's your daughter's."

She sighed. "I've known this whole time she was dead. I knew it right away. This is a tangible sign of that." Agnes took a few steps back, reaching out her hand to her chair. She lowered herself down. "Where did you find it?"

I explained how we had come into possession of it. "Is there any reason Kathleen would have been in the back of a police car? Any relatives or friends who were cops at the time?"

Agnes closed her eyes as she shook her head. "Are you telling me that a cop killed my daughter?"

"We don't know anything," I said, trying to slow her down. "It's one more piece of the puzzle. When we leave here, I'm also going to research some records to see if I can find what officer might have been driving the car where this was found."

"Thank you," Agnes said with hope in her voice. It was the first time I heard it. "Maybe, finally, justice will be served."

The same hope Agnes had, I had as well. I didn't want to give her false hope only to disappoint her once again. "I promise you we are going to do everything we can."

CHAPTER 27

L uke stood in the back corner of the conference room, the evidence tacked to the board, its surface riddled with pushpins and scribbled notes. He gripped a marker in his hand to write more notes. His breath had been shallow since learning from Scarlett that the man had a badge. The reality of it had crept in like a splinter under his skin – small, sharp, and impossible to ignore.

It could have been a fake badge to lure kids into his car. Luke had read about cases like that. There was something that gnawed at his gut and told him that it might be more. It was the way that Walter Fields had been murdered and disposed of so efficiently.

The image Scarlett and the sketch artist were able to create stared back at Luke. He was certainly older than any beat cop on the force today. The bushy hair almost looked like a wig and the glasses were too big for his face. The beard concealed his facial features. Even with all of that, there was something about him that was familiar.

Luke was sure he wasn't among the SWAT officers or the detective bureau. He knew all of them personally and this man wasn't among them. That didn't mean that the man hadn't been a cop with the Little Rock Police Department. Luke had sent the image to other local departments to see if the man was familiar to anyone else. There were several other departments in the surrounding area. If the man was from out of state or even far outside of Little Rock, it would take considerably more time to track him down.

Luke ran both hands over his face, then down the back of his neck, trying to shake the cold certainty that had begun to settle there like a second spine. It made sense in all the wrong ways.

He stepped back from the board, now seeing it with new eyes. He muttered a curse he didn't expect anyone to hear.

The knock at the door jolted him. He turned sharply. "Yeah," he shouted, gruff and caught off guard.

"It's us," came Riley's voice, muffled.

Luke moved to the door and opened it.

"We need more than a few minutes of your time," Cooper said, moving into the conference room. "I'd ask if you have the time, but even if you don't, you're going to have to make the time."

Luke had rarely seen Cooper so direct or forceful. He raised an eyebrow at Riley for an explanation. She gave him a look that told him he might want to sit down for this. He closed the door behind him, then went to the table, leaning against it.

Cooper pointed to the photo he had brought up on his phone. "This is Kathleen's pink sneaker that she was wearing on the day she went missing. We confirmed it with Agnes, her mother. Then I called the crime scene techs and confirmed that the sneaker found in the back of the cop car, being processed at the lab, had the girl's name written on the tongue far into the sneaker."

It was unfathomable to him that a cop could have taken those girls.

Riley pulled out a chair and sat next to him. She craned her neck to look up. "I still need to find who arrested Pat Jenkins. It's whoever arrested him that night that we need to find. He's a suspect, Luke."

The information hit Luke like a hammer. The pieces were coming together now. "I can't believe this evidence has been out there all these years."

"He was afraid to come forward, Luke," Riley explained. "I can't blame him. Look at what the system did to Randy. Pat assumed that if he came forward with the sneaker, the attention would turn to him. He has a record."

Luke's fingers tightened around the marker. "I guess we should just be glad he finally came forward." Luke gestured toward the sketch hanging on the board. "Does this guy look familiar to either of you?"

Both leaned forward to get a better look. Cooper shook his head while Riley said, "There's something familiar about him, but I can't place it."

"Same," Luke said. "I think he's wearing a disguise. But from his eyes and what we can see of his face, I'd put him right around sixty."

Cooper and Riley agreed.

Luke told them about Scarlett's statement about the badge in the car.

Riley's eyes got wide. "Luke," she said his name in a rush of breath. "Do you believe that you're looking for a cop now? He murdered Walter Fields, then took the girls?"

Luke sat down at the table. "I don't know what I think other than this case is confounding in every way conceivable. Why take the girls, then let Scarlett go? Why kill Walter Fields and try to frame him for the kidnapping? What's this guy's plan? I don't understand any of it." He could see the wheels turning in Riley's mind. She was good with puzzles like this. But she didn't offer up anything she was thinking. It was Cooper.

"Randy Stock is about to get out of prison. There have been threats against him. He's been moved to a safer facility," Cooper reminded them. "Why would someone be threatening him?"

"To keep him quiet," Riley offered.

"Right," Cooper agreed. "So why move him?"

Luke was following the logic. "To protect him because someone wants the truth to come out. Someone in the system with power wants

Randy Stock alive. Someone knows the truth that he didn't kidnap those girls back then." The words came out of Luke's mouth before he had a chance to process what he was saying. If it were true, it meant that a great injustice had occurred and an innocent man had spent decades in prison for a crime he didn't commit.

Riley noted what he said but didn't make a big deal about it. For that, Luke was grateful. She asked, "Who would have had the power to make a call like that? Who'd be able to get Randy Stock moved from state prison to the local jail? We know that's not typical even for someone about to be released. Also, who was the one threatening him?"

None of them had the answer for that – not even Luke. "Let me make some calls to the prison to ask. I can't imagine anyone from the police department or the prosecutor's office would be making that call. It had to have come from someone higher up."

"Or someone who faked being high up," Riley said as both turned to her. "This guy is a phone creeper. We already know this based on his ongoing calls to harass Gail Herin. He's been able to keep track of her no matter what phone number she has, even going from a home phone to a cellphone. If it is a cop, that makes sense. Who else would have that kind of access? Unless he knows her personally and she hasn't connected the two."

That was another terrifying reality that Luke hadn't considered. "Do you think this guy is the one threatening to harm Randy before he gets out of prison or the one protecting him?"

They were able to make an argument for both.

It was finally Riley who said, "Who knows. For all we know, this man didn't like that Randy got credit for a crime he committed. These creeps want credit after a while. If Randy was killed, the secret of his innocence dies with him. No one is going to be looking into it. Most people will assume justice has been served. With him alive and getting out of prison, he can claim he's innocent."

Cooper glanced over at her. "Are you suggesting that this kidnapping is to help prove that Randy is innocent?"

"Possibly," Riley said evenly. "I do think it's more than that. I think the timing might be to prove Randy Stock is innocent and draw attention away from the fact that he's getting out of prison. I don't think the kidnapping is totally about that. I think whoever this person is either has a real grudge or fascination with Gail."

"Could she have been the intended victim all along?" Cooper asked.

Luke hadn't considered that. "She was a few years older than her sister. She might have been more difficult to kidnap. Maybe he took her sister to make her vulnerable with the intent to come back for her later."

"That is what he said in the calls to her," Riley offered. "He threatened her all the time. We have to consider that he's obsessed with her in some way. He called the other families, but the threats to Gail were different."

Luke hadn't seen the cases as connected before, not in this way. Now, with the sneaker and what Riley said about Gail, there was no other way to look at it. He wasn't sure that Riley had it right. He didn't think the killer would be protecting Randy. But someone else, someone who might suspect the truth, might be making sure Randy made it out of prison alive. He watched both Cooper and Riley, wondering whether he should keep it to himself or not.

Cooper didn't give him the option. "There's something on your mind, Luke. You might as well say it."

Luke took a moment to formulate this through before he said it aloud. "While I can appreciate Riley's perspective that the killer might be protecting Randy so he doesn't get credit, it makes more sense to me that the killer might be the one threatening Randy, and someone who knows the truth is protecting him. There is a thirty-year gap between these cases. We don't have any other cases in between like this that haven't been solved. There's a gap for some reason. Maybe he was in prison for something else or lived out of the area."

"That's entirely possible," she conceded.

Luke asked, "Do you think you can find the man who arrested Pat?"

Riley shrugged. "I found the other information in the files. I don't see why not. If the arrest record is there, I'll find it."

"What if the kidnapper removed it?" Luke asked, knowing files that old were paper copies without backup.

"We don't know that he even knew about the sneaker being in the back of the car. I think if he knew, he would have removed it," Riley reasoned. "It sat there for a long time. It was there when Pat was arrested then later that evening when William retrieved it. I think if the kidnapper knew it was there, it would be long gone. If he knew someone took it and connected it to Pat, I think the man would be dead."

That Luke could agree with. "We have every resource out there right now looking for Jenna. There's nothing more I can do on that front. Walter Fields seems to be a literal dead end. He was a private man who few people knew. He has no connection to law enforcement that I know of right now. Someone with a connection to him killed him."

"Or he was targeted," Cooper offered. "Like Randy took the fall, the killer set him up to take the fall for this, which would bolster your claim that he isn't protecting Randy."

Luke nodded in agreement. "That's exactly what I was thinking. He's trying to cover his tracks. Not well, but he's trying." He glanced over at Riley. "Can you head back to the records room and continue your search? I'll call over and make sure you have all the clearance you need for as long as you need."

"Is that all you need me to be doing right now?"

"That's it," Luke confirmed. "The most important thing we can do right now is find out who the man is that had the sneaker." He took a breath and asked again, "You're sure that it wasn't one of the two men who are pointing a finger at the cops?"

"I'm sure," Riley said quickly.

Cooper was a bit more measured. "Pat came to me, Luke. If this killer is covering his tracks, there's no reason to come to me with it. The fear of becoming a suspect is why Pat held onto it for so long. And to be honest with you, neither he nor William seemed like a master criminal capable of pulling this off. Pat's record is mostly petty crimes and drugs. William has been straight with no arrests outside of his early twenties. I don't see either of them involved in this."

"What Cooper said," Riley added. "Even if I didn't think Pat was credible, William was. I don't think he'd lie about something this important."

Luke was satisfied with that. Not to mention that Jenna was still missing and had either of them been involved, they probably wouldn't have let Cooper and Riley in their homes.

"What do you want me to do, Luke?" Cooper asked.

"Get me all the background you can find on Walter Fields. I might have missed something in my search. While I'm dealing with the prison issue, find me anything you can. Let's close all the loopholes and corner this guy."

With the plan in place, Luke called the records department to make sure Riley had access. On the way out, she asked him if he was okay. Luke assured her that he was even though he felt like any moment he might crack. The hardest cases for him were the ones involving children.

CHAPTER 28

Cooper would do exactly as Luke asked and explore Walter Fields's background. First, though, he wanted to go back to the jail and speak to Randy. He had questions about the man's past that he hadn't asked before – there hadn't been a reason to ask.

The warden wasn't happy to see Cooper again but had no reason to deny him an interview. A prison guard escorted Cooper to a meeting room and left him there to wait. The beige cinderblock walls and metal table gave Cooper little stimulation while he waited more than half an hour for Randy to be escorted to him.

The man shuffled in with the guard, his eyes going wide when he saw Cooper. "Has something happened?"

Cooper wouldn't speak until the guard uncuffed him and Randy sat down at the table. He knew there were eyes and ears everywhere but he had little choice. Cooper filled him in on the investigation about the missing girls. "Scarlett has been returned. Jenna is still missing. She's Gail's daughter. As you know, we suspected this guy has been targeting Gail. But there's been a development."

Randy leaned forward, resting his arms on the table. "Is the girl who was returned okay?"

"Shaken up but unharmed as far as we know."

"What's the development?"

Cooper dropped his voice even though he knew he could still be heard by the guard and any audio recording. "We believe the case has a law enforcement connection."

Randy shook his head in confusion. "What do you mean?"

"Scarlett said the guy who took her had a badge." Cooper leaned in closer and told Randy about the sneaker and his interviews with Pat and William. He watched as Randy tried to process the information. "It's significant because it means that sometime after Kathleen was taken, her sneaker was found in the back of that cop car. There's no reason for that unless the cop driving that car was involved."

Randy didn't see it that way. "Couldn't he have been searching and found the sneaker?"

"No," Cooper said, his voice loud enough to make the guard turn to him. "Everyone was looking for those girls. If a cop found that sneaker, it would have been seen as evidence and processed properly. It was found wedged under the back mat." Cooper asked if Randy knew Pat or William.

"The names aren't familiar to me. I knew a lot of people back then. I wasn't friends with any criminals. That wasn't my life, you know that."

Cooper held up a hand to stop him. "No one is accusing you of running with a criminal crowd. I'm here to learn who you were friends with. Who did you know? Was there anyone in law enforcement you were friendly with or might have hassled you in the past?"

Randy listed off a few of his friends. "It was mostly guys I worked with. We'd have a few beers after work and hang out on the weekends watching TV or going to a football game in the fall. I led a pretty quiet life up until that point."

"What about cops?"

"None that I was hassled by or anything like that. I wasn't friends with any cops." Randy grew quiet, looking down at the table. "I'm trying to think of the guy's name. One of the guys I worked with had a brother who was a cop, a rookie not too long on the job when I got picked up for the kidnapping."

"Did he ever hassle you?"

"No. We met on one or two occasions, but nothing significant. I don't think we exchanged more than pleasantries."

"Do you remember his name?" Cooper was holding his breath waiting for the answer. It was a long shot and probably would not prove anything.

"My friend was Skip Jackson. I can't remember his real name. He always went by Skip, but I assume that wasn't his real name."

Cooper didn't think it would be either. "When was the last time you had contact with him?"

"About a month after my conviction. I got a letter from Skip telling me how sorry he was and that he knew I didn't do this. He said he tried to tell the cops but they wouldn't listen. I do recall him saying that his brother encouraged him to stay out of it. I can't blame him. I was innocent and look what they did to me. He was probably just trying to protect Skip before attention turned to him."

Cooper asked him a few more questions about his friends back then and the interactions they had. There was nothing of note that could help him. He had one last question. "Do you remember where Skip lived?"

Randy shook his head. "No. I wouldn't be surprised if Skip was working at the same place or someplace similar. He wasn't the ambitious type. He even used to say he was going to put in his time at the place and retire. He didn't have a lot of motivation for more back then."

Cooper got the name of the company and told Randy that he'd meet him in less than forty-eight hours upon his release. "Freedom is close. Just hang on." He waited until the guard escorted Randy out, then

Cooper made a few notes in his phone and exited.

On his way out, he called Luke and asked if he knew of any officers with the last name Jackson. Luke rattled off a few names that he knew. Only one of the men was close to the age of Skip's brother. Rob Jackson was in his fifties and had worked his way from patrol through the ranks and was now one of the police department's hostage negotiators. He wasn't far from retirement, which made sense to Cooper given the decades that had passed.

Cooper drove directly to the police station and asked for Rob Jackson at the front desk. "He's not expecting me, but Det. Luke Morgan asked me to meet with him quickly about a current case." It was a lie that hopefully wouldn't come back to bite him.

He made his way up to the office and found an overweight man with graying hair sitting behind a desk. He glanced up before Cooper could knock on his door. "Can I help you?"

Cooper introduced himself. "I have a couple of questions, but I'm not sure you can answer them."

Rob gestured to the chair in front of his desk. "Come on in and I'll try."

Cooper sat across from the man, assessing him. Rob didn't seem like the kind of man who'd kidnap and murder young girls. That didn't mean much. It boded well that he was here at work, as Cooper assumed the kidnapper was currently still with Jenna. "Is your brother Skip Jackson?"

A faint smile spread across his face. "I haven't heard anyone call him that in a long time. Not since we were in our early twenties. But, yeah, my brother was Skip. Did you know him?"

Cooper picked up the past tense. "Is your brother deceased?"

Rob offered a curt nod. "Two years ago, from cancer."

Cooper offered condolences. "I'm not here because of your brother exactly. I was trying to find the brother of Skip Jackson and now I know that's you. Did you know Randy Stock?"

"I think everyone knows that story," Rob said non-committedly. "I can't recall if I ever met the man. I assume you know my brother was friendly with him for a time."

"That's why I'm here. I'm curious what you thought of the case?"

Rob sat back and folded his arms over his chest. "I guess I didn't think much of it either way. I was a rookie at the time. I was brought in during the searches to help find the girls. We all took a shift either manning the phones, at the volunteer center, or out on the street helping. It's a tragic end. Those girls were never found."

"Given your brother knew Randy, did he ever confide in you that he didn't think he was guilty or express concern that he had been arrested?" Cooper was trying to gauge the man's reaction, but Rob wasn't giving him much. He was a blank slate, probably from years of police work. Cooper wasn't accusing Rob of anything. This was a long shot in the dark.

Rob expelled a breath. "Eric," he paused, "Skip to you, was surprised that Randy was arrested. He said he didn't know that side of him and was having a hard time believing Randy would kidnap three little girls. My brother couldn't wrap his mind around it. It was too horrible for a lot of people to understand. That happens in a lot of cases. It's not surprising. Predators often hide in their day-to-day lives. It's why they get away with it for so long."

Cooper couldn't debate that point. "I was a detective on the force here for a while. I'm good friends with Det. Luke Morgan. What you're saying is a fair point. Something I've seen myself a time or two. I don't believe that Randy was guilty of that. There is another case happening right now."

"Jenna Herin," Rob said, interrupting. "I'm aware of it. We all are. I know Luke and thought you looked familiar too. Bottom line it for me, Cooper. Why are you here talking to me? I don't think it's about what my brother might have said or thought about Randy thirty years ago. Unless you're just fishing."

"Fishing," Cooper said and sat back. He glanced around the man's office, taking in the awards that plastered the man's walls. Rob Jackson had a long, successful career in law enforcement. Cooper didn't get any sense from him that he might have been involved. That wasn't why he was here. Now that he was sitting in the man's office, face-to-face with him, Cooper realized what a foolish errand this had been.

He focused back on Rob. "Randy told me that a friend of his had a cop brother. There's a cop connection in this case. I was hoping you might know something, given you're the only cop connection I have to Randy. I admit, I'm shooting in the dark here."

Rob leaned forward, resting his arms on the desk. "What do you mean by a cop connection?"

"Luke has some information that the guy who took the girls might have a badge. They know he's not Walter Fields, whose body we found in the park. In the case of Randy Stock, witnesses have come forward with an item of clothing one of the girls was wearing on the day she disappeared. He found it in the back of a cop car."

The man jerked back as if Cooper had punched him in the gut. Rob raked a hand down his face and stared across the desk at him. He looked on the verge of saying something but didn't say anything.

"Rob," Cooper said, drawing out the man's name. "If you remember something, it's important. Randy served his time and will be getting out of prison. As you said, those girls are still missing. Something you know might bring closure to those families and might save Jenna Herin's life. You know who her mother is, don't you?"

Rob shook his head. "Only the father has been on the news."

"Gail Albright. Her sister was Samantha Albright, one of the missing girls. Her daughter has now been taken and she's been harassed by the kidnapper for years and years."

"That can't be true," Rob said, glancing toward the door and then back at Cooper. "Is that true?"

Cooper told him it was. "Look, I'm trying to figure this out in the hopes that we can get Jenna Herin back alive. Something stinks about this whole case and it keeps coming back to this police department." Cooper checked his watch. "I'm wasting time here if you don't know anything." He stood to leave, but Rob told him to sit back down after he closed the door.

Cooper walked the short distance to the door and closed it. He turned back to Rob. "What do you know?" He remained there near the door and didn't sit back down in the chair.

"I don't know that I know anything for sure." Rob gave him a knowing look. There was something on the man's mind, something he remembered from long ago.

"You know something," Cooper said as he slowly made his way back to the desk. He remained standing. "Rob, whatever it is, please tell me. A lot of lives hang in the balance."

"I haven't thought about this in years," he said. "I'm not even sure I'm remembering correctly." Cooper used silence as a way to urge him on. "You remember how it is being a rookie. You're seen not heard. You get the crap jobs and the worst shifts. You are the butt of every joke, but otherwise, invisible to the more seasoned guys."

That's exactly how it had been for Cooper. "Was there something you saw or heard?"

"A group of officers, more seasoned guys, were talking about what a creep another officer was around kids, especially young girls in that twelve to fourteen range. They never caught him outright doing anything, but it was the leering and the way he spoke. This went beyond locker room talk. It didn't sit right with them." Rob chewed on his bottom lip. "I remember distinctly when those three girls went missing, my partner at the time and another more seasoned officer wondered if this other guy could have been involved. They said those girls were the prime target range. They even said that he had known Gail Albright. That he was a friend of the family. He talked about her so much that one of the other guys reminded him she was a kid. He shut up about her after that."

Cooper realized then that his heart was racing. "Did anyone come forward with the information?"

Rob shook his head. "No one knew anything for sure. I swear, Cooper, it's not like anyone saw this guy hurting a kid. He was just a creep. I think it was shortly after the girls went missing that the guy left the police department. I don't know the circumstances around his leaving. I just know he was gone and no one talked about him again. I don't know where he went."

"What was the officer's name?"

"Trotter is what they called him. I never spent time with the guy. He was a big shot. He made a lot of arrests, particularly related to drugs. My partner at the time told me to never be like Trotter. I asked him what he meant and he told me that he bent the rules. He didn't play it by the book."

That sounded like the guy. "Is Trotter a first or last name?"

"I don't know," Rob said with wide eyes. "I was a rookie, Cooper. I barely even remember the guys I worked with back then. They are all retired. I don't even know who to tell you to ask."

Cooper cursed loudly. "Anyone that might still be around and willing to talk?"

Rob shook his head. "I haven't spoken to any of them in years. Please remember it was all talk. I don't want to waste your time. It might all be nothing."

Cooper didn't think it was *nothing*. He thought it might finally be the key to breaking the case wide open. He thanked Rob for the information and encouraged him to call if he remembered anything.

He asked for the names of the guys that Rob had worked with back then and left with a short list of the ones who might still be alive.

CHAPTER 29

I made my way back to the cold, damp records room, passing the officer on guard at the front. He waved me through, barely even looking up at me as I passed. The air smelled like old paper and dust – an aroma that clung to my clothes. I pulled a stack of folders from the shelf in the date range I needed. I dropped them on the table with a thud that rattled the wobbly leg.

I pulled out the chair and sat, staring briefly at the overwhelming pile. Needle in a haystack. Still, I had found the information on William that led me back here, so not all hope was lost. I pulled my hair back into a ponytail, tucking errant strands behind my ears. If these arrests had happened any later, I'd be able to type the names into the computer and pull back all the records with ease. I was grateful for the advancement in technology that we had now.

I pulled the top folder from the pile, feeling the brittle edges of the manila file as I rifled through its contents. The dim light above buzzed, making it harder to concentrate. The cramped, windowless room felt like a tomb. I couldn't hear any noise from above or outside the room. It was probably good as I couldn't deal with any distractions.

I scanned the contents but found nothing. I tugged another file from the pile and went through the same process. Pat Jenkins wasn't a common name. I flipped open another file, nearly tearing the tab. A mugshot from the '80s stared back at me – shaggy hair, an expression like a drunk man about to get hit in the face with a brick. My finger traced the name at the top of the report – Henry Ralston. Not the one I was looking for. I threw it aside.

Another one. A teenager, barely eighteen, caught in a brawl. The crime looked petty on the surface, but I'd learned long ago to look deeper. Most things, especially in the criminal underworld, weren't as simple as they seemed. I didn't even bother reading the arrest report fully. The name and details weren't right. I slapped the file into the finished pile.

I went through file after file, finishing a stack and returning it to the shelf. I'd take another pile and start the process all over again. My vision started to blur, but I got faster as I went, knowing exactly where to find the information I was seeking. Suspect name, date of birth, and arresting officer's name. They were sections of the reports now that seemed to jump off the page for me.

The sound of my fingers snapping the folder shut echoed in the silence, but the frustration was louder than any noise. My eyes darted to the clock on the far wall. I'd been at this for two hours and still nothing.

I grabbed another file. Nothing. Another. Nothing. My pulse began to speed up. I could feel it – the panic, the pressure. What if I couldn't find him? What if I couldn't piece this thing together? I'd prided myself on not giving up, but this? This was starting to feel like one of those things that just didn't have an answer.

I slammed the next file down, my knuckles white from gripping the edge. A jolt of anger rushed through me, almost making me throw the thing across the room. Instead, I inhaled deeply, feeling the tension thicken in my chest. I let my breaths come as they wanted, fast at first, then easing back, slowing down as I reminded myself of the importance of finding the information.

I pulled another file from the stack. "Please," I muttered to no one, flicking it open. I considered getting really Catholic in the moment, calling on one of the saints my mother prayed to so easily. St. Anthony. He was always good at calling on for lost objects. I considered whether he'd work on finding me a police report. I silently said a little prayer, laughed at myself for even considering it working and pressed on.

I was probably at it another thirty minutes when the name Pat Jenkins jumped off the page.

My eyes skimmed the report, matching the name and date of birth that I knew. I let my eyes drift up to the date – the day the girls went missing. It was a match.

I held my breath as I found the arresting officer's name.

Curtis Trotsky.

It wasn't a name I knew or any police officer that Luke had ever mentioned.

My heart skipped a beat. I felt like I'd just found a lifeline in the middle of an ocean of dead ends. My fingers tightened on the paper as I read the details.

I turned the page, reading the details I had already heard from Pat. He was arrested on 6th Street for possession of cocaine. The way Pat told it, he hadn't had any drugs on him that night, but the cop was hassling him and a group of other men standing on the corner outside of a bar. Pat said the cop rolled up on them, got out of the car, and told the men to get lost. When Pat was the last one remaining because he was waiting for a friend inside the bar, something he told the officer, it was then that the officer got in his face and pushed him up against the wall of the building and searched him. It was only after the officer searched Pat, a search that was probably illegal, that the cop came away with the small baggie of cocaine. The baggie Pat said the cop planted.

The report noted that Pat had been walking in the middle of the road and had appeared drunk. That was the reason for stopping him.

Trotsky indicated that Pat was slurring his words, had dilated pupils, and seemed on edge. He wasn't able to answer the officer's questions. Trotsky indicated that Pat had the baggie of coke balled up in his hand. The arrest was made.

I didn't know exactly whose version of events was to be believed. I didn't see why Pat would lie about it as he already admitted that he had been legitimately arrested on other occasions for things he had done. Dirty cop planting evidence on a suspect wasn't out of the realm of possibilities.

I flipped the page to continue reading when the smell of coffee reached me. Before I could get up to get myself a cup, Cooper appeared in the doorway with two cups in hand. He didn't speak right away. He just stood there, probably taking in the sight of me hunched over a mountain of paperwork, trying not to suffocate under the weight of it all.

Finally, he broke the quiet, his voice low, deliberate. "You won't believe this, Riley. I think I found something."

I glanced up, my heart still hammering from the cop's name. "Me too," I said, almost too excited. By the look on Cooper's face, he wanted to go first. He handed me my coffee, moved the pile of completed files to the side and sat. "Go on then. You go first."

Cooper spent the next twenty minutes filling me in on the meeting with Rob Jackson and how he had come to find the man. "I believed him when he said he didn't remember it until I brought up a cop being involved. He was a rookie and described it exactly as I remembered. The seasoned guys wouldn't have told him anything outright. But he was around. He would have overheard things and knew better than to ask more. Trotter isn't someone he worked with, wasn't his partner, but had a reputation as being a dirty cop. He was known to talk about young girls in a way that made the other cops uncomfortable. He talked about Gail. Said he knew the family. Do you have any idea how hard it is to make a bunch of cops uncomfortable, Riley?"

I had an inkling. "I'm assuming it had to be pretty bad and direct."

"Exactly."

"Why not go to a supervisor? Why not share their concerns?"

"Cops don't rat out other cops. They especially didn't back then. I don't know if they had anything tangible other than what the guy was saying. He was being a creep, not giving details of a crime."

"No one said anything, even after the girls went missing?"

Cooper nodded. "For all we know, someone did go to a supervisor. He left the police department shortly after. I called a few of the names that Rob gave me for guys who might remember him, but I didn't get anywhere with that. Most didn't answer and the one guy who did didn't want to talk."

I pinched the bridge of my nose. "He didn't want to talk because he didn't remember Trotter or he didn't want to say something bad about a fellow officer? What was the vibe?"

Cooper gave me a knowing look. "He said there was no reason to dredge up the past and he had nothing to say. I wasn't even able to ask if Trotter was a first, last, or nickname. Rob wasn't sure. I guess it's something we will be able to search for or maybe Luke knows."

I couldn't know for sure, but I had a strong suspicion I might have already found Trotter. I slid the file over to Cooper and pointed to it. "Curtis Trotsky. He was the one who arrested Pat that night. Trotter was probably a nickname."

Cooper's eyes were wide as he bent his head over the file and reviewed it. He confirmed aloud each of the details I had already read, then got to the arresting officer's name. When Cooper was done, he looked up at me. "Now that we've found him, what do you think we should do?"

"Let's bring it to Luke and see if it's a name he knows." I pulled out my phone and texted it to him. I wasn't sure if he would be able to get back to me quickly enough. I glanced up at Cooper. "Did you explore Walter Fields's background at all?"

Cooper shook his head. "I didn't get to any of that yet. I had a hunch that if there was a cop involved, he might have had some connection to Randy. I wasn't sure how or why. He didn't have anything for me other than his friend's brother was a cop. One thing led to another and this is where I ended up – with Trotter. It's not solid, Riley. What we have is a lot of speculation about some locker room talk from thirty years ago. We can't even be completely sure that Trotter is Curtis Trotsky."

"We don't need to make that connection," I reminded him. "We were looking for the cop who arrested Pat, and I found it." I jabbed my finger down on the file. "This is the guy who brought Pat in that night. It also looks to me like he lied about the arrest. His version of events contradicts Pat's, who didn't have any reason to lie to us."

I got up and started putting the files back when my phone chimed. One text, then two, then a third came in. I dropped the files and picked the phone up, opening the text from Luke. I read the text as my stomach dropped and my hand shook.

"What is it, Riley? You've gone pale on me. What did Luke say?"

I heard Cooper asking the questions but couldn't register a response for him. I was reading and rereading Luke's texts. I shifted my attention to Cooper. "Luke only knows one Curtis Trotsky, who had worked at the police department that long ago. Luke can't remember the date the man left, but he left for law school. He was gone for a long time before coming back here as a sex crimes prosecutor. The man was highly decorated for his work and retired about five years ago."

"It can't be the same person," Cooper said, all the air let out of his lungs in disappointment. "There is no way a dirty cop became a prosecutor and also kidnapped and murdered three little girls and now took another two."

"Why not?"

Cooper didn't have an answer for me. "It doesn't make any sense to me that a man like that would do something so horrible. It's definitely not the Trotter that Rob was referencing. He couldn't go from making crude sexual comments about young girls to being a sex crimes prosecutor."

I had worked sex crimes cases before where Cooper had been hesitant to take them. I knew sex offenders came from all walks of life and all backgrounds. Most of them in the cases I had were straight, white men often holding well-paying jobs. Many of them are in positions of power in churches, schools, and the criminal justice system. I reminded Cooper of all of that.

"He could have prosecuted any crimes, Riley? Why focus on the crimes he was committing?"

I didn't know the answer to that for sure. "The thrill of fooling everyone. Access to young victims who had already been victimized. Maybe the fact that he knew so well how the crimes were committed meant he chose what he knew for work. It leaves him in the perfect position of trust and power."

Cooper held his hand up to stop me. "We aren't even sure this is the same guy. Maybe there is another Curtis Trotsky." Even as he said the words, Cooper faltered. We both knew there was no one else with that name.

I also knew that Luke was cautioning me not to jump to conclusions and make a rush to judgment. His last text to me had been to *go slow and find the evidence.*

That's exactly what I intended to do.

The clock was running out.

Jenna was still missing and in the hands of a dangerous man.

CHAPTER 30

The late afternoon light cast long shadows across the sidewalk as Luke parked in front of a grand colonial tucked behind a thicket of trees in their shared Heights neighborhood. The Evans' home was tidy, white-trimmed, and had a fall wreath on the door. They lived blocks apart. Luke often saw Amelia running in the early morning hours before work.

Luke cut the engine but didn't get out. He sat there for a beat, knuckles tight around the wheel. His pulse drummed. He replayed the conversation he just had with Riley. They had texted about Curtis Trotsky, and he had told her not to jump to conclusions. What she didn't know was that his heart had been racing as he read her text at his desk at the police station. There hadn't even been anyone around for him to talk to about it. Granger was out in the field coordinating searches, and Tyler was in a meeting with the mayor, trying to convince him that the police department was doing everything they could.

Luke had sat with the information as the minutes passed slowly by. It wasn't that he didn't believe Riley or even that a cop or prosecutor couldn't commit such heinous acts. He had been at Curtis Trotsky's retirement ceremony. Luke hadn't worked with the man much over his career. Trotsky wasn't a homicide prosecutor. He was a sex crimes prosecutor. Those weren't the cases Luke normally took – unless the homicide had a sexual assault element.

Luke had pulled up the sketch and the photos from the video surveillance. He wasn't able to definitively say it was Trotsky. But the more he studied the images, he couldn't rule it out either.

By all outward accounts, the man was a pillar of the community. He had never married, had no children of his own, but had dedicated his life to taking sex offenders off the street. Luke knew he had started as a cop decades ago before moving away for law school. He worked in other states as a prosecutor before returning to Little Rock later in his career.

He had worked his way up to the head of the sex crimes unit. The man spoke at international conferences and there had even been mention of him writing an educational book on his long-storied career, sharing with other prosecutors what made him so successful and how they too could replicate that.

The last Luke had heard about the man was probably a year ago. Trotsky was on a podcast giving his expert opinion about a serial rape case in Seattle. That's what he was – an expert in the field in some of the most heinous crimes imaginable. That's why it was knocking the wind out of Luke to even consider that the man might be a person of interest, let alone a suspect. It's what brought him to the front curb of Amelia Evans's home. He needed to talk this through with someone who knew Trotsky and had worked with him.

But Luke wasn't ready for this conversation. Not ready to say aloud that the pieces were starting to fit together. He wasn't ready for the truth he could feel writhing beneath the surface.

Scarlett Evans had seen the man who took her. She'd said he had a badge.

Luke had no idea if Scarlett had ever met Trotsky. If she had, she could clear the man, which Luke needed before he went down the rabbit hole. If she had never met the man, the time wouldn't be wasted because Amelia could either tell him he was insane and to drop the idea or she might know something that could confirm it.

Either way, he wasn't going to accomplish anything spinning over it outside.

Luke stepped out of his SUV, made his way up the driveway, and climbed the porch steps. The front door opened before he knocked.

Amelia Evans looked exhausted. Her hair was pulled into a loose knot that had half-collapsed, strands clinging to her temples. There were dark rings under her eyes. She wore a faded long-sleeved shirt and jeans, bare feet on hardwood. Her composure, always her armor in the courtroom, was thinning.

"Luke, I saw you pull up. I didn't want to rush out there. Thought you might be on the phone or something," she said as she stepped aside for him to enter. "Has Jenna been found? The man caught?"

"No, not yet," Luke said, hope still in his voice. "There is something I need to discuss. Something only you might be able to help me with."

Inside, the house smelled like lavender. Her home was tidy but lived in. It didn't have any pretense of impressing people. Amelia led him into the large eat-in kitchen. Groceries were piled high on the counter. "Sorry, I'm still putting things away."

Luke gestured to it. "Let me help you."

Amelia offered a soft smile. "The cold and frozen stuff is away. The rest can wait. Please, sit down. Can I get you something to drink?"

"Where's Scarlett?" he asked, eyes flicking to the ceiling above.

"Upstairs. Painting. The psychologist said to let her get lost in something she can control." She poured herself a glass of water, hesitated, then poured him one too, even though Luke hadn't responded to her offer. "You said it was important."

"It is."

Luke took the glass but didn't drink. "Scarlett said something yesterday."

Amelia folded her arms. "She's said a lot of things."

"This was different."

She looked at him, waiting.

"She said the man who took her had a badge. A real one. The kind cops carry."

"Right," Amelia said, knowing the facts already.

"That narrows the field."

"She's a child, Luke. She was traumatized. Maybe she didn't get it right. The badge could have been fake." There was an expression on her face that Luke couldn't read. It might just be denial that someone in their shared field might be responsible for something this terrible.

Luke had to make her see. "After we got her over her initial fear, Scarlett was precise. She described the car, their interactions, what they were all doing and saying, what the man said and did. I understand Scarlett was traumatized, but she was also detailed, more detailed than a lot of witnesses I've spoken to over the years. If Scarlett said she saw a badge, I believe she saw a badge. That's significant enough that we have to figure out what it means."

"What are you saying?" Amelia asked. "You think someone on the force—?"

He waited until her brain caught up to the implication.

She froze. "Oh no. No, Luke, not one of our own." He let her settle into the idea. Amelia slumped back in the seat, taking her water glass with her. She cradled it in her hand. "Do you have a suspect in mind?"

"I'm not accusing anyone. Yet." Luke took a sip, knowing what he was about to shatter as soon as he said the man's name. He put the glass down and locked eyes with her. "Tell me about Curtis Trotsky."

Amelia cursed and winced her eyes shut. "No." She repeated the word several more times.

Luke exhaled slowly. "His name came up."

She opened her eyes and fixed her gaze on him. "How?"

"He was the arresting officer thirty years ago for Pat Jenkins." Luke went on to describe the sneaker and the information that had been uncovered so far. "Those girls would have gone with a cop, Amelia. We both know that. They disappeared without a trace."

Amelia turned away, looking down at the floor. She took several deep breaths, seeming to either digest the information or get herself right with it. Then she turned back to Luke. "You think Curtis Trotsky could've taken those girls?" she said, voice tightening. "You're talking about a man who put away more predators than any prosecutor I've ever known. A man who mentored half of us when we were cutting our teeth in court. Including me."

"I know. That's why this is hard."

"Hard? It's grotesque."

Luke took a step closer, his voice low, steady. "We've got three missing girls and the wrong man convicted of the crime. Then, thirty years later, two more go missing with a stark connection to the first – Gail Herin. Her daughter is still gone and your daughter said a man with a badge took them. Cooper found evidence that it was a cop all those years ago, and Riley found that it was Curtis Trotsky who made the arrest that night. I'm not saying it's him, but I'm here to understand what you know about the man."

"Curtis is…what? A convenient coincidence?"

Luke's jaw ticked. "He was a patrol officer in the city. More recently, a prosecutor with prosecutor's connections. There is something I keep coming back to over and over again. Who'd have the inside information to know Gail Herin's and the other families' changing telephone numbers?"

Amelia's mouth opened. Then closed.

Luke knew she knew. "Someone in the prosecutor's office was responsible for contacting the victims' families. You guys keep those records on file for parole hearings and the like. I haven't spoken to Gail, but I'm sure that's the one place her phone number has been kept up to date."

Amelia couldn't debate the point. It was the one sticking point for Luke even when he had tried to talk himself out of it.

He asked, "Have you ever worked a case with him involving minors?"

"Plenty. He was protective. Thorough."

"Too thorough?"

Amelia hesitated.

Luke pressed. "Ever feel like he went above and beyond in a way that didn't track?"

She didn't answer. Instead, she stood up and started to move away from the table, only to return seconds later. Luke sensed she was trying to physically remove herself from what he was saying, but she couldn't any more than he could.

They fell into silence for a few beats. Then Amelia finally said, "There was a case years ago when he first came back to Little Rock. There was a child who had been molested by their soccer coach. Curtis was relentless. Showed up to every prep session. Sat in on the forensic interviews. I remember thinking that he cared too much. But isn't that what we want?"

"Sometimes predators hide behind the right kind of caring," Luke said. "It's a performance."

She doubled-back on herself. "Don't you think I would've seen it. I was close to him. We all were."

"Were you ever alone with him?"

Her eyes sharpened. "That's not relevant."

"Were you?"

She swallowed. "Once. Maybe twice. Drinks after work. Nothing happened that made me question him."

Luke watched her carefully. "You sure?"

Her silence bloomed in the room like a bruise.

"He never crossed a line with me," she said at last, voice brittle. "He was flirtatious, but he respected boundaries."

"Predators often do. Until they don't. If we are talking about a predator going after little girls, you weren't in his victim range."

"Luke," she said, like the air deflated out of her.

He softened, just slightly. "I'm not trying to paint you as blind. I'm trying to figure out if this is real. I don't want it to be him. But too much is pointing his way. I need help seeing if this is real or confirmation bias."

She crossed her arms again, pressing her palms tight into her sides. "There was something," she murmured. "A girl. A runaway. Fifteen, maybe sixteen. This was five years ago, not long before he retired."

Luke stood still, listening.

"She came into the office late one night. She said she wanted to file a report. She seemed scared but wired. Curtis saw her in the lobby. We spoke to her briefly. In the middle of it, he said he was taking her to the police station."

"Alone?"

"Yes. I didn't think it was a good idea. I wanted her to go into one of the offices and wait for a detective to come to us. She had said she had been assaulted the year prior, was still scared and wanted to tell her story. Curtis cut us off and said he wanted to go to the police with her."

Luke felt his throat tighten. "What happened?"

"They left but he returned maybe an hour later. I asked what happened and he told me the detective didn't find her credible. He sent her on her way."

"Did you check?"

"I didn't," she admitted. "I believed him. It happens sometimes, particularly with older cases."

"But?"

"There was something I couldn't quite explain about him afterwards.

He looked almost satisfied and I noted that his shirt was buttoned wrong. I couldn't remember if it had been that way prior."

"What happened after that?"

Amelia swallowed hard. "Curtis came to me a couple of weeks later and told me that she had gone back to the police to say that he had assaulted her in retaliation for the cops not taking her initial statement. He wanted me to tell the cops that she seemed unhinged in our office. He was going off about how he knew he had put himself in a vulnerable situation by bringing her to the police station, but that he was only trying to help her."

"Did a detective ever follow up with you?"

Amelia shook her head. "No. I didn't follow up either. I got busy with other case work and it left my mind. I guess I figured since nothing came of it that there was nothing to concern myself with." Amelia reached for the topknot and failed to straighten her hair. "It happens, Luke. Victims get angry. Some of them seek justice in their own way. I'm sure there have been accusations against you for things you never did."

"Not sexual," Luke said, his tone even. "Nothing ever like that. I'd venture to guess ninety-nine percent of us don't have false allegations against us of that nature."

"Yeah," Amelia said with weight in her tone.

They sat in silence.

Luke gave her a moment before he asked, "Has Scarlett ever met him?"

Amelia shook her head. "Not that I recall. I never took her to the office. The sketch she did doesn't look like Trotsky."

"No, but the man does look familiar. The hair, beard, and glasses. Remove all that and I can't rule out that's not him." Luke ran a hand down his jaw. "Do you have any recent photos of him? I just saw some older ones online."

Amelia didn't speak. Just moved across the kitchen to a built-in desk, pulled a stack of folders from a side drawer, and sifted through until she found one. Inside, there was a photograph from an office retirement party three months ago. Curtis stood with several others, smiling, a glass of champagne in hand.

Luke took it. "Can I borrow this?"

A noise from upstairs cut them off. Then soft footfalls on the stairs.

Scarlett.

She appeared in the doorway, small and pale in pink pajamas, clutching a ragged stuffed fox. Her cheeks were flushed. When she saw Luke, she blinked, then stepped forward.

"Mom?"

Amelia knelt. "Hey, sweetie. Are you okay?"

"I'm hungry." Before she could say anything else, Scarlett's eyes darted to the photo in Luke's hand. Her eyes got wide with fear. She pointed with a trembling hand. "That's him, Mom. That's him," she said more softly.

Luke went very still. "What did you say?"

Scarlett didn't flinch. "That's the man who took me."

Amelia paled.

Luke moved from the chair. Crouched next to her, bringing the photo lower, showing it to her again. "Scarlett. You're sure?"

She nodded. "His hair was messier, like I told that other lady. I know that's him."

Amelia's breath caught.

The walls of the kitchen seemed to tighten around them.

Amelia looked at Luke, shaken, eyes wet but not crying. "If it's him, he's been right under our noses. For decades."

Luke nodded. "I'm going to tear everything apart until I prove it."

CHAPTER 31

Cooper and I hadn't had too much time to react to the information about Curtis Trotsky because Luke told me to stand down one minute, then texted me later to tell me to head over to Gail's house to see if she was familiar with the man. The goal was not to arouse any suspicion but to find out if there was any connection there.

During that call, Luke explained that he had spoken to Amelia, who had a few stories to tell about Trotsky and that Scarlett had identified him as the man who had taken her.

Cooper headed back home to do some background work on Walter Fields because we still didn't understand how he fit into the whole thing. With Cooper doing that, I headed to Gail's.

Scott, her husband, answered the door looking like he hadn't slept. He probably hadn't. His shirt was wrinkled, a stain on the pant leg of his khakis still looked wet, and he had a streak of something orange across his cheek. "Has there been a break?"

"I'm sorry, no. I need to speak to Gail."

Scott glanced back into the house. "She's still in bed. I can't get her up. I've got two kids to handle." He hesitated for only a few seconds before opening the door wider. "If you can get her to talk, by all means. I can't manage this on my own. I'm worried about her. I called the doctor, but all he wants to do is give her drugs, which knock her out."

"She's been through compounded trauma," I said as I entered the home, sidestepping toys and what looked like the remnants of a half-eaten sandwich. It was obvious Scott wasn't used to managing his children alone.

"It's the second door on the right," he said as I ascended the stairs. The air grew stuffy as I reached the second-floor landing, like a window hadn't been opened in days. I tripped over a kid's toy truck as I made my way down the hall.

I knocked gently on the door that Scott had indicated. It was slightly ajar and inched open under the weight of my knock. "Gail," I said quietly, as I stuck my head in. The smell of sleep and sweat of stress hit my nose. "Gail," I said again, stepping into the room.

Gail was on her back, staring up at the ceiling. I could see that her eyes were open, fixed on the ceiling fan as it swirled above. She didn't turn her head to look at me, didn't acknowledge my presence in any way. If I hadn't known better, I might have assumed she had passed, given the stillness of her body. I barely even saw her chest rise and fall with a breath.

"Gail," I said her name, sharper this time, needing to get her attention. "I know that you don't want to speak to me, but I have to ask you something. Det. Morgan might be getting close to a suspect. We need your help."

When the woman still didn't stir, I clapped my hands loudly, hoping to jar her. I cursed loudly. "Did you hear me? We need your help. Jenna needs her mother's help, Gail. If you can't do it for yourself, do it for your daughter." I wished that I had the time to be more sensitive to the woman's needs but I didn't.

At the sound of her daughter's name, Gail shifted her head to the side to look at me. "What did you say?" she asked, her voice coming through a mouth of cotton as if she hadn't spoken in hours or maybe days.

There was a glass of water on the bedside table. I reached for it and offered it to her. She didn't take it. I stood there with my hand extended. "I said I need your help to find Jenna. Luke is exploring a suspect. He's making progress finding Jenna and we need your help."

Gail expelled a breath, tucking a strand of hair behind her ear. She struggled to sit upright, but once she did, she took the glass from me and drank a gulp of water. She shook off the comatose state and looked over at me. "What do you need?"

A part of me wanted to draw her out of bed to another room of the house. I resisted that urge. "I need to know your interactions with cops over the years. Has there been any who took a particular interest in your sister's case?"

Gail furrowed her brow. "I don't understand the question."

"You don't need to understand it. You just need to answer me."

She considered it for a moment. "There's been a few, I guess. My father was a donor to the Police Benevolent Association. He had a few friends on the force. It's who he went to the day my sister went missing. I think, in part, that's why they worked so hard to find the girls and took it so seriously from the start – he knew people."

"Do you remember any of their names?"

"Det. Lyle Tucker was one of them. He was the detective assigned to the case and the one who found Randy Stock."

I was not sure I had heard her correctly. "Your father was friends with the detective who arrested Randy?"

She looked up at me and nodded.

"Is that why you so staunchly believe that Randy is guilty?"

"My parents trusted Lyle Tucker and so did I. Why would he try to convince us of someone's guilt who wasn't guilty?"

I wanted to say because a cop was maybe involved, but I held my tongue. I asked her about the others and she offered a few names that weren't familiar to me. I needed to get to the most important thing without raising suspicion. "You must have had contact with the prosecutor's office over the years regarding Randy Stock. Did you have a particular contact there?"

"Oh yes, Curtis, a friend of my father's was the one who was handling everything. He even handled it while he was living out of state before he came back here. He was such a kind man. He's been with me every step of the way."

"Curtis Trotsky?"

"Yes, that's him." Gail smiled slowly at first then more brightly. "Curtis was one of my father's best friends. He was so lovely to us when the girls went missing then after the fact. He was our rock through the whole thing. Then he was there for me when I buried my parents. He's been keeping me updated after all these years. He's one of the people I talked to about the calls. When no one else was taking me seriously, Curtis was. He was never able to figure it out and told me that I couldn't tell anyone I was going directly to him. He said it was a conflict of interest."

My jaw tightened and my stomach knotted. "When was the last time you were in contact with him?"

"A few months ago, I guess. He moved out of Little Rock when he retired. He's got a place up on Beaver Lake that he built during the last few years when he was with the prosecutor's office. As far as I know, he's moved up there permanently."

I wasn't sure that I could form words, my heart was racing so fast. "Do you know the address of the place?"

"Why?" she asked, brow furrowed. "What does Curtis have to do with anything?"

I shook my head. "He was a prosecutor. I think Luke might want to speak with him but can't reach him by phone," I lied, hopefully convincingly. "We didn't realize you knew him. You can help us with that, too."

If Gail thought I was lying, she didn't press the issue. "I had a cellphone number for him, but it stopped working about a month ago. I haven't been able to reach him since. I assumed once he got settled and wanted to be in contact with me, he would be."

"That makes sense," I said and waited. "Does he know Jenna?"

Gail leveled a look at me and held the stare. "Riley, what aren't you telling me? Is there something about Curtis I should know?"

Luke didn't tell me not to tell her anything. In truth, Curtis was a person of interest, possibly more given Scarlett had identified him. "Tell me first if Jenna has ever met him then I'll explain."

"Not in years," Gail said with a shake of her head. "As far as I know, Jenna wouldn't know him if she tripped over him. Not for any reason other than there hasn't been an occasion for them to meet. Curtis mostly texts me and makes an occasional call here or there to check in. It's been some time since I've seen him face-to-face. He met her when she was a toddler, but she wouldn't know him now." Gail swung her feet to the floor, pushing herself up on her hands as she stood. "What does Curtis have to do with any of this?"

The way she was moving was not what I had expected – I had expected disbelief. I held my hand out to stop her, but she slapped it away. "I don't know anything for sure yet. Luke is looking into a few things about Curtis. There is some evidence."

"Evidence of what, Riley?" Gail asked, shoving past me, heading out of the room and down the hall toward the bathroom. If I had wanted her to take charge, this wasn't the information I had expected would do it.

I trailed after her. "It's not information I can release to you right now." I stood at the edge of the doorway while she splashed water on her face and reached for her toothbrush and toothpaste. She started furiously brushing her teeth. She turned her head to me. "Is he the one who took Jenna?"

"We don't know for sure. That's what we are trying to figure out."

She wiped her mouth on a towel and turned to me. "If that man has my daughter, I will kill him myself." Her flash of anger subsided as quickly as it had come on. She paused and took a breath. "I don't understand any of this. Curtis was always a good man. Why would he take her?"

"Tell me how he was a good man?"

"He stopped by after my sister went missing. He asked how he could help with the case. He was there constantly asking about her, what he could do, and what my parents needed. He'd take me for ice cream and ask me how I was doing. He told me that everything was going to be okay, even though I knew it wouldn't be. Over the years, he remained a constant presence in my life. Even when he lived out of state, he'd come back and visit me."

"He was the one you shared your fear with about the calls?"

Gail nodded. "I'd go to him with every call. Not that there was a way to put me at ease, but he'd try. He'd calm me down until the next call."

"He knew your number even when it changed," I suggested.

She nodded again. "Of course, I always reached out to him to let him know."

She still wasn't getting it. I needed to be more direct. "Did anything inappropriate ever happen between you when you were young? Hugs that lasted too long? A kiss? Secrets? There must be something you're not remembering."

"No. Never."

"Not even once? Not something that made you feel uncomfortable? Not something that happened that you wanted to tell your parents but thought better of it? Maybe you thought he'd be angry with you."

Gail stopped cold, staring past me. Her mouth fell open slightly. "How did you know that?"

"That's what they do. These kinds of offenders get close to vulnerable people. They get close to kids and then…" I let my voice trail off, not wanting to say the words.

Her hand went to her lips. "He kissed me once. When I was sixteen and he had taken me out to dinner to celebrate something I had done well in school. I can't even remember what it was now. It was after dinner and he was driving me home. He pulled over a few blocks before my house to talk, he said. Then he leaned over and kissed me. I froze. Didn't know what to do. He pulled back and apologized, just said that I looked too pretty and he couldn't control himself. Then he suggested it was better for me not to tell my parents. He made it sound like they'd believe I tried to seduce him. I brushed it off. He never tried it again. I thought maybe he was under stress, a momentary lapse."

"Did you ever allow yourself to be alone with him again like that?"

Gail's eyes got wide. "That was around the age I got busy with school and friends and even stopped spending time with my parents. He stopped coming around for a long time after that. He'd call, but I didn't see him for years."

I suspected that Curtis was afraid Gail might have told her family about the kiss. "Did he ever show an interest in your sister?"

She grew completely still, but her gaze never left me. "He talked about her all the time. He spoke like she was still with us. I thought he was doing it to be kind. But it always creeped me out a little. Do you think? He couldn't have." She didn't sound convinced at that point.

I nodded slowly. "You need to come with me to speak to Luke."

Gail put her hand to her heart and closed her eyes tightly. When she opened them again, she was a woman on the move – moving with the purpose of a mother out to save her daughter.

CHAPTER 32

While Luke was busy running down leads and Riley was busy speaking to Gail, Cooper had only one task and that was to see if there was a connection between Walter Fields and Curtis Trotsky. Before doing that, he wanted to stop by Adele's office and see her.

Her assistant had informed Cooper that Adele had taken a half day and gone home sick. Cooper stopped by their favorite coffee shop near the loft and picked up her favorite tea. He walked the short distance back to the loft and found her asleep in bed. She was curled on her side, breathing evenly. He pulled the covers up a little and left her there in peace.

He slipped quietly back out, closing the bedroom door behind him, and left her a note on the pad in the kitchen. He put the tea in the fridge and wrote her a sweet message on the cup, hoping she'd find it later.

He grabbed his laptop, shoved it in his work bag and headed to Cat's. He had worked there before and he could do so again. She'd probably appreciate the update. He walked the few blocks to Cat's office. Her assistant was gone for the day. Cat was in the middle of research about the case.

"I thought I could work here for a few hours. Adele is home sick," he said, gesturing to his workbag.

"You know the Wi-Fi code if you need it," she said, barely looking up at him. When she realized that Cooper remained standing there watching her, Cat slowly raised her head. "Sorry, I'm in the middle of full background research for the podcast. Did Luke find the other missing girl?"

"Not yet," he said as he pulled out the chair across from her desk and sat. Cooper told her a little about what had been happening, leaving out a few of the more confidential details. "Luke is zeroed in on a suspect. I'm supposed to be doing background research on Walter Fields to see if there is any connection between them. I already used my database and haven't found much. What he was doing with the creepy room in his house and all those photos of kids, I don't understand. I was hoping some internet research might help."

Cat scooted back her chair and reached behind her to a stack of files. She grabbed the third one from the bottom and tugged it free. She turned around and slid it across the desk to Cooper. "While you guys have been running around the city, I have already started some background research on Walter. That file has everything I could find on the man. I scoured the internet, every social media site, his reviews, and everything that mentions his name. There's not even a hint of a scandal or accusation against him."

Cooper flipped over the file and stared down at Cat's familiar handwriting. There were pages printed off the internet – mostly Walter's business social media profiles. Cooper scanned through the pages and Cat's notes enough to see what she was saying. There were only glowing reviews about the man and his professionalism. Everything that Cooper had seen when he'd interacted with Walter in the past. It didn't match up with the man's home.

Cat could see the confusion on his face. "As I was reviewing, I started wondering if his house was staged, knowing the cops might end up there. If someone set him up, then murdered him, they knew what they were doing. Even if the cops found his body and knew right away that he was a murder victim, the house would suggest that maybe someone had a reason to want him dead. Even more so, they were doing the community a favor by killing a predator. I could see the cops might not take that kind of murder so seriously."

It wasn't the craziest theory Cooper had heard. It kind of resonated with him at a gut level. He didn't see the house firsthand, so he had no idea how long staging the scene might take. All Luke told him was that the photos spanned a long time and that none of them were inherently sexual. Cooper wondered if someone had taken old stills from Walter and displayed them in a way that made it appear creepier than if the photos might be framed or found separately. He couldn't account for the hidden room, but old houses had spaces like that. For all Cooper knew, Walter might have used the space as a dark room before getting his office.

"It's as good a theory as any," Cooper said, thanking Cat for the file.

"What about his office? Has anyone gone through there?"

"The cops should have. At least that's what Luke told me they were doing."

"But this new suspect. Surely, they weren't looking for that connection," Cat suggested and she wasn't wrong. No one would have been looking for a connection between Walter and Curtis. Even if something in the house pointed to a connection, Cooper assumed that it would have been overlooked.

"That's a good point," Cooper said, reaching for his phone. He sent a quick text off to Luke asking if he could access Walter's office. He was only a block away but knew it had been roped off by police tape. He'd need permission and a way to access it.

Luke texted him back quickly enough. They had installed a lock box in the door, like real estate agents use, that was holding the key. A cop should also be in the vicinity watching the place. Luke assured Cooper he'd send the message that Cooper would be on his way over. Cooper thanked him and asked if Cat could come with him, sharing with Luke the information she had already pulled up on the man. Luke agreed but told them to watch their steps and not to remove anything.

Cooper glanced up at Cat. "Want to look through Walter's office with me?"

"I can," she said slowly, "but I don't know what I'm looking for. You haven't told me who the new suspect is. How am I supposed to help you if I don't know?"

Cooper explained that Scarlett had identified Curtis Trotsky and told her about his relationship to both the police department and the prosecutor's office. "If Curtis is the one who did this, then he's been hiding in plain sight for a long time."

Cat always seemed to be one step ahead. "He'd also carry the weight of scaring Walter with arrest or having access to children's photos from criminal cases."

Cooper was considering how much access Curtis would have in the community. Not only what Cat was saying but access to the prisons as well. Cooper could only assume that Curtis had been the one making the threats rather than having him moved. "Let's go," he said, full of confidence that they were finally on the right track.

Cat reached for her small recorder as she started to follow behind Cooper. He glanced down at it and told her that she probably shouldn't.

"I won't use anything unless Luke gives me permission," she assured him. "We are going to want to record anything we find, particularly if it ends up being used in court. This is going to protect us as much as it's going to help the podcast."

Cooper couldn't argue with that. "Do not release it until Luke gives you the go-ahead or he'll never speak to you again."

"Yeah, yeah," Cat said off-handedly.

They walked the short block to Walter's studio. Cooper waved to the uniformed cop sitting in the squad car just a few parking spaces down from the front door. The young cop didn't make a move, so Cooper assumed Luke had already told him they were coming.

Cooper reached under the yellow crime scene tape that crossed the doors and punched in the code to the lockbox. It opened and he pulled out a key. "Don't break the tape as we go through," he said as he unlocked the door. He pushed open the door. The air inside hit him like a forgotten basement – stale, damp, metallic.

Cat sneezed behind him.

The room was cramped, filled with mismatched furniture and old cameras lined up on shelves. The walls were papered with photographs – portraits, mostly. Headshots Walter had taken over the years and this was a showcase of his work. There was nothing to hide out there.

To the left, Cooper knew the short hallway led to smaller rooms. There was Walter's dark room, a studio space, a small bathroom, and the office.

Cooper flicked the light on as he entered the office. Not a lot had been disturbed from the police search. A few things were out of place. The items on the shelves were sitting askew. For the most part, the place hadn't been ransacked the way he'd seen with other searches.

"They cleared him," Cooper said aloud. "They didn't find any evidence in here. I don't know what Walter kept but anything that might show a connection to Curtis Trotsky is what we are after." Cooper spelled the man's last name for her. She headed toward the studio space while he explored the man's office.

Cooper went straight for the desk against the far wall. A pile of unopened mail leaned precariously beside a lamp. He opened the top drawer – loose batteries, old pens, and a pad of paper. Not much else. In the second drawer, it was much of the same. The third had a solid metallic lockbox. Cooper lifted it from the drawer and set it on the desk. There was no lock and the latch lifted with ease. Cooper opened the lid with disappointment on his face. The box was empty. He lowered it back to the drawer and dropped it the last few inches.

The hollow sound reverberated in the small space. Cooper paused and lifted the box, setting it on the desk again. He knocked on the wooden base of the drawer and heard the sound again. He used his fingertips to pry up the board.

Cooper came face to face with yellowing paper with jagged handwriting. Some folded, some torn.

The first one read: *You think no one sees, but I do. I see it all. If you don't stop, I'm going to bury you.*

Cooper's pulse jumped. He flipped to the next. *You think your secrets are hidden. I know what you are. You're a sickness in this city.*

This time, the note included the initials C.T. at the end.

"Cat," he called, and she was by his side in seconds.

She read over his shoulder. "Curtis Trotsky. C.T."

"Must be," Cooper said, flipping through more pages. "He threatened to expose him. Repeatedly."

"But never said for what," she said.

Cooper scanned another one. Same tone. Same menace. Curtis had written them with the confidence of a man who believed he was untouchable. Maybe he had been.

Cat pulled out her phone and snapped photos. It wasn't the photos that caught Cooper's attention. It was the cracked leather-bound book tucked under the arm. "What's that?"

She took the last of her photos, then pulled the book free, setting it on the desk. "I don't know. I only just found it tucked behind a box of expired film."

Cooper fingered the edges of the book, soft from wear. He flipped it open to the first page.

March 2nd – He was parked across the street again. Just sitting there. No badge. No uniform. Just watching. I don't know who he is yet, but he wants something from me.

The journal continued with more dates and similar notions of Walter observing someone following and spying on him. It didn't just happen at the office. It was happening at home and when he was in public too. Walter had no idea why this was suddenly happening and was gravely concerned. It was right around the time he was going to call the police that the first letter showed up, accusing Walter of having a secret that was going to be exposed. For whatever reason, there was no indication in the journal that Walter ever went to the police. He said over and over again that he had no secret. But he assumed the man sending him this was powerful.

Roughly two months later, the final note read: *May 4th – Followed him. Couldn't help myself. I tailed him to Beaver Lake. Remote. Creepy. He stopped at a cabin on the water. I thought about confronting him, but something stopped me. Fear? I don't know.*

Cooper's eyes narrowed. "He followed Curtis. To Beaver Lake."

Cat leaned in. "Is there an address?"

He flipped ahead, scanning for more entries but found none. Cooper got to the very last page. There was one short line that was underlined twice in pencil:

Beaver Lake – 197 Hawthorn Ridge. Lakeside cabin. Property of Curtis Trotsky

"That's it." Cooper's voice dropped. "That's where Curtis might have taken Jenna."

Cat stared at the page. "We need to give this to Luke. Like – now."

Cooper's phone buzzed in his pocket. He yanked it out, checked the screen. Luke.

He answered. "We've got something."

CHAPTER 33

Everything converged on Luke all at once. He'd gone from having nearly no leads to all of them coming in a flurry of activity. After Scarlett identified Curtis as the man who took her, Luke needed to see where the man had lived. He hadn't been at the first address, the one Amelia knew, and he wasn't at the second, the one Granger had found for him. The man was long gone from those homes. There were no property records for the man in all of the state.

Now that they had identified the man and he had received clearance from Tyler to go after him with the full force of the law, Luke put his foot on the gas and was going full throttle.

After alerting the SWAT team that they'd probably be needed as soon as he could find an address, Luke was sitting at his desk, head bent over the database searching for any scrap of information – license, car registration, voter registration – anything that might hint at where the man was located. Everything came back to his former address, where a young couple was living. They had bought the house from Curtis. When Luke visited them to see if they had any forwarding information for him, the young woman was annoyed that they occasionally received his mail. They had no forwarding, but she had handed Luke a stack of mail if he ever found him.

Luke had arrived back at the station, dumped the mail on his desk, and gotten back down to work. So far, still nothing. He cursed at the screen for not giving him the information he needed. He tipped his head back in the chair and was staring up at the ceiling, trying to think of ways to find the information, when the sounds of chatter and rushing feet caught his attention.

He sat upright at his desk in enough time to see Cat, Cooper, Riley, and Gail rushing toward him. He recognized Riley's flushed face as a sign that she had something important to share. He was just as surprised to see Gail not only upright but moving quickly.

It was Cooper who made it to the desk first. He shouted an address at Luke. As he started to ask him to repeat it, Riley grabbed Cooper by the arm. "Did you say something about Beaver Lake?"

Cooper glanced over at Gail. "Maybe we should speak in the conference room."

"No," Gail said, her voice strong and clear. She marched right up to the edge of Luke's desk and looked Cooper right in the eyes. "If this is about Curtis Trotsky and he has my daughter, you're not keeping anything from me. I know Curtis built a house on Beaver Lake. I know that's where he's been living. What I don't know is the exact address."

By this time, other detectives had started to watch what was unfolding. Luke got up from his desk, quieting them down and ushering them all into the conference room. Once they were all inside and seated around the table, he closed the door.

"One at a time. I can't understand what you're saying when you're all shouting at me." He moved to stand at the end of the table and looked down at Riley. "You go first."

Over the next few minutes, it wasn't Riley who told them about the connection between Gail and Curtis, but Gail who had found the strength. She explained how Curtis had come into their lives, the extra attention he had paid to her, the kiss at sixteen, and her pulling away after that. She detailed their interactions as an adult and where things stood now.

"Years ago. Jenna was a small child then," Gail said when she neared the end. "He asked about her all the time. He saw photos of her and I talked about her. I didn't realize that I was putting my daughter in any danger." Gail closed her eyes and took some deep breaths fighting the tears that wanted to come. She opened her eyes and looked over at Luke. "If you're going to tell me that Curtis also took my sister and those other girls and it wasn't Randy Stock, I'm ready to hear that too. I wasn't ready before, but I'm ready now."

Luke was proud of the woman for the strength she was showing. "I don't know for sure about your sister. There's enough evidence to suggest it wasn't Randy. My only focus right now is on getting Jenna back."

"As it should be," Gail said.

Luke wanted to tell the woman that she should go home and wait, but if she had that much of a connection to Curtis, they might be able to use that. Luke thanked her and turned his attention to Cooper. "What did you find?"

Cooper repeated the address and then explained how they had found it. He slid the leather-bound journal across the table to Luke. Inside, Cooper had collected the letters from the drawer and added them. "It sounds to me like Curtis zeroed in on Walter and was watching him. Honestly, more like stalking and harassing him. I assume he was trying to set him up." Cooper looked over at Cat and nudged her. "Tell Luke your theory."

When Cat seemed hesitant, Luke encouraged her to speak up.

Cat cleared her throat and speculated about Curtis making Walter's house look like what they expect a predator's home to look like. "If he was abusing that many children, Luke, there'd have been rumors or speculation. He has a thriving business with good reviews. Cooper said there were no photos of children being abused."

"There weren't," Luke said, recalling the collage on the wall. "There were so many photos."

"Because he's a photographer," Cat said, stating the obvious. "I can make a collage of normal-looking photos look creepy too with lighting and how they are arranged. You were in there looking for proof he was a predator. That small room could have been anything. For all you know, before Walter was murdered, it might just have been that Curtis staged the house to look like a kidnapper's lair."

"There is a notebook with children's names and dates," Luke said, still not sure how to make sense of that.

Cooper pushed the notepad he had found at Walter's across the table to Luke. "That we can assume is Walter's handwriting. Does it match?"

Luke went to the evidence that they had been storing in the conference room while working on the case and tugged out the notebook. He slipped on gloves and flipped open a page. He leaned down and looked at the pad of paper with chicken scratch writing. Luke was no handwriting expert, but it was not a match. It wasn't even close.

"Can I look at that?" Gail asked.

Luke carried it down to her and rested the notebook in front of her at the table. "We found this in Walter Fields's home. We don't know the meaning of it."

Gail bent her head and sucked in a breath. "That's Curtis's hand-writing. He's sent me enough cards over the years for me to recognize it."

"Are you sure?" Luke asked.

"There's no question in my mind."

Luke knew what they had to do. He turned to Riley. "I've already called SWAT. We can take it from here. You should take Gail home."

"No," Gail said, speaking up before Riley. "I'm going with you. That man knows me. If he's the one who has been harassing me for years, maybe I can speak to him. He might listen to me."

"He's not going to listen to you," Luke said without much conviction.

Riley locked her gaze on him. "Let us come with you. If you don't need us, we'll stay out of the way. If we can be of use, at least we'll be there."

Luke sat back and considered his options. Riley wasn't wrong and neither was Gail.

"Okay," he said, relenting. "But you follow my orders. Got it?" When they all agreed, he told them to be back at the police station in an hour. It was a little more than a four-hour drive to Beaver Lake and they needed to be prepared for a stand-off. Luke didn't say it aloud, but he was hoping that Jenna was still alive. It was the best-case scenario.

Hours later

Beaver Lake shimmered under the dying sun, its coppery reflection flickering across the still water. A windless hush hung over the cove, broken only by the faint creak of boat docks and the crunch of boots on gravel.

Luke crouched behind the thick trunk of a white oak, its bark biting into his shoulder as he scanned the lake house through binoculars. The house looked brand new compared to the others. Its modern, sleek design stood out against the older rustic cabins. The wide windows stared blank and dark except for one – upstairs, left side.

Luke noted the flicker of movement behind a gauzy curtain. He lowered the binoculars, heart pumping slow and hard against his ribs. "You see the upstairs window?"

Granger knelt beside him, the crinkle of his tactical vest loud in the stillness. "Saw it. It could be her. It could be him. He's keeping the lights low on purpose."

The SWAT commander stood a few feet behind, one hand on his

earpiece, the other gripping a rifle. Twelve men in full gear crouched in the woods and along the tree line, weapons trained on the house.

"He's boxed in," Granger murmured. "Nowhere to run."

Luke exhaled. "Unless he panics. Then we've got a dead girl on our hands." He rose and stepped into the clearing, slow and deliberate, hands away from his weapon. He took several steps toward the back of the house. He knew he was out in the open and the man could take a shot at him if he wanted. Still, what choice did Luke have? He wasn't going to walk up to the front door and he didn't have a number to call the man.

His voice cracked the silence. "Curtis! Curtis Trotsky! This is Detective Luke Morgan."

A pause. Then the curtain upstairs twitched again.

"We know you took Jenna. You can walk out of this with her alive. That's all anyone cares about now. Let Jenna come out. We know you have her."

Curtis offered no response.

Luke took two more steps, careful not to spook the sniper team in the trees. "I need to know she's okay, Curtis. Just show me she's safe." It was all still a gamble Luke was hoping would pay off.

A breathless beat stretched long and taut.

Then a voice floated down – reedy, hoarse, too calm. "She's fine."

Luke froze. The voice chilled him, not because it was angry or wild – but because it wasn't. Curtis sounded like a man giving a weather report. And he recognized the man's voice. If there were any lingering doubts about the case, it was gone for Luke then.

"I need to see her," Luke called. "Let her come to the window."

No answer.

"You want me to believe she's safe, you show me."

A minute passed. Two.

Then the curtain pulled back just enough to reveal a narrow sliver of light. A small shape appeared, silhouetted – shoulders, a flash of blonde hair, a pale hand raised to the glass.

Jenna.

Luke's chest clenched. She was alive. The curtain fell shut.

"You got what you wanted," Curtis called. "Now leave."

"Let me come in and speak to you."

"Never!" Curtis shouted back and the light in the upstairs room extinguished.

Luke backed away toward the trees, his neck prickling with the sense of being watched.

Granger's jaw flexed. "He's unraveling. This is his endgame, and he knows it."

Voices crackled over the comms – teams adjusting, moving, recalibrating their aim.

He still had his ace. He turned to see Gail and Riley standing just beyond the perimeter tape, a uniformed deputy trying – and failing – to hold Gail back. Her face was pale but resolved, her eyes red but dry. Riley stood beside her, hair pulled into a tight braid, arms crossed over her chest.

"Do we let her try?" Luke asked Granger.

"We don't have a lot of options. Either storm the place with SWAT and hope he doesn't kill her in the process or try to negotiate. With no phone and him backing away, I don't know how we do that."

Curtis wasn't going to talk to Luke, but he might talk to Gail. He waved Gail and Riley over.

Gail pushed past the deputy. "He'll talk to me."

"You're not going in," Luke snapped. "You can shout from down here like I just did."

Without any trace of fear, Gail stepped into the clearing. "Curtis!" She shouted his name three times before the light flickered on. "I know you can see me. We've been friends a long time, Curtis. I know that you don't want to hurt Jenna. Maybe you just took her to get my attention. I'm here now. Talk to me."

The voice shouted from the shadows. "Come in the side door, alone. No cops."

"Absolutely not," Luke said from behind her.

"I'm not asking permission," she said as she turned to him. She stepped close enough that he could see the tremble in her fingers. "He's been obsessed with me since I was a child. He consoled me about my sister, who he probably murdered. I'm going in to save my daughter."

Granger cursed under his breath. "It's a trap. He'll only kill you both."

"Not if I'm in there with them," Riley said, raising the hem of her shirt to show that she was armed.

"No," Luke said again with a shake of his head, knowing that it was going to happen whether he wanted it or not. He had known deep in his gut this was how it was going to end. The lake house had no landline as far as they could tell and they weren't able to get a cellphone number for Curtis. Granger was right, they had few options other than storming the place. Curtis was too smart to get close to windows and give a sniper a chance at him.

Granger and Riley were still bickering about going in.

"Of course it's a trap," Riley shot back. "You don't think I've handled worse?"

Luke's mind raced. Riley was tough and smart but could be reckless. "I can't lose you in there," he said to her. He pressed his hands to his temples.

Riley came to his side, wrapping her hands around his waist. "You're not going to lose me."

"Give me five minutes," Luke said finally and stalked away to get them bulletproof vests. He knew the fight was a losing battle. They were going in, but he wasn't sending them in unprepared.

After he suited them both up, he radioed the SWAT lead. "Hold position. No shots unless ordered. Stand down perimeter patrols by the house entrance. We have civilians approaching."

Granger stormed after him. "Luke, this isn't a good idea."

"Of course it's not, but you said so yourself that we don't have a lot of options. I knew that coming up here," Luke said, voice hard.

"You think Curtis will let them back out?"

Luke didn't answer.

Back at the staging area, he found Riley checking a pocketknife hidden inside her boot. She zipped it up and met his eyes. "He's not going to expect me to be armed. And even if he bets on me having a gun, he's not going to assume I have another gun at my ankle and a knife in my boot. It's backup for backup. I have my phone in my pocket too. I'll be recording everything."

He couldn't say she didn't think things through.

Gail stood nearby, silent, trembling – but her gaze was locked on the lake house like a mother wolf watching the tree line.

Luke moved to Gail's side, instructing both of them. "Don't make him any promises. You buy time. You look for exits. You find Jenna and you get her out of there."

Gail nodded once.

"I'm going to have a sniper on you the whole time," Luke added. "If he even looks wrong, I'll take the shot if you can get him near a window."

"No," she said. "You shoot and he kills Jenna."

"I'll trust you in there. Trust me to do what I have to out here." He reached for Riley and wrapped her in a hug. "Be smart in there."

The two women started toward the lake house.

The light was fading now, the woods casting long shadows over the shoreline. A loon cried from somewhere across the water, its lonely trill threading through the thickening dark.

"Curtis, I'm bringing my friend Riley," she shouted. "I've been very upset by this whole thing. She's here to support me. But no cops. They are standing down. Please let us in!"

They continued toward the house, walking right up to the side door where Curtis had told Gail to go. Riley looked back only once before disappearing into the house.

Luke – helpless behind a tree line, behind a badge, behind rules Curtis had never once followed – watched his wife walk into a lion's den.

CHAPTER 34

The lake house reeked of cleaning products and something else I couldn't identify, maybe floor polish. The hardwoods were spotless. There wasn't a thing out of place inside. The space inside was a masterpiece of modern design – sleek, minimalist, and untouched. From the polished glass windows that framed the view of the shimmering lake outside to the smooth, pale hardwood floors that creaked underfoot, everything about the place exuded pristine perfection. It was a stark contrast to the chaos its owner had created.

The side entryway was lined with tall, sculptural vases, each holding fresh-cut flowers that looked as if they'd been placed with a ruler's precision.

I took a few steps into the home, keeping Gail at my side. "We are here, Curtis, show yourself." There was a hitch in my voice I didn't like. The fear permeated my body, but I couldn't show him that. Gail reached for my hand and squeezed it tight. I whispered reassuring words as best I could.

The soft light from recessed ceiling fixtures bathed the living room space where we stood and waited in a warm glow, casting shadows that only emphasized the sharp lines of the furniture. A gray sofa sat against the wall, each cushion fluffed and aligned, the throw blankets folded in perfect thirds at the edge.

A moment later, Curtis stepped into the living room, one arm wrapped around Jenna's shoulders, the other holding a revolver with the casual grip of someone who'd carried a badge for as long as he had.

"Lock the door." His voice carried the authoritative tone he'd probably used in the courtroom. There were dark age spots on his wrinkled hands. His icy blue eyes stared back at me.

I turned back to the door, expecting him to shoot me in the back. My fingers trembled as I reached for the deadbolt. The metallic click echoed through the cramped space, sealing us inside with a man who'd spent three decades perfecting the art of deception.

I walked back to stand near Gail, looking at Jenna as her dark eyes met mine – wide, terrified, but not broken. Not yet.

"Curtis, please." Gail's voice cracked as she stepped forward, her hands raised in surrender. "Let her go. You have me here. That's what you wanted, isn't it?"

He laughed, a sound devoid of warmth. "I have both of you now." He gripped Jenna's shoulder tighter. "I'm not letting either of you go."

I shifted my weight, cataloging escape routes. The kitchen was to my left, with what I assumed would be the back door, but I'd have to get past Curtis. Windows on either side of the room, but if we came crashing through, SWAT might shoot us.

Gail's voice grew stronger, though her hands trembled. "My father trusted you. He thought you were his friend. I trusted you. All these years, I trusted you, Curtis. After what happened to Samantha and the other girls, I was broken. You were there for me. I just don't understand why you took Jenna."

"You were never very smart, Gail. So pretty but so utterly stupid." Curtis tightened his grip on Jenna, who whimpered softly. "Your father was always so righteous. He knew what was best for everyone. Including his daughters."

The way he said *daughters* made my stomach clench. I thought of photos of three young girls who'd vanished thirty years ago. Samantha

Albright. Kathleen Elliott. Violet Yeaton. I whispered their names.

Curtis turned toward me. He caught what I had said, but he asked me to repeat it.

"You killed them." The words left my mouth before I could stop them. I repeated their names again. "You made a mistake that day. Kathleen Elliott left her sneaker in the back of your squad car and the guy you picked up that night, probably framed that night, found it. We have that sneaker and it's tied to you."

Curtis's eyes found mine, and for a moment, the mask slipped entirely. I saw the predator underneath, calculating, remorseless, and proud. For a split second, I thought he might deny it, but then a slow, sinister smile spread across his face. "Very good. Though technically, I only killed two of them on purpose."

Gail's sharp intake of breath filled the silence. "Samantha."

"Samantha should have been mine." He tilted his head, considering. "It was an accident. She fought harder than I expected. I was young then, inexperienced. The other two, well, they were just loose ends."

Gail shrieked and lunged forward, but I caught her arm, pulling her back. Curtis's gun swung toward us. Jenna started crying.

"It's going to be okay," I tried to reassure her. I kept my voice level, professional. "Nobody needs to get hurt here."

"Don't they?" His laugh was bitter. "I've spent thirty years watching from the sidelines while everyone praised the Albrights for how strong they were while their daughter was missing. Such a stellar family. But Jim wasn't that bright, was he? If only they knew their hero had been too blind to see what was happening right under his nose."

"You were there," Gail shouted. "At our house. My father trusted you. I trusted you."

"Sunday dinners. Holiday parties. Birthday celebrations." His voice took on a dreamy quality. "I watched Gail grow up. Watched you become a woman and how I wanted you. But you were aloof. Always out of reach for me. I tried to take you first. Did you know that?"

Gail stepped back, shaking her head. "You should have taken me instead of Samantha."

"I tried but you were always out of reach, so I took the next best thing."

"She was a child. She wasn't a thing." Gail's voice was barely a whisper.

"She was perfect." Curtis's grip on the gun tightened. "Until she started asking questions about where I was taking her. Started screaming and fighting me."

I measured the distance between us. Maybe eight feet. Too far to reach him before he could pull the trigger, but close enough to see the madness burning in his eyes. The rational prosecutor was gone, replaced by something primitive and hungry.

"Where are they? What did you do with their bodies?" I asked, keeping my tone even. "We know you took them after they left the store that day. What did you do with them?"

Curtis smiled. "Who doesn't want a ride in a police car. Samantha came willingly. Why wouldn't she? I was a friend of the family. The other two girls came too but were guarded, especially Kathleen. She got the sense of what I was going to do before the others. I guess that's why she slipped off her sneaker. I didn't even notice it in the frenzy."

He went on to describe how he had approached them on the street. Pretended to put the girls' bikes in the trunk but tossed them into the grass instead. He drove them to a wooded area and strangled the two girls, putting their bodies in his trunk.

It was only then that Samantha became frantic. Curtis said he had punched her and knocked her out cold for the rest of the drive.

"Where did you take them?" I asked again.

"You're looking at it," he said with a smirk.

"Where?" I asked, not getting it at first. Then the truth settled in and turned my stomach. "This land. Before you built the house?"

"I like to keep them with me."

A sound like a wounded bird escaped from Gail but she held her ground. Even Jenna had stopped crying, but her breathing was shallow. Shock, maybe, or the beginning of hyperventilation. I caught her eye and told her again that it was going to be okay.

"Did you frame Randy Stock?"

Curtis laughed. "I didn't frame him. I just nudged the detective in the right direction. I was just a beat cop then, but I told him there were rumblings out there in the city that Randy had done it. Then, after his conviction, I kept an eye on him. I was going to finish him off before he got out, but I don't know what happened. Someone moved him."

All I could imagine was that someone, either at the jail or in law enforcement, knew the truth and was protecting Randy. At least half of that mystery was solved. The threats had come from Curtis.

"You harassed me and the other families," Gail reminded him. "Why did you do that? What did you gain?"

"That was just fun. A way to make you need me. A little icing on the cake. Then, when you rebuffed my advances, it was revenge. I enjoyed seeing the terror in your eyes when you came to me. I had to keep up the ruse for the other families, too. I didn't want anyone to suspect it was a show just for you."

Gail balled her fists. "I was sixteen when you tried to kiss me. You were a grown man."

"More than old enough."

"Why take Jenna?"

"This is about showing you the truth." Curtis shifted his weight, and I tensed, ready to move. "Your husband is useless. You need me. You need someone to protect you. You've always needed me. Jenna needs me too."

"I never needed you." Gail's voice was steel now that all fear had been burned away by fury. "I was a child when you murdered my sister. A child who looked up to you, who trusted you. And you used that trust to torture me."

"I loved you!"

"You don't know what love is." She stepped forward again, ignoring my restraining hand. "Love doesn't kill. Love doesn't harm innocent children to get attention."

Curtis's face flushed red. "Don't you dare lecture me about—"

A soft thud came from somewhere deeper in the house. All of us froze, listening. Curtis's eyes darted toward the hallway leading to the bedrooms, then back to us.

"That's just the SWAT team," I lied smoothly. "You know how this works, Curtis. You've been on the other side of these situations."

"Shut up." The gun wavered between Gail and me. "They can't get a clear shot through these windows."

He was right, and we both knew it. But doubt was creeping in, making him sloppy. I shifted my weight again, this time toward Gail rather than forward. If he pulled the trigger, I wanted to be able to shield her.

"What's the endgame here, Curtis?" I kept my voice calm, conversational. "You can't hold us here forever. The cops know what you've done. They aren't going to let you just walk out of here with Gail and Jenna. What's the plan or didn't you think that far ahead?"

His laugh was sharp, desperate. "You think I'm stupid? You think I didn't know this would be the end?"

The certainty in his voice chilled me. This wasn't a man planning an escape. This was a man planning a finale.

"Curtis, think about this." Gail's voice was gentle now, almost pleading. "Jenna hasn't done anything wrong. She's just a little girl. Let her go, and we can figure this out."

He jerked Jenna closer, and she cried out. "What are we going to do?

Talk about our feelings? Work through my issues? I've been carrying this secret for thirty years. I'm tired and this needs to end."

Another sound from the back of the house – footsteps this time, careful and measured. Curtis heard it too, his head cocking toward the hallway like a hunting dog scenting prey.

"Someone's here," he whispered, almost to himself. Then louder, his voice cracking. "Someone's in my house!"

"Curtis!" I shouted to get his attention.

"Shut up!" The gun swung wildly between Gail and me. "Just shut up and let me think!"

Thinking was the last thing he was capable of. I could see the breakdown happening in real time – the careful control he'd maintained for decades finally shattering under the weight of exposure. His hand shook as he pressed the barrel against Jenna's temple. She whimpered, tried to pull away, but he gripped her tighter.

"Don't." The word tore from my throat before I could stop it. "Please. She's a child."

"I know exactly how old she is." His voice dropped to a whisper. "The same age Gail was when I first realized how perfect she was."

The footsteps were closer now, moving down the hallway with practiced stealth. Curtis heard them too, his eyes wild with panic and rage.

He muttered, "After all these years, they're finally coming."

"Yes," I said quietly. "They are. It doesn't have to end like this. You can still do the right thing."

"The right thing?" He laughed, high and hysterical. "The right thing was supposed to be Gail choosing me. The right thing was supposed to be us being together, like I always dreamed. I worked so hard to show you I was a good man. I kept the predators at bay. I was the good guy."

"You were never good and that was never going to happen." Gail's voice was steady, final. "Even if you hadn't killed my sister, even if you hadn't terrorized me, I would never have chosen you. Because you're not a good man, Curtis. You never were."

Something broke in his face then. The last pretense of sanity, of control, crumbled away. He raised the gun, pointing it directly at Gail's chest.

"Then what's the point?" His finger tightened on the trigger. "If I can't have you, why should anyone?"

Time slowed to a crawl. I saw Curtis's knuckle whiten as he began to squeeze. Saw Gail's eyes close, accepting her fate. Saw Jenna's terrified face as she realized what was about to happen.

I lunged forward, knowing I was too far away, knowing I'd never make it in time. The gun was already firing, the muzzle flash bright in the dim room.

But the shot went wide as Curtis suddenly pitched forward, driven to the ground by a figure in black tactical gear. Granger, moving like a linebacker, drove Curtis face-first into the hardwood floor, taking Jenna with them to the ground. The gun skittered away across the room as they hit.

"Gun!" Granger shouted, shoving Jenna out of the way and wrestling with Curtis as the older man bucked and thrashed beneath him. "Riley, the gun!"

I dove for it, snatching it up just as Curtis broke free of Granger's grip. He rolled onto his back, blood streaming from his nose, his eyes searching wildly.

"It's over," I said, pointing his gun at him. "It's done."

Curtis stared at me for a long moment, then at Gail, who had thrown her body protectively over Jenna's. The little girl was sobbing now, deep, wrenching sobs that seemed to echo through the silent house.

"Thirty years," he whispered, his voice barely audible. "Thirty years I waited."

Granger grabbed handcuffs from his tactical vest and slapped them on Curtis as he dragged the man to his feet. "Curtis Trotsky, you're under arrest for the murders of Samantha Albright, Kathleen Elliott, and Violet Yeaton. And for the kidnapping of Scarlett Evans and Jenna Herin."

As Granger cuffed him, Curtis looked up at Gail one last time. "I loved you," he said, as if that explained everything. As if that made it all worthwhile.

Gail knelt beside Jenna, wiping blood from her face, a scrape on the chin from hitting the floor. Otherwise, she seemed okay. Luke and the others rushed in around us. Gail didn't look at Curtis as they dragged him away.

She didn't need to. The nightmare was finally over.

Epilogue

Six weeks later

Over the years, my house had become a gathering point for all my favorite people in Little Rock. I had bought the place when I lived in the city, when I was working as a journalist. I had kept the home after leaving Little Rock to go back to New York, only to return. It was then that Luke and I reconciled, and he moved in, making it as much his home as my own.

Emma, her husband Joe, and their two children were great neighbors and long-time friends. While there was a fence between our backyards, Joe had cut a hole in the fence to add a gate so Emma and I and the kids could go back and forth more freely. Whether Luke and I would have children down the road was something still to be determined. We were both fine with the decision, no matter which way it went.

That's why on that late fall afternoon when we were all gathered between the kitchen and the backyard for a cookout, we couldn't have been happier when Cooper and Adele announced that they were expecting. I can't even say that it took me by surprise. Adele had been feeling sick more days than not over the last few weeks, but her skin had a glow of pregnancy about her.

Cooper could not keep the excitement to himself. Adele had told him the night that Jenna had been rescued. He told Luke the next morning but swore him to secrecy. Luke had managed to keep the secret from me. I couldn't even be angry with him. The news was too exciting, and I was far too happy for Cooper and Adele to worry about it.

Cooper was overjoyed with the news. He couldn't wait to be a father. The news came on the heels of him finally extracting the information from the warden about who had issued the order to protect Randy Stock.

The night of the confrontation in Beaver Lake, Luke had asked Cooper to go back to the jail to find out who was the one protecting Randy. Given all the information that had been gathered about Curtis, Luke hoped the warden would finally reveal who it was that had been protecting the man. Cooper had shown up, provided all of the details, and demanded answers.

The warden finally relented and pointed Cooper back to the police department. Two cops who had worked with Curtis thirty years ago had always been suspicious of the man, nothing solid that they could do anything with, but not for lack of trying on their part. They had been working in the shadows. When they heard word that there were threats against Randy as he was about to be released from prison, they had greased some wheels and ensured that Randy was transferred from state prison to the jail for the last few weeks of his sentence. The inner workings of how all of that played out were still a bit of a mystery, but one favor turned into another and it had happened, which was the only point. It turned out they were also the ones to send Cat an anonymous email with the podcast suggestion. They were determined to get the truth out.

After the truth came out, Det. Lyle Tucker finally admitted there was no Brad Hogan who had given him the tip about Randy Stock following the girls. That had come from Curtis. Tucker thought a fellow officer was doing him a favor. Tucker was too lazy to ask too many questions. It explained why there was no official witness statement and Mary had never been able to interview that witness.

With Curtis's confession about all of it, including killing Walter Fields and staging his home to look like a predator, there was no hope he'd ever be released from prison. Fields had been shot behind his home, which is why the crime scene had been so hard to find. Curtis even admitted to using an old wagon to drag the man's body to the woods.

With all the things he admitted, what he wouldn't do was tell Luke exactly where the girls' bodies were buried.

Luke had an entire crew examining the man's Beaver Lake property, including going through the flooring and foundation as part of the search. With the use of cadaver dogs and some highly motivated cops and forensic teams, the girls were discovered in the far northeast corner under the home. He had built a small section of the home - his bedroom - right over their graves.

The discovery was a sad day but one that at least brought some peace of mind to the families. They had answers and could give their loved ones a proper resting place. Luke, Cooper, and I attended the services for all of the girls.

Curtis was currently sitting in prison awaiting his sentencing.

After Randy was released from jail, he started working with Adele for a full exoneration and compensation for the thirty years he spent in prison for a crime he didn't commit. She had taken the case after all, mostly because it was a sure thing and Randy had insisted that he wanted to work with her. He had been grateful for Cooper and, by extension, trusted his wife.

Luke, as a spokesman for the Little Rock Police Department in collaboration with the brass, issued a formal apology for his arrest. Not that an apology was worth much that many years later, but Randy appreciated it.

We were all there the day he was released from jail. The full exoneration was working through the court system. It would take time, but it would happen. Adele worked with a local nonprofit to get him a place to stay, something better than the halfway house he had initially chosen. The nonprofit also provided help to him to get his life back on track until the money from the settlement came in. Randy was clear that once that happened, he was leaving Little Rock forever and not looking back. He said the first thing he was going to do was spend time with his sister. I couldn't blame him for never wanting to be in Little Rock again.

In the meantime, he was meeting with Cat to tell his story on the podcast. With resolution in the case, the podcast was taking a far different direction than Cat had initially planned. It was good being able to tell Randy's story, knowing he was innocent but also knowing the real responsible party.

Cat told us that all the families were participating, and Gail was doing everything she could to help. When I found that out, I called Gail and asked her to lunch. I wanted to see how she was doing and make sure that she was comfortable with the podcast. Not that I thought Cat would do anything wrong, I just didn't want Gail to feel pressured.

When I sat down at the restaurant that day, a woman I barely recognized walked through the door. Gail held her head back, shoulders high, and she walked with a confidence I had never seen in her. She was bright and smiling. She had even dyed and cut her hair. Her makeup was flawless and her clothes were stylish and pressed. She said knowing for sure what had happened to her sister and getting Jenna back had given her a new lease on life.

Jenna was meeting with a child psychologist but was bouncing back from the trauma of the kidnapping. Gail was impressed with her daughter's resilience and had used it as a motivator for her own. She confided in me that sharing her story on the podcast was empowering for her. She liked finally having a voice. I wasn't going to take that away from her.

Amelia had Scarlett in counseling to process what had happened to her. She had also found out that Christopher was getting counseling of his own. That's where he was sneaking off to during the workday. Feeling defensive, he wasn't going to admit it to law enforcement. In the end, he didn't bother going after her for full custody, citing that Scarlett had been through enough trauma.

All in all, the case had wrapped up better than we could have expected. There isn't always hope that a thirty-year-old mystery would be solved and justice would be served. It was even better that we were able to bring some resolution to the families.

Cooper and I talked about possibly taking on more cold cases as well as our current workload. Luke had finally settled into a place where he was okay with the work I was doing. And some days, he even saw me as an asset to the police department.

I leaned against the dividing wall between our kitchen and dining room, watching out our back sliding door at Luke at the grill. He was talking happily with Joe and Cooper. Cat and Emma looked like they were conspiring together at the garden table. The kids were running and playing in the yard. Granger and his family and Tyler and his family would be joining us soon.

A great sense of peace washed over me. Life was good.

I had created an entire family of people who loved me and that I loved. My family back home was doing well, too. I couldn't ask for anything more.

"You look nostalgic for something," Adele said as she put her hand on my back.

I looked over at her and smiled. "Just happy and even happier that we are going to have an addition to our family soon."

Adele rubbed her still flat stomach. "I'll be glad when I can start keeping food down. This little one is making me sick daily. I thought it was only supposed to be in the morning."

I laughed and shrugged. "I have no idea. But soon, hopefully." I glanced over at her. "What's going to happen with your practice after the baby?"

"I'm bringing on two other attorneys to work with me. I'll work but cut back a little. With Cooper working from home and you both bringing on other investigators, there will be plenty of coverage for childcare."

"Our businesses are growing," I responded, pleased that Cooper and I had taken our respective investigative firms and combined them. Now that it was growing, it would allow both of us to cut back on some of the more labor-intensive investigations to pick and choose the cases we worked.

With beer in hand, Cooper waved at us through the sliding door. He motioned for Adele to join him outside. She kissed me on the cheek. I promised I'd be out soon.

Luke saw me still standing there alone and put Joe in charge of the grill. As he came toward the house, he stepped out of the way for Adele to leave. He closed the sliding door behind him. "I can't believe the weather is this nice. What are you still doing in here?"

I leaned into Luke. He tipped my chin up and kissed me sweetly. "I was just thinking about how grateful I am for all these wonderful people in our lives."

Luke nodded. "I feel it every day."

"I love you."

"I love you too," he said and kissed me again, deeper this time. "Come outside and join in the fun."

I realized in that moment, I had everything I ever wanted.

If this was a dream, I didn't want to wake up.

About the Author

Stacy M. Jones was born and raised in Troy, New York, and currently lives in Little Rock, Arkansas. She is a full-time writer and holds masters' degrees in journalism and in forensic psychology. She currently has four series available for readers: the completed cozy paranormal Harper & Hattie Magical Mystery Series, the hard-boiled PI Riley Sullivan Mystery Series, the FBI Agent Kate Walsh Thriller Series and the new Connor Fitzgerald Thriller series. To access Stacy's Mystery Readers Club with free novellas, visit StacyMJones.com.

You can connect with me on:

- http://www.stacymjones.com
- https://www.facebook.com/StacyMJonesWriter
- https://www.bookbub.com/profile/stacy-m-jones
- https://www.goodreads.com/StacyMJonesWriter

Subscribe to my newsletter:

✉ http://www.stacymjones.com

Also by Stacy M. Jones

If you liked the PI Riley Sullivan Mystery Series, check out the FBI Agent Kate Walsh Thriller series next.

Access the Free Mystery Readers' Club Starter Library
PI Riley Sullivan Mystery Series novella "The 1922 Club Murder"
FBI Agent Kate Walsh Thriller Series novella "The Curators"
Harper & Hattie Mystery Series novella "Harper's Folly"

Sign up for the starter library along with launch-day pricing and special behind-the-scenes access. Hit subscribe at http://www.stacy mjones.com/

Please leave a review for The Missing Link. Reviews help more readers find my books. Thank you!

Other books by Stacy M. Jones by series and order to date:

FBI Agent Kate Walsh Thriller Series
The Curators
The Founders
Miami Ripper
Mad Jack
The Fuse
Dead Senate
Close Killer
Diamond King
The Magician
Helix Syndicate

Midnight Lilies

Connor Fitzgerald Thriller Series
Midnight Judge
Sparrow Down

PI Riley Sullivan Mystery Series
The 1922 Club Murder
Deadly Sins
The Bone Harvest
Missing Time Murders
We Last Saw Jane
Boston Underground
The Night Game
Harbor Cove Murders
The Drowned Boys
What He Saw
Fear City
What Stays Buried

Harper & Hattie Magical Mystery Series
Harper's Folly
Saints & Sinners Ball
Secrets to Tell
Rule of Three
The Forever Curse
The Witches Code
The Sinister Sisters
Scandal Knocks Twice
A Treasure Most Deadly